AS LONG AS YOU'RE MINE

OTHER TITLES BY NEKESA AFIA

THE HARLEM RENAISSANCE MYSTERIES

Dead Dead Girls

Harlem Sunset

A Lethal Lady

AS LONG AS YOU'RE MINE

A NOVEL

NEKESA AFIA

This is a work of fiction. Names, characters, organizations, places, events, and incidents are either products of the author's imagination or are used fictitiously.

Published by Lake Union Publishing, Seattle

www.apub.com

EU product safety contact:
Amazon Media EU S. à r.l.
38, avenue John F. Kennedy, L-1855 Luxembourg
amazonpublishing-gpsr@amazon.com

ISBN-13: 9781662524080 (paperback)
ISBN-13: 9781662524097 (digital)

Cover design by Faceout Studio, Tim Green
Cover image: © Ilina Simeonova / ArcAngel

Printed in the United States of America

Hi, family! Please do not read this book.

CHAPTER 1

1934

The song is cloying enough to get stuck in my head. I learned it three months ago, and ever since, it's been on a dull repeat. I sing it while getting ready. I sing it on the drive to Sunset Studios. I sing it in the makeup chair, as my hair is set, as I'm put into costumes.

It's always in my head until right *now*. The words won't come. All of them are piled up at the back of my throat. I'm unsure which one is supposed to come first. Now that I'm on set, lights on me, makeup caked over my face, I cannot remember the lyrics.

Kenneth Webster has risen from his director's chair, his wide, flat hands waving in the air. Everything he does is punctuated by a gesture. "Can we do this scene again? And can *our star* please keep it together? We're wasting time and money today." Kenneth is in a mood. He's glaring at me. I've been on set since two in the morning. Some of that time was in hair and makeup; more of it was in costumes. But the majority of it has been spent running the same scene over and over again, trying to live up to Kenneth's exacting standards.

I place my hands on my waist, feeling beads of sweat bloom under the stage lights. A flurry of activity happens around me; a woman brushes makeup on while another adjusts the skirt of my dress. The girls behind me, a flock of colored dresses that look muted against mine, prepare to restart the scene.

This is a big deal for me. Everyone on set knows that. Every time we finish, Kenneth finds something wrong. I'm sure my feet are bleeding, but that's something to worry about later.

"Reset," Kenneth says. This is my sixth film with him, but it's the first one I'm starring in. I understand the risk he's taken for me. Risks. Plural. "Action!"

He sits back down. My flock of girls lines up behind me, and we do it again.

Ramona Penderghast stands right next to me in a brilliant blue dress that contrasts with my red. The colors don't matter. The film will be in black and white. Ramona smiles at me, part encouraging, part threatening. The flock of girls dances behind me. All our moves choreographed to perfection.

I need to convince the audience that I'm a woman worthy of love.

Sunset Studio's pictures are all the same. Girl meets boy, boy meets girl, and, through a number of lengthy and complicated dance numbers, boy and girl fall in love.

It's a successful formula.

"Cut," Kenneth yells. We hold in place at the end of the number. He rises from his chair again, takes one long look at us. "Print. Moving on."

Relief.

He turns away from us. Characters are broken; background girls go back to talking about what they're going to do when they're done for the day.

"Good work, kid." Ramona remains by my side. She's maybe my only friend at Sunset, and that's saying a lot. We started at the same time, in the same acting and voice and etiquette classes.

"You think?"

"Stop being so modest." She's every bit the vixen. Her dark hair falls into her emerald eyes; her voice is low and throaty. She's the perfect 36-24-36 hourglass, measurements I have to constantly work to achieve.

And yet I'm starring in this flick, while she plays the best friend.

"Thanks." I smile.

Ramona blinks her big green eyes. "Why don't we change and go to lunch?"

"Would love to but can't. I need to go run my lines. Next scene," I say, trying to look apologetic.

Ramona slinks off, tossing her hair over her shoulder.

It's true I want to get off my feet, but I have something else.

Something better than Ramona Penderghast.

~

He's waiting for me when I open the door to my dressing room. I've just been moved to Star Row, where all the big Sunset stars have dressing rooms. I'm aware that I have the smallest one. I'm just happy to be here.

I flick on the radio and turn on the lights to find Tommy Ross sitting on my couch. "You're early," I say. He laughs. I kiss him and then disappear behind my screen to change.

"Did old Kenneth keep you?" Tommy asks. "You Do Something to Me" is playing on the radio. I can hear him humming along.

"Ran it twenty times." I slide on my dressing gown and reappear from behind the screen.

"Well, you were wonderful every time." Tommy wraps an arm around me as I settle in next to him. I'm exhausted. I close my eyes.

"You were watching?" I ask.

"Of course. Why wouldn't I? Maybe I wanted to hear you say you loved me over and over."

"Ha."

He kisses me before I can say anything else, and I melt into him. This, right now, makes all those hours under the hot lights worth it. He pulls me onto his lap.

"Those are just lyrics, you know," I say with my lips against his.

"Are you saying you don't love me?"

"I'm saying we have to work some things out."

I can smell him; our heat collides as he slides a hand up my bare thigh. His fingertips make ripples on my skin as he touches me. His kiss is disorienting, throwing me off kilter when his lips meet mine.

Tommy and I met on my first Sunset film. He played the lead, and I was a featured dancer.

And now, we're doing this.

He's my costar now. I know he's married. I've never overstepped boundaries like this before. I've met his wife twice at parties, a stunning thing. Mrs. Ross is cold, reserved.

Being this close to Tommy distorts my thoughts. I meant to tell him here and now that we can't continue doing this, but when his tongue parts my lips, I lose all sense.

And I don't ask him to stop, because I don't want him to.

CHAPTER 2

1934

I can't breathe.

I'm supposed to be on set, filming. Instead, I'm in a crumpled satin ball. The entire weight of the world is on me, and I can't breathe.

It came on suddenly and with no warning, as these things usually do. One moment, I'm humming along with the radio; the next, I'm pressing my cheek on the carpet of my dressing room, tears streaming down my face. The radio is still playing, and it sounds like it's a million miles away. I'm grasping at the dress that cages me in, and I think I'm about to vomit.

I can't let anyone see me like this, but it's inevitable; someone will come looking for me. I just hope it won't be Tommy. He doesn't know about my little episodes. I've done everything I can to hide them.

I can't let Kenneth see me like this either. If I can't make it to set, we'll have to push the schedule another day. We're already out of time and out of money. If this movie fails, I'll lose everything.

There's a knock on the door. When it opens, I can see a swirling skirt. I squeeze my eyes shut.

A hand presses to my forehead. I lie still.

"Lorelei." It's Ramona. I'd recognize her low, smoky voice anywhere. "Are you okay?"

It's a dumb question, but I think I'd ask the same if our roles were reversed. I open my mouth, and sobs escape.

Ramona kneels down, pulling my head into her lap. I'm shaking, dripping tears and snot on the skirt of her dress. She pushes my hair from my face. "You're okay," she whispers. Realizing that just makes me cry harder. "I know, I know," Ramona says over and over, her voice soft and low.

Slowly, I pull myself together. I stop crying, and I release the skirt of my dress. It's a supple douppioni, which means that I've put wrinkles in it. "I have to get to set." I get up, as unsteady on my feet as a newborn deer, and lean into the mirror. I'll have to redo my makeup, but I can do that quickly and then go.

"There's no way you're going to set." Ramona stands, her arms crossed over her chest. "If Kenneth gets mad, then let him. You're much more important than he ever could be." She steps toward the mirror, undoing the buttons that run up the back of my dress. I take a deep, grateful breath, in and out, as the world settles around me.

"He's going to . . ." I can't finish the sentence because I don't know *what* he'll do. He holds every part of my life in his hands, and he could ruin me if he wanted.

He knows more about me than anyone in my life, and that's not a good thing.

I look at my reflection in the mirror. With her hair pressed and eyes stained with mascara, this woman just looks sad. "You need to take a day off. Maybe two," Ramona says. I can tell she won't take no for an answer. Deep down, I know what she's doing. She's angling. She wants what I have, and she'll do anything to get it.

But I don't care.

I can't.

Everyone in Hollywood has their own goals, their own agenda. I want to be great, but Ramona does too.

"You stay here." She presses a kiss to my temple. The gesture is so maternal, so gentle, that I'm stunned, frozen for a moment. "I'll tell Kenneth."

I know what will happen. I've had too many days like this. The reason *Live, Love* is behind schedule is because of me. And they—maybe Kenneth or someone higher than him—will tell the press it's my fault. And then I'll be trapped at Sunset because no other studio will have me.

But I don't have it in me to argue. I don't have it in me to fight. I don't have it in me to report to set and pretend to . . .

I can't even remember what scenes we're doing. So it's better that I don't film.

I'm starting to spiral again; I can feel my breath hitching in my chest. Before she leaves, Ramona helps me slip out of my dress, hangs it neatly, and gets me on the couch.

I close my eyes, trying to stop the swirling thoughts from intruding again. I take my time; the radio is still on, invading my senses. I want to turn it off, but to do that, I have to stand up.

And I try. With my heartbeat thrumming in my chest, I try.

I take a half step and feel myself collapse.

And then the cycle starts all over again.

~

I hide out at home. My absence pushes *Live, Love* back another few days, and on the third, I'm lying in bed when there's a knock on the door.

I'm not about to move. I'm not about to let someone into this house. I've sent the maid away twice, and I can't do it again.

"Lorelei, you shouldn't keep your spare key under the mat."

I freeze. I pull my blanket over my head, curling up into a ball. It's Tommy. He's supposed to be on set.

"Kenneth didn't send me." His voice breaks the silence of the house, and it's like he knows what I'm thinking. "Lor, you disappeared for three days. Say something so I know you're not dead." I can hear him walking around. I'm wondering how long I can lie here, how long it will take him to go away. I squeeze my eyes shut, hearing him move from room to room. He's getting closer to my bedroom.

The door squeaks as it opens. I can feel him watching me.

If I pull myself out from under the blanket, he'll see that my face is red and puffy from crying. I haven't been able to stop sobbing since I left set. I'm still wearing the same bra and slip from three days ago, the bands pinching into my waist and back.

But I can't move.

"When I was ten, I bet my brother I could hold my breath for longer than he could," Tommy says. "We timed it. He went for ten seconds. I went until I passed out. You're stubborn, Lorelei, but I am too. Make this easy on the both of us."

I can hear his laugh, slightly amused. I can't take it. Also, it's hot under the covers, and I'm starting to sweat.

I pull myself out. My hair is tangled in knots. I keep my brassiere covered, even though he's seen me in less. I paw at my eyes, trying to do something to make myself more attractive.

He says my name. His voice is so soft, and he kicks his shoes off, climbing into bed with me. He wraps his arms around me. I'm out of tears. "I'm . . ." He trails off. He doesn't know what to say. "You don't have to go through this alone."

He surprises me.

I was imagining the worst—his reaction, how he would see me—so focused on it that I couldn't begin to think that things would ever be okay. "You need to go back to sleep. Lie down." He moves with me, letting my face rest on his chest. I close my eyes and feel his arms around me. As I succumb to the twilight of sleep, Tommy pulls away and says, "I'm sorry." His voice is soft, barely a whisper on my skin. It feels as if I've been hit by a car, run over, and dragged behind it for miles.

I don't fight it; I need to sleep.

And when I wake, Tommy has cooked. Except he's a man and he doesn't know how to cook. He's put bread in the toaster, smeared it with butter. He brings it to me in bed, and I start to believe that everything will be okay.

CHAPTER 3

1954

Thea Ross was intensely watching her father soak up attention. Tommy Ross had his hand on a woman's shoulder. He leaned in and said something, and the woman's laugh rang through the ballroom.

It was the middle of a long night. Thea wore an ornate black gown with gold peacock feathers embroidered on the bodice and skirt. She had to be stitched into the dress and could barely breathe, let alone eat. Her dinner sat in front of her, untouched.

She'd already taken two turns around the dance floor, her injured foot wrapped in a way that it didn't bother her. She wasn't even supposed to be dancing at all, not even a rigid waltz.

But her father had asked. And this evening was all for her father.

It was another Constellation Pictures event. The studio her father had founded. Thea had been attending these parties since she was a child. He'd moved from acting to directing, and now he owned a film studio.

Hollywood at large was finally honoring Tommy and his achievements, after decades in the film industry, and Thea had remained by his side for most of the night.

To Thea, Tommy was *Dad*: the man who had raised her, indulged her whims, educated her at home until she graduated early.

To the rest of the world, he was the actor and director who led films to financial success.

They sat at a table with her father's old friends and business partners: Jake Turner and his daughter, Willa, and Ingrid Belle and her son, Max Armstrong.

"He's just loving this, isn't he?" Willa jutted her chin toward the table where Tommy was, standing over film executives Thea thought she knew or at least recognized.

"This is the greatest day of his life," Thea said. "There's nothing Thomas Ross loves more than attention."

Willa smirked. Her lips were drenched in red, her dress daringly low cut, revealing her swanlike neck and well-defined clavicle. She reached into her purse and took out her silver cigarette case. She lit a cigarette, and the moment she did, Thea took it from her for a long drag.

"Why don't we dance, Thea?" Max asked. This was rare for him. He normally tried to avoid the dance floor, and every other bit of attention, as much as he could. "Consider it your birthday present."

Thea checked the time on her elegant, art deco–style wristwatch. It was almost midnight, which meant it was practically her twentieth birthday.

The band started up an old Cole Porter song. Thea took Max's outstretched hand.

Like her, Max had had years of ballroom lessons. He'd been her escort at her debut four years ago. And although he hated the spotlight, he was the best dancer she'd ever been paired with.

"Happy birthday, Thea," Max whispered in her ear, under the music of the band.

"Thank you," Thea whispered back.

From her vantage point, as Max whisked her across the floor, she watched her father make the rounds. He was nearing sixty now but still spry and bright—charming as ever. He was leaning over a table, talking to a couple.

"I should go. My father might need me," Thea said.

"He's a big boy." Max didn't stop moving. "He can handle himself."

"You're right," Thea said. But Tommy was waving her over, and what choice did she have?

~

Thea found it easy to hide at these parties. Attention was rarely on her, always on her father, and there was always some commotion that allowed her to rise from the table, slip from the ballroom, and step outside into the courtyard.

The night air was cool, and she could see the Hollywood sign in the distance.

"I've been looking for you." Thea turned to see Willa with the skirt of her dress balled in her hand, making it easier for her to move quietly.

Thea didn't pause. She closed the gap between them as quickly as she could and kissed Willa.

Hard.

Willa pressed her forehead against Thea's. "Happy birthday." Her voice was soft. From their spot in the courtyard, they could hear everything going on in the ballroom.

"Thank you," Thea said. She'd been looking forward to this all night. Just five minutes alone with Willa.

Willa fumbled with her purse and pulled out a flat box.

"You didn't have to get me anything," Thea said. She lifted the lid, revealing a bracelet with topaz stones linked together with yellow gold. Her birthstone. "It's beautiful."

"I *wanted* to do this," Willa said. She clipped the bracelet around Thea's outstretched wrist, on top of her black evening glove. "And I want to do this too." Willa leaned in and kissed her again. Their bodies were as close as they could be, with their voluminous skirts between them.

"Well, thank you," Thea said. Every time they kissed, she got a little lightheaded, the bubbly feeling of a little too much champagne mixed with Willa's intoxicating charm.

Willa pulled back, a mischievous glint in her eye. "And there's something I want to talk to you about. But later." Willa winked, blew her a kiss, and turned to go back into the ballroom. They had to get back to the party. Thea looked at the bracelet on her wrist.

This little rendezvous was what Thea had been looking forward to all night. They had to steal their moments together. It was always worth it to sneak away.

She waited two minutes, then returned to their table. Thea slipped back into her seat, Willa's kiss still hot on her lips. Her father was making the rounds, now with Ingrid next to him.

The attention was on her father. That was how Thea liked it.

CHAPTER 4

1954

The night, or early morning, ended the same way these parties always did: Thea and Willa in Willa's bed.

They couldn't spend time together at Thea's house, with two present parents. But Willa's house, with an absent mother and an unobservant father, was perfect.

They had left Jake at the party, and he was probably doing the same thing Thea and Willa were, albeit with an actress half his age.

They climbed into Willa's ridiculously large bed, pulling the velvet curtains around them and shutting out the world. They were tangled together: limbs, fluffy chiffon peignoirs, and not much else.

"I thought that would *never* end." Willa sighed.

"And now you want to talk?" Thea asked. They were so close together; Thea ran her middle finger over Willa's bare thigh. Willa smelled like sweet alcohol and perfume, an intoxicating combination.

"No, I don't," Willa said. "But I have something to ask you." She moved, Thea's hand outstretched as she did. Willa sat straight up, and Thea did too.

"This seems serious," Thea said.

"I'm a very serious girl—you know that." Willa's smile was bright; it lit up her heart-shaped face. She was so beautiful. Thea found it hard to look at her directly. Thea pushed her hair from her face. They sat in the center of the king-size bed, a breath away from each other. Willa's eyes found Thea's in the dim light. "We need to leave together."

"What?" Thea asked.

"You're what I want," Willa said. "We can't be together with my dad and your dad and Max and—"

"You're getting married," Thea said.

"Unless you give me a reason not to," Willa said. She looked at her engagement ring, a Prohibition-era baguette diamond surrounded by smaller diamonds. The ring had been Ingrid's and, thus, was an almost-family heirloom. "Unless you think there's something else we should do."

Thea had seen their relationship as a sexy little secret between the two. It wasn't supposed to last. "Is that how you see us?" Thea asked. They never talked about it. They didn't talk about much at all.

"How do you see us?" Willa asked. She pulled back, putting space between the two of them.

"Fun?" Thea asked. "I like having fun with you. I can't *leave* my life. You can't either." She was violently sober now—aware of every nerve in her body and the dark look crossing Willa's face.

"I love you," Willa said, quiet and confused. Thea got up from the bed, pushing the curtains back. "I want to be with you, and we can't do that here."

"What life would we have?" Thea asked. Maybe she wasn't brave enough. Willa was brave enough to do whatever she wanted. "Our parents would disown us. Max would never talk to us again. He's wild about you."

Willa exhaled. She watched Thea collect her things. "I don't love him," Willa said.

How could they be so out of sync? Thea stopped, her arms full of the black gown she had worn. It was deceptively heavy, hard to lift. "I just thought we were a little more than friends."

"Really?" Willa asked. She looked hurt, her perfect lips in a pout. This was not the conversation Thea had thought they'd be having. She didn't think they'd be talking much at all. She didn't like having hard conversations, and now Willa had blindsided her with her proposal.

"I thought you knew I didn't want anything serious," Thea said softly. She was still wearing the bracelet, and now she fumbled, trying to take it off. "This was really kind of you, but I shouldn't keep it."

Willa didn't look at her. Thea succeeded in releasing the clasp and placed the bracelet on the bed. "I'm going to take a guest room, and I'll leave in the morning," Thea said.

The guest room she chose was at the opposite end of the house, cold with little use. The sheets were stiff, and as Thea climbed in, she wondered if she had made the right decision.

She liked Willa. Willa understood her body and what Thea wanted better than anyone else. But it wasn't love. It was physical.

She wasn't going to upend her life because something *may* work out. She wasn't going to leave her mother and father to be one of Willa's whims. She closed her eyes, pressing her fingers to her lips, still burning with Willa's kiss.

Willa would see Thea had made the right choice.

She slept alone and left, driving home before Willa woke up.

~

Every meal in the Ross house was a *production*. Every Sunday, Sophie sat down with Ilsa, their cook and housekeeper, to build a truly decadent menu for each evening.

But this Sunday was special. It was Thea's twentieth birthday, and she faced a table full of her favorite foods.

Thea wore a bright-pink dress with a skirt so voluminous she needed two petticoats underneath, a boatneck, and a scoop back, finished with a rosette at the waist. Her outfit was Sophie's choice. Sophie chose everything for Thea—what she did and wore and ate.

Her parents were also dressed up, Tommy in a tux and Sophie in a powder blue strapless dress, as if this was a fancy night out rather than a dinner at home.

They also were hosting Sophie's family. Grandmother Osbourne, Aunt Natalia, Uncle Reginald. Thea's cousins: spoiled only son Gordon and twins Catherine and Caroline. Thea sat across from the Osbourne family, noting, for the millionth time, how Sophie's beautiful, cold looks fit in perfectly. Sophie, her mother, and her sister shared blond hair, big blue eyes, and a small nose. Even Reginald and his son had dark-blond hair and the same unreadable eyes.

Dinner with her mother's family never changed. Her mother and Aunt Natalia fussed over Grandmother Osbourne while Reginald and Tommy talked business and politics. Gordon didn't care enough to talk to his cousins, and the twins always had each other. They didn't have to pay attention to Thea.

Thea had always known that she had been adopted about a week after her birth. That her mother couldn't have children biologically. That her grandmother saw her adoption, and Sophie's inability to have children, as some sort of moral failing.

The last course was a four-tier cake. Ilsa brought it to the table, with two flickering candles, and placed it in front of Thea. The Ross family didn't do anything as undignified as sing when Thea closed her eyes and blew her candles out.

She did make a wish, even though she was too old for it now. It was the same wish she always made on pennies and fountains and shooting stars.

She wanted to know where she came from.

Then Ilsa took her cake back into the kitchen, and Sophie stood. Her mother was beautiful and intimidating. Sophie was the youngest of the Osbourne siblings, and her controlling, competitive spirit drove everything she did. "I have something for you," Sophie said. She disappeared into the kitchen and returned with a box, large and flat. Thea thought about the bracelet Willa had given her the night before.

"You didn't have to get me anything," Thea said.

"You're my daughter, and I will do what I please," Sophie said.

"Me too," Tommy said. He reached into the breast pocket of his suit jacket and brought out an envelope. "Don't open it now. Later." He kissed Thea on the cheek, and Sophie sat back down.

"Thank you," Thea said. Ilsa passed slices of cake on small pink dessert plates, Thea's favorites.

"You can open mine now," Sophie said. Thea did as she was told, opening the black velvet box.

Nestled inside was a necklace from another age. The delicate chain held a silver art deco star pendant with a single emerald in the center. It was beautiful. Next to her, Tommy had gone still. "I was saving this for your twenty-first, but I want you to have it now," Sophie said.

"That isn't one of ours," Natalia said. She was squinting; she probably needed glasses. Sophie's cool smile didn't budge as she eyed her sister. The Osbourne family didn't have any heirloom items. The Osbourne family was decidedly not rich.

"It's from Thomas's side," Sophie said. She always used his full name around her family. It was strange to Thea, and she'd been hearing it for twenty years.

"It's amazing," Thea said. She looked between her parents, who were having a silent conversation. They'd been together so long that they could speak volumes with a few facial expressions.

"What about ballet, Theodosia?" Grandmother Osbourne changed the subject.

"Going slowly, Grandmother," Thea said.

"She's in the running to be in a Coca-Cola campaign," Sophie added excitedly. Thea was the only one of her cousins with an actual job, a real career.

But in her grandmother's eyes, she was other.

She would never be a real Osbourne. Thea didn't want to be.

CHAPTER 5

1954

The day always began and ended with ballet. Thea did her first plié at age three, and by three and a half, she was in training to be the next great prima ballerina. Her parents inspired and expected greatness. Thea had spent every free minute in a leotard and tights, learning the ultimate control she needed to succeed.

At seventeen, she joined Ballet Los Angeles as the youngest corps de ballet member to date.

At nineteen, five months ago, her partner in a pas de deux, Dorian, a man she'd danced with since she joined, dropped her. A freak accident, but it fractured her left foot. She needed months of rehabilitation before she could return to her regular schedule.

She was still healing.

Which meant instead of doing five hours of company class and rehearsals in the afternoon, Thea was teaching until her doctor cleared her to return. It was hard watching her friends, her coworkers, her competitors move on. She hated being sidelined.

But she was making the most of it.

Thea got to the studio early. Her parents' silent conversation over dinner had turned into a screaming match the moment the Osbourne family had left. The Ross house was large, and Thea could still hear the barbs and bites traded by her parents from her private dance studio. Tommy had left early that morning, and Thea had followed, not wanting to end up in Sophie's crosshairs.

Thea turned the studio lights on, pulled the barres out into orderly lines. She wore a light-blue leotard to match the five-year-olds she taught and had made sure her hair was in a tight, neat bun. As a teacher and a company member, Thea knew these little girls looked up to and wanted to be her. She had to lead by example.

There was a knock on the studio door, and a man she didn't recognize entered wearing a tweed jacket. "Are you . . . Thea Ross?"

"Yes."

He cleared his throat. "I'm Julian. Jessica said my freshman acting class could join in your class today. I said I'd play the piano as a favor. I teach at Gershwin College."

Jessica, the studio secretary, hadn't informed her of this. Thea cleared her throat, turned away from him. "You want your students to take a ballet class meant for children?"

"I thought it would be funny," Julian said. He was handsome and looked to be around her father's age, brown hair with touches of gray at his temples. He had warm brown eyes, hidden behind circular glasses with tortoiseshell frames, and he held himself with grace and poise. "They need to learn movement, and this is the best way to do it. I can reschedule, if you like."

Rescheduling would put everyone out, and the one thing Thea liked least was putting anyone out. "They can come," she said.

He took off his jacket and rolled the sleeves to his elbows. "Thank you so much. I promised them extra credit, and they would hang, draw, and quarter me if I went back on that now."

She'd have to talk to Jessica about telling her these things.

"You look so familiar," he said.

"Everyone tells me that," Thea said. "I think I just have one of those faces? The type that everyone thinks they know."

Julian paced around the floor, looking equally as lost as she felt. "Maybe. But it's going to bug me until I figure it out. I haven't seen you in any films, have I?"

Thea wanted to ask why it mattered so much. She inhaled. "I'm a ballerina."

"Who are your parents?"

"Sophie and Tommy Ross."

"Tommy Ross?" Julian repeated.

Thea nodded.

He snapped in recognition. "You look exactly like Lorelei Davies."

~

"Who is Lorelei Davies?" Instead of going home after her final classes, Thea went to Uncle Harry's house.

Teaching had been easy. She'd liked having Julian at the piano. Her girls had loved the idea of having adults in the class who didn't know what they were doing and shined because they were showing off. Julian's students were awkward, reserved. Julian, from the piano, had reminded them to *relax* every five minutes.

Harry wasn't her uncle, not really. He was her father's best friend and the one link Tommy kept to his life before Thea, the life he never talked about. Harry was sort of a second father to Thea. He attended all her recitals, all her shows. When she was younger, he'd watched her when her parents went on trips.

Thea found Harry sitting at the kitchen table, a large bouquet of roses in front of him. He had a talent for plants. He had a greenhouse out back and tended to roses and zinnias and irises and hydrangeas and sunflowers. His award-winning roses were beautiful, big and red. He brought her a Coke, and Thea sat across from him. She had had a long day of teaching classes. Not being able to do the thing she loved but being so close to it was making her cranky.

"Why do you ask?" Harry asked.

"An acting teacher brought his students to one of my classes. He said I looked like her," Thea said. "Julian something?"

"John Weston?" Harry stopped messing with the flowers in front of him. His brown eyes met Thea's, and there was a frown on his face.

"Maybe." Thea realized that Julian hadn't mentioned his last name. Or, for that matter, his middle one.

Harry's eyes narrowed. "Lorelei Davies was an actress who worked with your father."

"What happened to her?" Thea asked. "Julian looked like he'd seen a ghost when he saw me."

Harry looked back down to his roses, avoiding answering her question. He was indulgent with Thea; she was the child that he'd never had. "She died. She died a long time ago. She killed herself. She and Julian were close." He stopped fussing with the roses, leaning back in his seat. He wasn't telling her something. She knew it.

"Did you know her?" Thea asked.

Harry lit a cigarette, taking his time before he answered her. Thea stared at her half-full bottle and waited. "I didn't know her well," Harry said. "We weren't friends or anything."

"Do you think I look like her?" Thea asked. She had so many questions, and she hoped that Harry would patiently answer every one of them.

"I have something for you," Harry said as he stood up from the table. "For your birthday."

Her birthday felt like ages ago, even though it was yesterday. "You didn't have to get me anything," Thea said. "If you do want to do something, you can answer my questions." Harry sat back down at the table, handing her a small wrapped box. She took it from him.

"Why was Julian John Weston in your class?" Harry asked.

"Ballet is good for movement in acting," Thea said with a nod. Her usual pianist, a man named Boris, was quiet, invisible. Julian had enthusiastically helped her instruct. Harry pushed the glass vase into the center of the table. "Do I look like her?" Thea asked again. "Lorelei Davies?"

"A little," Harry said. "I never thought of it until now."

"But she killed herself?" Thea didn't care about the present in front of her. Sophie would tell her it was rude to not open it immediately.

Harry's face was unreadable, quiet, and still. "That's the story."

Thea pulled her knees to her chest. She wasn't sure what else to ask. "How come I've never heard of her?"

"Not all of them make it," Harry said. Harry had worked with her dad at Sunset Studios, but he never talked about what, exactly, he did. Whenever Thea had asked, he always changed the subject. All Thea knew was that he wasn't an actor like her father. "All of them try. All of them want to," Harry said. "Not all of them do."

CHAPTER 6

1934

Every Wednesday, Kenneth and I have a standing appointment. We meet after everything else has finished for the day, so sometimes it edges into Thursday.

It's early enough tonight that his secretary is still sitting at her desk, reading a magazine and painting her nails. "Is he in?" I ask.

Eva doesn't look up. "He just got in. You look lovely today." I know I do not, but I also know that Kenneth has instructed Eva to compliment all of us in the same way. At our core, we're all just hungry little girls, looking for attention. "Can I go in?" I ask.

"Of course," Eva says. I push the heavy door open. My hands shake as I do, even though our standing Wednesday appointment has been routine since I was signed to Sunset.

"Lorelei." Kenneth doesn't look up either. "Please, take a seat." I do as he says, sitting on his sofa, girlish and demure.

When Kenneth settles down next to me, I try not to look at him. He pushes a stray hair from my face. Then he kisses me, hard and unrelenting.

I let him paw at my blouse, unbuttoning it and letting it fall to the floor. The skirt and bra and slip are next.

The garter belt and nylons stay on, panties pulled down as far as they can go, just how he likes it. I know way too much about Kenneth Webster's sexual preferences.

As a lover, Kenneth is selfish and concerned with himself. He bats at my body, as if he might hit a magic button that will make me explode in shivers of ecstasy. When he fails to find it, I fake it. Well, I'm an actress.

After he's satisfied himself, Kenneth falls asleep, an arm still over my stomach. There's barely enough room for two on this couch. My stomach growls, and I remember that I've not eaten today. His ejaculation cools on my thigh, a hole ripped in my nylons. And they were a brand-new pair.

Once he starts snoring, I pull out from under him, and I use his tie, discarded in the lukewarm throes of something far less than passion, to wipe my thigh. After dropping the tie to the floor, I put my clothes back on and make my way to his desk. He has a view of the main street that runs through the studio grounds. It's quiet now; only a couple of films are shooting at night. I don't sit at his chair, but I lean over the desktop.

He has scripts and proposals scattered all over the place. He's never been very organized.

On top is a proposal for *The Taming of the Shrew*. I flick through the first few pages.

This would be Sunset's first straight film: no musical numbers, no tap-dancing, no singing.

And I cannot believe how much I want it.

CHAPTER 7

1934

I don't get to go home as much as I would like. Once a month, or twice, I try to take the train to see my family.

I dress down, in a shapeless dress, my hair curled to the nape of my neck. I read script pages or look out the window on the train, feeling guilty whenever a Black passenger or porter passes me. I have to lie to be who I am. They don't, and they're free. The train ride isn't long, and the moment I'm back in Watts, I become her again. I remove my hat, my gloves, feeling the cool breeze run through my hair.

When I turn down the block, I see my youngest sister, Phyllis, sitting on the steps. She's turning sixteen, wearing a housedress that I think was once mine, a black unflattering thing. She looks up when she sees me. Her hair is in tight braids to manage her curls, and her smile lights her face up. "MILLIE!" She shouts it, and soon, my whole family crowds onto the porch to greet me.

My mother hugs me first. "Millie, you haven't been eating." She tuts. I haven't been, and she knows it. I hug my father, my brothers—Walter, Ralph, and Calvin—and Phyllis last. It would be perfect, but someone is always missing.

It's the same house we've always lived in, bursting at the seams. Walt, Ralph, and I have moved out, which means Calvin and Phyllis get rooms to themselves, the luxury. I'm just in time for dinner. I sit at the table next to my mother. I look around at my family. I've always stood out, five shades lighter than everyone else. I inherited no traits from my parents, everything passed down to me from earlier generations.

My siblings share my parents' dark skin with sunny gold undertones. Their dark eyes that glow in the sun. And now, with the slight red tinge to my hair, still pulled to the nape of my neck, the higher quality of my clothes, even the sack I'm currently wearing, I feel out of place. I give them as much money as I can every month, and it never feels like enough.

"Millie," Walt says. He's the second oldest, right before me. He's very good at telling if something is wrong with me, but I never talk about my work at home.

And I never talk about my home at work.

It works out rather well.

"How are you, Phyllis?" I ask to turn the conversation away from myself. I love my family, but I don't want Walt trying to dig into my life. They all know the bare minimum of what they need to know. They know that Kenneth found me singing in a nightclub, that the changes to my hair and name are necessary for my new life.

They do not know what I do with Kenneth every Wednesday, the caveat to keep it all. They do not need to know.

"I'm great," Phyllis says. "I think I'm going to start working at the dressmaker's." She's a talented seamstress. She's changed for dinner, and I know the dress she's wearing, one obviously made from a feed sack with an abstract print, is one she made. We have an age-old sewing machine upstairs, and she's been attached to it since she was old enough to use it.

"I'm proud of you," I say.

"I want to see your next film. I must see it," Phyllis says.

Everyone is more reserved at family dinners than they used to be. Everyone but Phyllis, who still yaps away. I feel the disconnect. I'm too white for my family now.

After dinner, after Phyllis and I wash the dishes and clear the table, Momma says, "Let's talk."

We sit on the porch, watching the sun set. I can hear the general family noises. Phyllis is in the kitchen, cleaning up, and Ralph and my father are talking inside.

"Momma," I say. I need to catch the train back home soon. I'm not ready to go yet.

"You don't look well." She's never been one to hold back. She always says exactly what she's thinking. May Dawson knows all, sees all.

"I haven't been sleeping well," I say.

"Not eating, not sleeping. What are you doing?" my mother asks.

Dancing. Fucking Tommy. Taking a lot of pills. None of those things are the right thing to say. I look up at the sky. I think about my train ride home.

"I'm okay, Momma," I say. I don't know if she believes me. It's impossible not to want to cry when I'm sitting with my mother. Every so often a neighbor waves in passing. Mother always waves back. I don't know if anyone recognizes me—or if I want them to.

"You know I worry about you," Momma says. "After Joanna."

She's the subject we rarely discuss. Even though there are no photographs of her in the house—not that there are many photographs of us Dawsons anyway—her presence hangs over us like a shroud. She was the oldest of us, born before Walt and me. I think about her all the time. I miss her all the time.

"I know, but I'm not Joanna." I tilt my head back, closing my eyes.

We sit in silence against the setting sun. No one in my family has ever been much for talking, except for Phyllis. Through the open kitchen window, I can hear her singing, almost perfectly, a song from *Mrs. Donahue*.

"You don't let her see my films, do you?" I ask.

Momma scoffs. "No one tells that girl what to do."

"Still, Momma. I don't want her to see me like that." My mother bites her tongue. From inside the house, Walt joins in, playing the piano for Phyllis. "The piano needs a tune."

"Tell Walt that," Momma says.

I bite back a laugh and lean into my mother. She smells like home. Her calloused hands run over my arms. I close my eyes. The problem with coming back is that I never want to leave. A part of me wants to climb upstairs, crawl into Phyllis's bed, and pull the covers over my head. A part of me wants to become Millicent Dawson again, even though that would mean once again singing in clubs at night and waitressing during the day.

I don't know what I want anymore.

"I miss you," I say. "I need to try to get back more."

"Your money sent Phyllis to school so she could really learn to sew. I know we never talk about it, but we're grateful." I exhale. They are the reason I became Lorelei Davies.

Every move I make, every decision, is driven by them. I want Phyllis to have a better world than Joanna and me.

I never wanted to be an actress. Never gave it a second thought. I loved singing. Loved performing at Cloud Nine. Acting isn't easy. It's not even a particularly enjoyable job. I'm constantly poked and prodded and yelled at. I'm stared at, watched. But it pays well, better than anything else I could do. And it means I can help my family, so it's worth everything.

Home is the only place where my thoughts calm, where I can breathe.

Home is the only place where no one is out to get me.

~

Driving to Watts would be faster, certainly, but I've always liked taking the train. It's one of the only times I get to be no one. It's always quiet this time of night. Tonight, I'm sitting alone, my head against the glass. I'm thinking about Phyllis, about Joanna. I'm loaded with food that Momma insisted I take because she thinks I'm too thin.

I won't eat it, but I'll say I did.

I'm trying to ignore the group of men sitting across from me. I'm focused on my pages for the next week. It feels like we've been filming *Live, Love* for ages, and it's been three months. We still have a month to go. It's the homestretch. I know that. And I can't wait for it to be over. Every so often, one of the men looks over, and they whisper. The hairs on my arms rise, and I turn myself farther away from them.

I close my eyes. The movement of the train threatens to lull me to sleep. I need to stay awake. I think about taking an awake pill, but then I'll be too awake.

It's all about balance, really.

When I think none of them are looking, I take a peek. They're young and randy, maybe a little older than me, and they're passing around a flask. They look like college boys, but I can't be sure. They're wearing identical navy suits, and one, a redhead in an aisle seat close to me, laughs loudly. They're drinking too much. I pull my gaze away, just as the redhead and I make eye contact.

I swallow hard, lamenting my choice to leave my journal at home. Without it, I'm unsure of what to do with my hands. I can't focus on my script pages. All I can think about is those four men just a few yards away from me. My heart thrums in my chest. I squeeze my fingers, then flex, trying to maintain feeling. I look around, noting the plush red velvet curtains that cover the windows, the seat I'm sitting on. I concentrate on breathing, in and out, holding myself together.

"Hey!" The redhead speaks. "Hey, you look familiar." I close my eyes, feeling tears start to prick.

"I don't know what you mean," I said.

"D'you want a drink?" He's bold. Other girls may like that. Or, of course, they may hate it. He reaches over and shakes the flask in my peripheral vision. I hold my breath, hoping that he'll lose interest and turn back to his friends. He slips into the seat across from me, still holding the flask. "C'mon. Me and my friends are gonna go dancing. You should come with us."

"I can't." I can barely summon the words from my throat. He has piercing green eyes, full lips, and a weak chin. "I'm going home."

"You can go home after the Trocadero," he says. He leans forward, his eyes finding mine. "We could use a pretty girl with us."

"I can't." He won't take no for an answer, too used to getting whatever he wants. I pull away from him.

"Come on, sweetheart. We can pretend you're . . ." He trails off, getting a good look at my face. "Lorelei Davies." His smile widens, filling his whole face. "Boys! We've got a film star here."

"I'm not who you think I am." My words are low and shallow.

"Lorelei Davies."

Ramona would lap this attention up; she'd go to the Trocadero with them.

But I can't move.

"Where are you coming from, Lorelei Davies?" The five syllables of the name seem foreign to my ears. I'm watching the entire exchange from out of my body. I see myself, surrounded by four men I don't know, all insisting I'm the woman they think I am. Even when I try to be invisible, people still spot me.

I wish Tommy was with me. He'd defuse the situation with his casual, easy charm.

But it's just me. I just have myself. I have to depend on myself.

I want to tell them all to leave me alone. The words stick on my tongue. I can't do it; I can't think of one thing to say to these men to get them to leave me alone.

So I turn her on. I smile, lean forward. "It's so wonderful to meet you all," I say. Lorelei emerges before I really know what's happening.

The redhead relaxes, his gaze and posture secure in knowing he's right. "Miss Davies, we're big fans."

"Thank you, ever so," I say. I'm shaking; I move my hands between my knees. They surround me until the train stops, and then they leave me alone.

Once I'm at home, safe in my bed, I start to cry.

CHAPTER 8

1934

Knowing I'm an outlier and seeing it are two different things.

This party, which is supposed to be a fundraiser but is just an excuse for every high-profile Sunset employee to dress up and drink, has been going on for two hours.

I've spent every minute of those two hours against the wall of the hotel ballroom, watching couples take turns around the dance floor. After spending all day dancing, I can't fathom doing it for fun. People's eyes are on me; I can feel them staring.

I know studio politics are important, especially here and now. No one trusts me, because they don't know me. Across the ballroom, I can see Ramona Penderghast, in a navy blue dress, holding court and letting bit players fawn over her.

That should be me.

I've been nursing the same drink since I entered, trying not to get drunk. I watch Tommy and his beautiful wife making the rounds. Sophie Ross sparkles. She's dressed in white; her hair is ice blond, and she's tall, perfectly matching Tommy's height.

Tommy and I lock eyes across the room. I drop my glass, feeling the delicate champagne flute slip from my fingers.

I almost curse but don't. Attendants in black and white hurry me away and sweep the glass up. I'm practically whisked right into

Kenneth's arms, no agency of my own. I know he's been looking for me, and I was doing a great job hiding from him until I broke that glass. Another faux pas.

Kenneth looks good, considering he spent most of today yelling at Tommy and me.

"You're needed," Kenneth says. His voice rings in my ear. "Sing something." It's not lost on me that I was the only star volunteered to work this evening. I climb the steps to the stage. The lights blind me, and I realize the demure black dress I chose for the evening wasn't the right choice. I scan the crowd, filled not just with Sunset players but also with photographers and writers and people who have sneaked in to try to be one of us.

I clear my throat as the opening tones of "Let's Misbehave" starts.

I love this song. I try to find Tommy in the crowd as I sing it, feeling myself fall into place as I do. It's a song I sang almost every night when I was still a club girl, and it feels like it's a part of me. I know I don't belong here, but I am going to make them want me.

When I finish, they applaud and call out for another. I look toward the bandleader, the only other Black person at this party and a man I know well. He nods. We've worked so closely together that he knows the song I'm about to launch into.

I lock eyes with Kenneth, and he raises an eyebrow.

Two songs later, I'm relieved when Ramona comes and whisks me from the stage. "Lorelei! You were magnificent. Come, come." She loops her arm through mine, half leading, half dragging. I pass Tommy, sans Sophie, and I almost reach out to him.

"Excuse me," I say, pulling away from her. One more moment in this hot, overcrowded ballroom, and I will scream.

I turn and exit as fast as I can.

~

The night air is dewy on my skin. It's warm, and I'm grateful to be alone on the grounds. I can hear the band playing, and it seems a million miles away. The city lights dance below me, and I can see the Hollywoodland sign beckoning all toward it. I blink, trying to remember who I was before Lorelei Davies.

I exhale, trying to put myself back together. I didn't think Tommy would bring his wife, and I feel foolish for pining after the man.

I know I've passed Kenneth's little test. Tomorrow will be another mountain to climb, doing the tap number over and over again. When I ultimately fail, I'll have to log more practice hours.

"Lorelei." I know it's Tommy without turning around. I know his voice, and I know that he's alone.

"Can you please go back inside? Isn't your wife waiting for you?" The words are bitter on my tongue. In the myriad rules we have for our affair, not mentioning his wife is number one. Not sleeping over is number two. Not falling in love is number three.

The others are so we feel less tawdry about having an affair.

"She left. She's not feeling well." I hear the click of his lighter, feel him step up toward me. I haven't gotten a good look at him all night. I know he's wearing a navy suit, his hair slicked back. Up close I can see he shaved, and his sharp jaw is perfectly smooth.

Earlier, during filming, I spent all day placing a perfect red lip print in the middle of his left cheek.

Marking him as mine.

He looks around—careful, surreptitious—and kisses my cheek. With a cigarette between his lips, he pulls me into an embrace. I can smell his cologne: French, expensive, and intoxicating. I haven't had another drink, and I'm glad to have my wits about me. "What are you doing?" I can't bring myself to talk louder than a whisper. He guides me in a semiwaltz, something in time to the music, and I close my eyes, letting myself revel in being in his arms.

He kisses me, and my knees go weak. I'm grateful that he's holding me, or I would have fallen to the ground.

"We can't do this," I say against his lips.

"We can do whatever we want." His rebuttal is always the same. I'm too distracted to argue. We know that he can do whatever he wants.

He spins me, a hand at the small of my back to guide me. I don't mean to sound clichéd, but it does really feel like it's just him and me, dancing under the moonlight. Every touch radiates electricity through me.

I was supposed to end it today. I was supposed to say that we could not, should not, do this anymore.

In the indigo night, his dark-brown eyes gleam, and I have to wonder if I'm mistaking something, ambition maybe, for lust.

I look back toward the party. It's so crowded, we could sneak away and not be missed.

Ramona is watching us. She's in front of the big double doors, backlit from the party. She's holding a champagne flute in her hand, and she's smiling.

CHAPTER 9

1954

Every morning, Sophie woke Thea at five thirty. Thea went through the motions of stretching, warming her body for the job that she wasn't currently doing. Her mother sat and watched her as she stretched.

Then they had breakfast and discussed Thea's plan for the day.

Thea sat at the table, taking a sip from her water glass. Breakfast usually meant coffee and water. Neither Ross woman ate that much in the morning. "You have a photo shoot today," Sophie said. Her father ran a movie studio, but managing Thea's career was Sophie's career. This morning, in a tailored shirtdress with pink stripes and a full skirt, Sophie looked positively dewy. Thea envied her. Her mother was always perfect, neatly dressed, and well put together. Next to her, Thea always felt messy.

"Do I have to?" Thea asked. She hadn't had much free time since she was six. Every moment of her life was devoted to the art of ballet. Sophie had added modeling when Thea turned thirteen, another avenue for stardom. Thea had drawn the line at acting, and her father agreed. Thea wanted to be a ballerina.

"Thea, stop." Sophie's eyes locked on Thea. Thea loved her mother, but sometimes, she wished she could have a break. "You have a doctor's appointment too. He's supposed to clear you for dancing."

"What's the photo shoot for?"

"Mascara," Sophie said.

That was the last thing she wanted to do. "I'm going to Constellation later too," Thea said.

"No," Sophie said.

"I'm teaching; then I'm having dinner with Dad at his office," Thea said. Thea had been spending time at Constellation Pictures since she was a child. She would sit with Tommy in his office, take dictation during meetings. When she was a kid, Tommy's secretary, Lauren, would sit Thea at the desk, and they'd take phone calls together. She had loved it.

"Whenever you go, you have some greasy, heavy takeout, and then you get mad that you gained weight," Sophie said. "No."

"You never let me have any fun," Thea said. She knew she was dangerously close to sounding like a petulant child.

"Thea, I'll see you later," Tommy said, making both Ross women turn. He strode into the dining room, adjusting the cuffs of his sleeves. His tie was loose around his neck.

"I thought you were staying home today," Sophie said coolly. Tommy and Sophie didn't look at each other. Their argument from Thea's birthday was still simmering, a slow boil. Tommy always burned slowly, and Sophie was quick to anger. Their fights lasted for days. It had been a week now, and they were still snapping at each other, full-out yelling when they thought Thea couldn't hear.

Sophie often tried to use Thea as a pawn to get what she wanted. In this case, Thea didn't know what her mother's aim was.

"Why would I stay home?" Tommy asked. Sophie didn't answer him. She sipped from her coffee cup instead. "Thea and I are having dinner tonight. Ilsa will have to make dinner for one," Tommy said.

"Unless you wanted to join us, Mom?" Thea asked.

"Please," Sophie said with a roll of her eyes.

"I have a vote today, and I need to make sure Jake knows what I'm thinking," Tommy said. He leaned over Thea's shoulder, picking up a slice of toast. Thea never thought that Tommy liked Jake, and vice versa, despite being business partners. They both got along with Ingrid, who managed to keep the peace between the two men. But if Jake wanted something, then Tommy would want the opposite.

"Dad," Thea said. He kissed Sophie and then Thea.

"I'll see you tonight for dinner, Thea," Tommy said. There was no convincing him to do anything he didn't want to do. Sophie and Tommy were alike in that way.

"Of course, Dad," Thea said. "Love you."

Tommy stopped, kissing her forehead again. "I love you too."

~

When Thea reached her dance studio, Julian was waiting for her. He was grinning, carrying a stack of old magazines.

Thea was in a foul mood. She was still wearing globs of mascara from the photo shoot, her eyes itched, and the doctor hadn't cleared her for dancing. Three more weeks, and they'd reassess.

"My students hated it," Julian said as Thea turned the studio lights on. He began to pull the barres out, placing them in lines. "I tried to explain, again, how movement will help them in acting, but they didn't believe me. So I said anyone who came again today didn't have to take my final."

"What is it?" Thea asked. She liked him. There was something soothing about him; something about his general demeanor made her feel relaxed. That was nice. Thea wasn't sure she'd ever felt relaxed in her life. Her thoughts were constant; she was always thinking of the worst thing that could possibly happen, the worst situation, the worst outcome.

"I make them do a monologue," Julian said.

"You were an actor? Do you know my dad?" Thea asked.

Julian's smile was almost invisible. "We're old enemies." He paused for a moment, his dark eyes on Thea's face. She wanted to ask what he meant, but he continued. "I wanted to show you these."

He sat down on the wood floor, and Thea sat across from him. He passed her the stack of magazines. A 1934 issue of *Life* was on top, featuring a photo of a woman she'd never seen before.

The woman was smiling, her face lit up. She wore a simple floral dress. Her hair was pushed over one shoulder, and she was lounging on a couch. Thea looked closer. LORELEI DAVIES AT HOME. Thea flipped the magazine open, trying to find the interview.

"Lorelei Davies was a friend of mine," Julian said. "My best friend." Thea flipped to a headshot of the woman and inspected it, trying to find the similarity that Julian said they shared.

"I've never heard of her," Thea said.

"She used to be the brightest rising star in Hollywood." Julian was silent for a moment, his eyes on the photograph. "She died that year."

"I was born in 1934," Thea said. She ran her eyes over the black-and-white portrait. Big eyes looking over her shoulder, her nose long and straight, her chin raised. Her softly curled hair fell over her shoulder, and she seemed to gaze right at Thea, as if she knew all her secrets. This woman, Lorelei Davies.

"What happened to her?" Thea asked.

"They said she killed herself," Julian said. "Overdosed in her bed."

"You don't believe it?"

"Never did." Julian raised an eyebrow. He took the magazine from her. "She would never take her own life. I knew her better than I knew myself, most days."

"Why do people say that?" Thea asked. Her voice stuck in her throat.

Julian laughed, although nothing was funny. A sharp exhale from his nose. "Everyone thought she was crazy."

"Was she?" Thea asked.

Julian's eyes remained on the photograph. The whole stack of magazines had articles about Lorelei Davies. Thea flipped through them all. LORELEI DAVIES AND HER DAILY ROUTINE; LORELEI DAVIES ON THE SILVER SCREEN; LORELEI DAVIES AND THOMAS ROSS, TOGETHER AGAIN.

That last one made her stop. It featured a photo of her father and Lorelei Davies, in the middle of a waltz step. She wore a long dress, her hair in a braided crown on top of her head. She was in her father's arms, looking up at him. From this angle, Thea could see Lorelei had a small dimple in her cheek. "Can I keep these? Just to look at."

"I have multiple copies," Julian said. "They're yours."

"Thank you," Thea said.

"I hope you'll see why you remind me of her," Julian said. Thea doubted it, but she hoped so too.

CHAPTER 10

1954

The call came halfway through Thea's class.

They hadn't moved from the barre when Jessica knocked. Julian was at the piano, playing them through the exercises. Thea was pacing through the class, giving corrections as needed. Julian's students seemed to adjust well, no matter how much he swore they had hated it before.

"Don't forget your turnout," Thea said to one of Julian's students. She stopped for a moment, watching him do a grand plié. "Try one more time." The rest of the class giggled. Her little girls were loving it, watching older students get more corrections than them.

The spell was broken when Jessica poked her head into the studio, saying she'd watch the class while Thea took the call. It was her mother on the phone, calling her to tell her to come to the film studio and refusing to elaborate further.

Thea left class and drove to Constellation Pictures. She did so with her heart in her throat, gripping the steering wheel tightly, worried she'd lose control.

Sophie was waiting for her just outside the building that housed the offices of her father, Ingrid, and Jake. Police cars crowded the parking lot, their blue and red lights shining. Ingrid was talking to a man in a suit, and Jake stood with her mother. Thea got out of her car. She was still dressed for ballet, Julian's suit jacket over her shoulders.

Sophie crossed over to her and hugged her as tightly as possible. Thea hadn't had a hug from her mother like this in years. Sophie was crying, sobbing. Thea felt her mother's body shake against hers.

"Mom? Mom?" Thea asked. "Mommy?"

"Thea." Sophie pulled away, holding her at an arm's length to look her in the eye. "Your father died. They're saying it's suicide."

Thea's knees gave way, and Sophie supported her when she fell. They both sat on the curb, mother and daughter together.

"Oh, sweetheart," Sophie said. Jake turned to talk to a detective.

"Suicide?" Thea asked, watching herself from above.

"He left a note . . . confessing to the murder of Lorelei Davies." That name again, ringing in the back of Thea's head like a gong. She thought about the picture of Tommy and Lorelei Davies she had *just* seen.

Had Tommy killed her?

"Thea," Ingrid said. Thea had always adored Ingrid. "I am so sorry, sweetie. I know how hard this is." When Thea was sixteen and Willa and Max were seventeen, Ingrid's husband had died in a car accident. It was the only funeral Thea had ever been to. She remembered hovering behind Max, devastated that he'd lost his father, wanting to do anything to feel useful.

"He was fine," Thea said. It was the one thing she couldn't get over. She had seen him that morning.

"Sophie, the detective wants to talk to you again," Ingrid said softly. "I'll stay with Thea." Ingrid pulled Thea to her, rubbing her arms. "Sweetheart, I'm so sorry. They found him with chloroform." Ingrid pulled Thea in close, Thea not caring that her makeup was going to smear on the front of Ingrid's white blouse. "It's the strangest thing," Ingrid said, almost to herself. "Same day Lorelei Davies died."

"We were going to have dinner," Thea said.

"I know, honey," Ingrid said and held Thea gently as she finally started to cry.

~

Tommy Ross didn't have a real funeral. Sophie insisted that he would have wanted to be cremated, have his ashes spread over the ocean, so they held a celebration of life instead. Their little ranch house overflowed with people. Most of the visitors were people who wanted to look, see, and snoop. They weren't actual friends and family. Tommy had one brother, whom Thea had last seen seven years ago. Her Ross grandparents were dead. Harry was there, and maybe he was her father's only friend.

Thea hated it. From the moment she greeted the first guest, in a black dress that itched, with her hair wound in a bun so tight it gave her a headache, Thea was uncomfortable. Mourners swept in from everywhere, descending on the house like a rainstorm.

Sophie was at the center of it, wearing a slim black dress. She made grief seem beautiful. Sophie shook hands, talked to people, thanked them for coming.

Meanwhile, Thea sat on the landing of the stairs, watching everything happen, unwilling to move.

"Thea," Willa said. She, too, was dressed in black and holding a plate. Max followed with two glasses.

He looked grim. Thea couldn't imagine what he was feeling right now.

Willa placed the plate on Thea's lap. "You need to eat."

"Water first, then the wine," Max added, handing her one of the glasses.

Thea wondered if she looked terrible. She'd been up all night, intermittently crying and staring at the wall.

That morning, she had pressed a cloth to her face to reduce the puffiness under her eyes, then gone through her entire routine—ballet warm-up, bathing, dressing, hair and makeup—just for some sense of normalcy. She took a sip of the water, closing her eyes as she swallowed.

"I'm so sorry," Max said. He awkwardly put a hand on her shoulder, something Thea thought was supposed to be comforting.

Thea didn't let her eyes leave her mother. She watched as Sophie circled around the room, her face stony and beautiful.

"Thea, please say something." Willa had settled next to her, leaning on her shoulder.

"I'm exhausted." It felt like she had run a marathon since Tommy's death. It had barely been a week, and she didn't know how she had coped. She'd taken some time away from teaching to be with her mother. But, in reality, Thea mostly lay on the couch, staring at the television, absorbing nothing while the shows played.

"We should get you to bed." Willa took the glass of wine from Max.

Thea shook her head. "I need to be here for my mother." Sophie was currently talking to Ingrid. "She hasn't slept. She hasn't eaten. She's going to collapse any second now."

Max exhaled. He was good in these types of situations, calm and steady. "I'll watch out for Sophie, and Willa will take you to bed."

Before Thea had time to demur or acquiesce, she wasn't sure which, a yell broke out through the mourners. "How dare you come here? You're the one person not welcome in this house. Not now, not ever." It was Sophie. Upsetting the plate in her lap, Thea was on her feet and at her mother's side in an instant.

And she was surprised to see that her mother's fury was aimed at Julian.

"Sophie, please." He looked slightly shell shocked. The mood in the room had changed. Everyone had taken a step back from Sophie, afraid that she'd turn her anger on them next.

"Mom." Thea put a hand on her mother's arm. "This isn't the time or place. Just let him—"

"Do you know who this is?" Sophie asked. Her eyes didn't leave Julian's face.

"We've met. Mother, just drink this." Thea tried to press the water glass into her mother's hand. Instead, it fell to the floor.

"Your father hated this man. He does not get to come here. Get out."

Julian took a step back. Sophie turned, her cheeks flushed with anger. "All of you," she snapped. "Out. And never talk to my daughter again."

With that, Sophie spun away and headed toward her bedroom.

All eyes went to Thea. She looked around. "Thank you for coming, everyone. The celebration is over."

CHAPTER 11

1934

In the days following the party, I do my best to avoid Ramona. And it works until I get off set, having finally completed the tap number to Kenneth's exacting standards, and I'm still sure the scene will be cut.

An extra named Richard helps me off set, and Ramona takes over. She's not in this scene, but I knew she was watching.

"I don't need your help," I say. It's not true. It hurts just to stand. I've been dancing for several hours straight, and I'm sure my feet are bleeding.

I'm grateful to have the rest of the day off. I'm getting bored. *Live, Love* is my sixth Sunset movie. I'm glad to get a regular paycheck, but I want more interesting roles. If I have to be an actress, I want to be more than the love interest.

That's never who I wanted to be.

It's not who I want to portray.

Ramona guides me to my dressing room. We sit across from each other on the couch. She is beautiful. Her hair is black; her eyes are a brilliant green, in an oval face with a pert little mouth. She's long and lithe, but I know it took time and money to make Rachel Smith into Ramona Penderghast. The same time and money that made Millicent Dawson into Lorelei Davies. Ramona exercises constantly, trying to maintain her perfect hourglass figure.

I just don't eat.

Work smarter, not harder.

She reclines on my couch, as if this is her dressing room. "I'll just cut to the chase. I know you know I saw you and Tommy at the party."

"Dancing. We were dancing," I say. I can feel my heart in my throat. The possibility of our perfect little world crashing down because of *Ramona Penderghast* is too much to bear.

"And kissing." She talks to me like I'm a child. Like I don't know what Tommy and I were doing. I want to smack her as hard as I can.

"You must have been seeing things. Tommy and I are costars. Everything is aboveboard." The lie is sour on my tongue. But I am going to deny everything.

"You're a shit actress," Ramona says, with her lips curled into a sneer. "I know what I saw. And now you're going to make sure I don't accidentally tell Sophie."

I snort. It's unladylike. "Are you trying to blackmail me?"

"I am blackmailing you."

If she were half this good in front of a camera, she wouldn't have to resort to a clumsy blackmail attempt to get what I have. "You're just jealous of me. It'll pass," I say. "Now, if you could go, I would like to take a nap."

Ramona stands. Her eyebrows are perfectly arched, her eyes glimmering with barely concealed anger. "Just you watch, Millicent Dawson. I will destroy you." With that, she flounces from my dressing room.

Every time she uses my real name, I'm stabbed with regret. I should never have told her my whole life story.

I thought I could trust her.

I sit on the couch in my dressing room. I press my head to my hands, willing the room to stop spinning. Everything around me shifts. I'm fighting so hard to stay where I am, where I think I want to be.

What I know about Ramona is that she's smart. She's dedicated. Anyone who gets up at three in the morning, devotes herself to her exercise and diet regime, and then comes to the studio every morning determined to be the greatest star in the world is committed.

But I'm smarter. I do things she would never imagine.

CHAPTER 12

1934

When I arrive at Cloud Nine, after a long week of filming, I'm grateful to find it busy. That means that no one will pay attention to me.

I can see Tommy, sitting with Julian John Weston and two other men from Sunset. They're deep in conversation, intermittently trying to flirt with the woman on stage, who is doing her best to ignore them. Julian is seated farthest from Tommy, his body leaning away, as if Tommy has something he could catch. They do hate each other, and it's not just Cheryl Lawrence at *The Courier* saying so.

Julian and Tommy spend time together for publicity's sake. They fundamentally do not get along. Tommy sees acting as more serious than Julian does. Julian makes everything he does seem so easy. Tommy hates that too. Nothing Tommy does is that effortless. Julian finds Tommy lazy and spoiled. Julian thinks Tommy is simply a good haircut: untalented and pretentious.

I stop to get a drink first. The kid behind the bar has been there since I started at the club. Johnny looks up and says, "Millie." He never calls me Lorelei, like he can't get used to the idea of me having a new name.

"Johnnycakes," I say, allowing him to kiss me on the cheek. "How is everything?"

"You know." He doesn't stop moving, starting to mix me a sidecar.

"How's Ma?"

Johnny's only a couple of years younger than me, and I think of him as a little brother. I've been able to occasionally help his family out while he completed high school. "Asking when you're coming to dinner next."

"I'll have to check my calendar, but I wanna see Ma!" I grin.

Johnny returns my smile. "She wants to see you too." He hands me my glass, and I take a seat at the back, trying to remain invisible.

This is where it began.

I was that singer, on stage, providing the backing track to conversations. Cloud Nine is close enough to Sunset and Paramount and Twentieth Century for it to be a haunt for major film people. I look around now and, aside from Tommy and Julian, see execs from all the studios.

The night Kenneth discovered me, I was wearing a red dress. I'd saved up almost a month's wages to buy it. When I put it on, I felt magical. Kenneth sat at the front center table with other Sunset men, but his eyes never left me.

When I went on break, he followed me into the break room. He wasn't supposed to be there, but he gave me his card and told me to call him if I wanted to be an actress.

I didn't want to be an actress. I wanted to make it out of Watts. It was the same thing.

The first time he asked me to his office, I was elated. I thought he wanted to talk about my career.

It was a surprise when, instead, he fucked me. And after, as I lay underneath him with his ejaculation between my breasts, he told me I was beautiful, I was lucky, that not every girl got to visit his office.

He thought I was a white woman. A lot of people did.

When a Cloud Nine club manager told him my race, he was delighted to find out the truth. Something to hold over me.

Presently, I sip from my glass, watching the singer. I think she's wearing my red dress, liquid satin falling to the floor. I wasn't allowed to take anything when I left. It felt like a waste of money to buy it in the first place. She moves slowly and languidly as she sings "Night and Day." No one is listening, not really. They're having their conversations, and she's just background noise. I remember being up there. It isn't as glamorous as it seems. The lights are on you, the microphone is in front of you, and, theoretically, your voice carries through the whole little club. Cloud Nine is a hole in the wall, small and dusty, with uncomfortable tables and chairs. The one I'm at now wobbles, one leg too short. I keep a hold on my glass as the singer segues into "But Not for Me." It's a slower set than I would have chosen, but it seems to work. Her voice is smoky, well suited for crooning. I wonder where she's from, if Kenneth would snap her up if he were in the audience. She's beautiful, a pale blonde.

I wonder if she reminds Tommy of his wife.

I finish my drink. I worry that people are looking at me. My skin itches with the pressure of attention, even though, logically, I know everyone is focused on the pale blond singer. The red dress looked better on me.

I want to get up on that stage, sing something, and show her up. But I also want to go home and pull the covers over my head. I do neither. I sit, frozen to the chair that wobbles a little. There's sticky alcohol underneath the sole of my shoe. I pull it free. I think people are whispering about me; I see a man cast a look my way.

Cloud Nine is who I was.

Not who I am now.

~

I devote every other Sunday to the care and upkeep of Lorelei Davies. I've never felt that she's a real person, that Lorelei Davies exists outside the desires of men.

Before I started at Sunset, I was given painful electrolysis to reshape my hairline and remove my widow's peak. My hair was dyed a shade that looks brown in the artificial light but gleams red in the sun.

Kenneth thought about having my chin changed and my nose reshaped. In the end, all he did was have the gap between my front teeth removed.

I was given lessons: elocution, personal style and grooming, and etiquette. Kenneth watched over every aspect. He had his hands in every part of my creation.

He's the one who named me. I wanted to be Joanna, but that, apparently, is too common. Not a name for stars. Lorelei Davies: A woman who is everything and nothing.

On these Sundays, I get up at eight in the morning and have coffee. Then upkeep begins.

The hair appointment is first. I sit in a studio-approved salon, getting my hair redyed, then straightened, and then curled. I smoke cigarettes while I sit. Lorelei Davies is never allowed to have Millicent Dawson's natural curls. Those could imply that Lorelei Davies is anything other than a white woman.

Obviously, we can't have that.

The salon employees fawn over me. They whisper when I walk in and practically fall over themselves genuflecting. It's embarrassing, but I let them. Other clients don't even look at me, too scared or polite to say anything.

So I flick through magazines as my hair is set. Quiet conversation hums around me. My eyebrows are plucked, as is my upper lip. With every pull of my hair, I can feel myself becoming her a little more. The eyebrows are my least favorite part, but Kenneth is convinced I have a unibrow, and whatever he says goes. He gives directives on my hair, my body, my clothes, my comportment.

Everything about her has to be perfect.

After my hair, I have my nails and toes painted. They're always a soft shade of pink, one that seems nude on screen. My body aches for Tommy; his lips against my skin; his hands on my waist, hips, and thighs; and the way our bodies fit together. I pass time by writing in my journal. I think about my scenes coming up for the week. I want *Live,*

Love to wrap, and we're nowhere near there. My breakdown didn't help, nor the fact that I hid from set for several days.

After lunch, which really happens at three or four, I go back home and gaze at myself in the mirror. I never really believe that I'm Lorelei. It's like I'm wearing the body, living the life of a completely different woman. It always shocks me when she copies my movements in the mirror.

I'm living a fantasy.

I read my script pages. I finish my journal entry. And when Kenneth's secretary knocks—it's always her—I let her in.

"Miss Davies," Eva says. She slips her shoes off. I pour her a glass of water. She sits on my couch. We do this every other week. Pretend to care and ask how the other is doing. "Mr. Webster wants to know how you're feeling."

Kenneth never asks me this himself. I don't know if he cares, actually. I don't know if how I feel actually matters.

Then Eva reaches into her purse, pulls out the bottles of pills. "He's added a new one. After your little . . . episode." He knows. Of course he knows. She sets the bottles in a row on my coffee table, smiles, and nods. "There's a fortnight's worth of pills here, Lorelei," Eva says. She talks like she's my mother, even though she can't be more than five years my senior. "Mr. Webster wants you to be careful with them."

"Thank you," I say.

I take a variety of pills throughout the day depending on what I need. They're all prescription, although I'm not sure whose. I barely recognize the words on the labels. Pills of all sizes meant to keep me awake, put me to sleep. Pills to keep me thin. Pills to keep me happy. And now, the new addition, pills to calm the waves of hysteria that flow through my body.

I think about the little girls who see these films, who want to be just like me one day.

If there was one thing I wish I could tell them all? It would be to choose any other career.

CHAPTER 13

1954

Within days of her father's death and celebration of life, Thea was back at work. Julian hadn't returned, and she found, as her five-year-old class finished and her seven-year-olds began, that she missed him.

Thea had to walk her students from the studio to their waiting parents, thirteen little ducklings following her every step. When they reached reception, her girls rushing forward to find their parents, Thea locked eyes with a strange woman who waved, and Thea waved in reply. Her dark hair was up in a bun, her smile slight. She was beautiful. "Thea, this woman has been waiting for you," Jessica said. She was on the phone, her hand over the receiver. Jessica nodded toward the woman, and Thea beckoned her over.

"I've been looking for you." Her voice was low and warm under the squeals of excited children with their parents.

Thea looked around, then nodded toward the staff office. "Why don't we talk in there?"

Thea ushered her inside and closed the door. She sat behind the desk, and the mystery woman sat across from her. Thea pulled a notepad in front of her. "How many children do you have? Have they taken ballet lessons before?" Because of her parentage and the magazines and television commercials she was in, it wasn't unusual for parents to seek her out to teach their children.

Her fame was good for the studio and the company. But since her injury, Thea didn't know if she was worth any of it.

"God, no." The woman's voice was soft and husky. She had big brown eyes. Her skin was warm gold with gorgeous red undertones. "I don't have kids. I'm twenty-five. I'm Amy Evans. I work for *The Courier*. I'm the gossip columnist." She reached into her purse and pulled out a business card.

"What is this about?" Thea asked.

"You're a really easy woman to find," Amy said, digging through her purse. "One second. It's about Tommy Ross." She emerged with a notebook. She was flipping through her pages. "Your father. He died." Amy exhaled. She talked at a quick pace, and she pulled a pen out from her bag.

"I know he died," Thea said. The loss of her father was raw. She was grateful to her job for a distraction, but she remembered him with every heartbeat. "I don't know why you're telling me this."

"Oh, I . . ." Amy said. "I messed up. I started in the wrong place; I do that sometimes. I'm writing a story."

"About my dad?" Thea asked.

Amy's pen scratched away. She held up one finger, and then when she finished writing, she looked up at Thea. "Mostly about Lorelei Davies. But your father is a major part of the story too. Do you know about Lorelei Davies?"

She had the magazines Julian had given her, but she hadn't had time to look at them. She had been distracted. And truthfully, even though Julian insisted she was this dead woman's twin, Thea didn't see it. "I've heard of her," Thea said slowly.

"I think she was murdered." Amy leaned forward, lowering her voice even though they were the only two people in the office. "And I think Tommy Ross was murdered. But I don't think Tommy killed Lorelei."

"Why would you say that?" Thea asked. "Why would you come here, to my place of work, to tell me this? What am I supposed to do about it? *You* do something about it!" She sounded angrier than she meant to, but Thea was furious.

Thea and her mother had received letters in the time since Tommy's death. Letters of consolation, letters claiming he was still alive somewhere. They'd also received countless phone calls, incessant and constant, at all hours of the day. Sophie told her not to respond, bade Ilsa to throw everything out. How was Thea supposed to grieve with all that going on?

Amy leaned back and frowned, considering her next move. She ripped some pages from her notebook and slid them toward Thea. "Read these, and think about it, okay? I want to do something about this." She got up, leaving her business card, and hurried out the door. Thea's first instinct was to throw the pages out. But she folded them.

Maybe it would be worth taking a look.

~

When Thea got home, she went right to her father's office. He didn't use it often, but knowing her mother never went in there, Thea had hidden the magazines inside.

The small office still smelled like Tommy. She dropped her dance bag next to the desk and sat down in his chair, something she was never allowed to do as a child, sinking into the plush leather of the seat. She opened the bottom drawer. There was a bottle of rye and a couple of glasses. Thea poured herself a glass. The room was small, and it had the best views of the property. This house had always seemed too big for three people.

But her parents had wanted to fill it with children.

Thea had stashed the magazines in the middle, biggest, drawer. She pulled them all out, sipped at the rye, and coughed as she swallowed.

She opened the issue of *Life* and flipped to Lorelei's article. In the glamour shots, Thea saw a smiling woman. The interview revealed

Lorelei was quick to laugh and introspective. Thea wondered who Lorelei was before fame.

Thea had never seen a film starring Lorelei Davies. She hadn't seen much of her father's canon, and he'd insisted he did his best work after she was born. She hadn't seen any of his earlier work. Tommy had wanted her to see him as her father, not as the world-famous actor. He wanted distinct boundaries between his home life and work life. That didn't stop him from dragging her to every party his studio held.

The boundaries had always been a little blurry.

Thea sipped from her glass again, gradually getting used to the rye.

She got up, stretching slowly. She put a record on the turntable, needing something to kill the silence around her. Ilsa had long gone home, so it was just her and her mother. Like it would be for the rest of her life. Ella Fitzgerald filled the little office, and for a moment, Thea stood, swaying side to side, picturing her dad with her. She used to dance with him, her feet on his, around her dance studio. Her favorite, most formative memories of him. She'd never get to do that again.

Thea sat back down at the desk, her heart aching. She looked at the open magazine pages of Lorelei Davies. Thea took Amy's notes out of her bag and examined them. Amy's writing was almost illegible, sentences squished together. Thea read them over, picking out phrases like "underappreciated actress," "Overdose = poison?," "Sex with Webster? Weston? Ross?," and "Crazy?" She looked through Amy's notes, wondering if this woman had something or if she was reaching.

Thea took a sip from her glass.

She'd be damned if she wasn't curious.

CHAPTER 14

1954

Following Tommy's death, Sophie granted one television interview.

The press had been clamoring for some sort of response: camped out in front of the house, wanting to talk to Sophie about her murderer husband.

How could she not have known?

Overnight, Tommy's reputation had gone from all-American star to murderer. It was tawdry, and Sophie was trying to keep Thea from seeing most of it. Sophie's response to the press never changed: "I will make a statement when the time is right. I am focused on caring for my daughter."

Now, Thea supposed, the time was right.

Sophie wore a demure black dress, her hair and skin immaculate. Thea was dressed to match, even though she would be off camera. The television studio was much like every stage on which Thea had modeled for an advertisement, big and bright and loud. There were people everywhere; Thea couldn't keep track of all of them.

And at the center of it was the reporter.

"Sophia." The reporter, a man in a black suit, came to kiss her mother on both cheeks. He had brown hair, brown eyes, and too bright a smile. He was tall and broad shouldered, a dimple in his square chin. He was the same type of man Thea saw everywhere: generic and boring.

"Colin," Sophie said softly. She was shattered with grief. Thea was too. It was all she could do to keep herself standing. "This is my daughter, Theodosia."

"Ah, I know Theodosia," Colin said. He extended a hand with a warm smile, as if they were talking about weather. "You may not remember me, but I did an article for *Life* about you when you were adopted. I held you for five minutes, and you threw up on me."

"Oh." Thea didn't remember. She shook his hand.

"I accept your apology," Colin said with a wink. "Sophia, I'm so glad you decided to do this." He turned back to her mother. It was a given that if Sophie Ross was in the room, no one was going to pay attention to Thea.

"You're glad I chose you, you mean," Sophie said, her remark simple and cutting.

Colin smiled, revealing nothing. "We went over the questions. No curveballs or anything. We're on in ten minutes."

Sophie went into makeup. Thea was given a seat near the primary camera. It was a talk show, in front of a live audience, and all Sophie had to do was talk about the death of her husband.

It occurred to Thea that Sophie had been in the public eye just as much as Tommy had. Until they adopted her, Sophie was at her husband's side at every event. The public knew her just as well as they knew Tommy.

The interview began. Colin turned to the cameras, saying, "For three decades, he shined on screen, and we were all saddened to hear of the passing of Thomas Ross. I'm sitting with his wife of twenty-four years, Sophia Ross."

"Thank you so much, Colin." Sophie gave him her most lovely, simple smile. "I would say it's a pleasure to be here, but I would prefer to have my husband with me."

Colin didn't laugh. He was sober, serious, as he faced her mother. Thea leaned forward in her chair, tried to relax. She wasn't the one answering questions. She leaned back, crossing her legs at the ankle.

"It is a devastating loss, one that my daughter and I will have to carry for the rest of our lives. I've been with him for longer than

I was ever without him. This will be a big change for both of us," Sophie said. She was turned toward Colin, addressing him as if he were the only person in the room. Colin leaned forward, drinking in Sophie's gaze.

"I am so sorry to have to ask, but what about Lorelei Davies? He confessed to killing her in his note."

The Courier had printed a copy of Tommy's suicide note. Sophie had banned all copies from the house.

But the world had seen it.

"As far as I'm concerned," Sophie said slowly. She was picking each word carefully. Thea knew that whatever she said now would reverberate through the country, on airwaves and in newsstands. Whatever Sophie was about to say mattered. "The subject is closed. It's true that my husband had an affair with Lorelei Davies. I knew about it. But we decided to strengthen our marriage for the sake of our daughter. I didn't know that he killed her. I didn't . . ." She trailed off, closing her eyes. Thea was on her feet, waiting to see what Sophie would do. Colin handed Sophie a white handkerchief, and she dabbed at her eyes, taking a moment to gather her composure. "I didn't see any of this in my future. I loved my husband. He was my best friend, my life partner. The life we built and the daughter we raised will always be the most important thing." Sophie took another second to compose herself. "I want to thank everyone who has sent their condolences. But I, and the police, believe the case to be closed. I would like to ask for privacy as my daughter and I try to rebuild our lives."

In the coming days, images of Sophie—sitting in the black chair, her body angled toward Colin, out of frame—would grace newspapers and magazines, glowing despite the black-and-white image. And Thea would see it. It wouldn't stop the phone calls or the letters.

Thea could see it for what it really was: an act.

~

Seeing Tommy's lawyer was an occasion that called for a dress, another black and uncomfortable one. Her mother let her drive, acquiescing so easily that Thea thought Sophie may have been ill.

Her father's lawyer was an older, graying man with a white mustache and a large collection of books. He met them in the lobby of the office, guiding them in.

"Sophia," the man said, kissing her on her cheeks. "And you must be Theodosia. I remember you from when you were just a little thing."

"Thea." Something stuck in her throat. Nerves, probably.

The lawyer sat down. The plate on his desk proclaimed him Owen Westfield. He pushed some papers around. Thea wondered how many of those papers he actually needed and how many were for show. Sophie pulled a cigarette from her purse. Mr. Westfield leaned over to light it.

"We don't have much time, Mr. Westfield," Sophie said.

"Well, there isn't much to go over. As you know, I've handled your husband's accounts for . . . three decades now. I have his will right here." He picked up a sheet of paper, slipping on a pair of glasses. "To my wife, Sophia Osbourne Ross, I leave the house and five hundred thousand dollars. To my daughter, Theodosia Adeline Ross, I leave my Corvette, one million dollars, and my shares to Constellation Pictures."

He put the paper down. Thea thought that he didn't need the sheet of paper for that simple will.

"What?" Thea asked. "He left me his shares of the studio?"

Tommy had spent much of her life—and his—shielding her from his work, and then he gave her the shares to the studio?

She couldn't wrap her head around it.

She was a millionaire.

"That's all?" Sophie asked. "The house and five hundred thousand dollars?"

"With some managing, you will be comfortable," Mr. Westfield said. He lit a cigarette. "I can answer any questions you have."

The office seemed big, cavernous, and echoey. Sophie pasted on her pageant smile. "Of course, Owen. Thank you. Tommy always spoke so highly of you."

Owen rose, shaking Sophie's hand.

Thea checked the time on her wristwatch. Ten minutes, and they were already being ushered from the office. She numbly followed her mother, clutching her purse under her arm.

Once outside, in the beating hot sun, Thea faced her mother. Sophie slid on a pair of sunglasses. "Of course," Sophie muttered. She was smoking frantically, using the butt of her first to light her second. "Of course." She was furious. Thea could tell from the way her hands shook. Thea knew that Sophie had expected more.

They both had received a surprise.

"Mom," Thea said.

Sophie was frowning. "Let's just go."

"I own the studio," Thea said. The news crashed over her again and again, the same wave breaking, and still she couldn't comprehend it. "I . . . own a company."

Sophie exhaled, lighting her third cigarette in a row. She never used to smoke this much. "You're not abandoning ballet, and I can't believe you think your father would ever let you do that. He worked hard for what you have. And you don't *own* a company; you own thirty-three percent of a company. And he didn't . . ." Sophie trailed off. Her dark glasses hid her blue eyes.

Thea said, "Why don't we stick to our plan? Go get lunch and talk about Dad?"

She looped her arm through her mother's. Thea had a sense that Sophie needed this more than she did.

"Okay, but you're back to work tomorrow," Sophie said, again sounding like Thea's no-nonsense mother. "Let me drive."

"I can't," Thea said. She pulled the keys to the gold Chevrolet Corvette, Tommy's pride and joy, from her purse. "It's mine now."

~

The last Friday of every month, Tommy would take Thea to Sal's for lunch. They sat at the same table, ordered the same dishes.

Thea thought that she'd have forty more years of lunches at Sal's with her dad.

So when she and her mother settled into their booth, a very small *TAR* marked in the worn, creased leather of the seats, she almost burst into tears.

Sophie concentrated on lighting a cigarette. "How did you and Dad meet?" Thea asked.

Sophie rolled her eyes. Thea had asked her this question so many times, usually while watching Sophie get ready for an event with Tommy.

Sophie inhaled. "Is this the story you really want me to tell?" When Thea nodded, Sophie closed her eyes. "I was at a speakeasy." It was hard to imagine her mother as a wild flapper girl. "I was dancing with my friends, and I spotted him across the floor. He was singing with the band. It was like the world stopped and the one man I saw was him. He was with another girl then, but I wanted him. He'd say I was *unladylike* in my pursual. But when I know what I want, I go for it."

Thea closed her eyes, trying to picture it all, like a film in her head.

"I loved him from the moment we met. And when he decided he wanted to be in movies, I had to support him. Then we had you . . . adopted you . . . and he was the greatest husband I could ever ask for."

Her mother's face never betrayed any emotion. But now, Sophie wiped a tear away as the waiter approached the table. "Miss Thea." Dean was their regular waiter, always greeting Tommy with a bright smile and a handshake. "I am so sorry to hear about your father."

Thea stood, letting Dean pull her into a hug. "Thank you," Thea said against the scratchy fabric of his uniform.

"He was wonderful," Dean said. He was older than Thea by a couple of years, a dark-haired college kid. Her father had taken a quick liking to him; they shared a sense of humor. Dean let her go and turned to Sophie. "Mrs. Ross. My condolences to you as well." He set down two menus.

"Thank you, Dean." Sophie tapped her cigarette on the ashtray. "A Coke for her, and a mimosa for me, please."

"Of course." Dean nodded and departed.

Once they were alone again, Sophie exhaled. "I know you wanted to talk about your father." She closed her eyes. "I miss him every day. And when I look at you, I see him."

"What did you do while he went to work every day?" Thea asked.

Sophie wrinkled her nose. Dean approached with drinks, and Sophie waited until he was gone to answer. "We had a girl for housework and to cook, so mostly I waited for him. I had lunches with other society wives. I ran committees, hosted benefits. I read *a lot.* I wasn't used to it. It was only after you were born that I realized I wanted more. Then, when Constellation had gotten off the ground, I was scared to lose myself in his shadow. I didn't want you to get lost behind him either. He was so magnetic, but you are too." Her mother picked up her glass. "It's why I'm glad you didn't want to be an actress. If you were, you'd only ever be Tommy Ross's daughter."

That's how Thea felt. That she had to be amazing at everything because Tommy was her dad, and he was amazing at everything. If she were an actress, the comparisons would be nonstop. If she was successful, people would say it was because of her father.

"You know what I'll miss most?" Thea asked. "Dancing with him." She thought about how she and Tommy had danced at every Constellation event. It was when she had really felt close to him, when they were both doing what they loved the most.

"Me too," Sophie said. She sipped from her glass, always elegant and ladylike. "It's how I won him over."

She exhaled. Thea tried to picture her mother and father this way, before she even existed, young and free.

It was impossible.

"What about Lorelei Davies?" Thea asked. She watched her mother's reaction, but, as always, her face gave nothing away.

"She was a mistake," Sophie said coolly. "A moment where . . . your father and I hadn't been having the best of times then. Lorelei was just a temptation. An accident," Sophie said.

"He killed her," Thea said.

The man who had raised her, who had pushed her to be spectacular in everything, was a killer. He had left Thea behind with nothing but a note.

She wasn't willing to believe it.

Sophie wouldn't look at her, intensely focused on the table between them instead. "I don't know. I didn't know. She killed herself." Sophie's voice was soft. "That was the story."

"But you knew about the affair?" Thea asked.

Dean returned to take their orders. Sophie didn't answer her question. They hadn't looked at the menu, but they knew what they wanted. She and Sophie so rarely did this—spent time alone. It was always her and Tommy, Tommy and Thea.

Sophie and Thea only ever talked about her career. Thea didn't really know what to say to her mother.

"He is—was—so proud of you. Proud of you for pursuing your dreams. And I am too. I know I haven't been the easiest mother—"

"Mom, you don't have to—" Thea said, but Sophie kept talking.

"All you need to know is that we wanted you. We wanted you so desperately. And because of that, we were hard on you. But you managed to grow into the greatest parts of us. And he couldn't have been prouder."

Thea sat with that for a moment, feeling warmth radiate from her chest.

She was lucky. So lucky.

Dean delivered their plates. Sophie waited for him to leave before continuing. "He wouldn't want you to stop dancing now. You're still young, and you already have a career."

"What if I don't want to keep the shares?" Thea asked. The question came out before she knew she was going to ask it.

"I can't answer that for you." Sophie lit another cigarette. Thea bit into her toasted cheese sandwich, the dish she had ordered every week since she was a child.

She thought about Willa. Willa would keep the shares, then lose interest within months. Max would keep them, too, and he'd be better at it than Thea would be. He had a head for business and numbers.

Maybe Sophie was right.

"I'm going to think about it." Thea thought that was the best decision.

Sophie nodded. "Of course. This is all very new. But you know what I want for you." Thea did know. What she wasn't sure of was what she wanted.

CHAPTER 15

1934

Ramona takes her time to decide what she wants. For the next couple of days, every time I see her, she winks at me, one perfectly made-up lid falling over her green eye, as if we share a secret.

Every time she does, my skin crawls.

I know she was pretending to be my friend. I was pretending to be hers. I wish we could be more supportive of each other, but Sunset is so cutthroat that I can't afford to have any friends.

I only have enemies and people I am neutral toward.

Ramona's in fine form today. We're filming a scene together. My lines are garbled in my head, and I keep getting them wrong.

This makes Kenneth angrier, which makes me more nervous.

This film is hemorrhaging money, and I know I'm to blame. I take a deep breath. The lights on me are starting to make me sweat. I can feel it blooming at the nape of my neck. Kenneth won't even look at me. We're taking a ten-minute break, and the extras and day players are talking among themselves. I hear Ramona laugh loudly, as if she *wants* me to hear.

Then she swans over to me. She puts her hands on her hips. "I know what I want." Her voice is low, near my ear. She's still smiling so it looks like we're having a casual conversation. "I want you to leave Sunset."

"No," I say. I squeeze my fingers together, stretch them out, concentrating on the action so that I don't reach out and smack her as hard as I can. It's hard enough keeping my cool as Lorelei Davies, and Ramona manages to get on my last nerve.

She pouts, as if I'm a silly man who will give her what she wants. That look may work on various Sunset executives, but not me. I cross my arms over my chest. We're getting ready to shoot the scene again. I want Ramona to leave me alone.

"Then I want to be the star," Ramona says.

"That's not up to me."

She narrows her eyes. She's one moment away from crossing her arms over her chest and stamping her foot on the floor. She's a spoiled, rich only child.

Ramona is conniving, but she's not stupid.

She could never be under Kenneth once a week; she doesn't have the stomach for it. "It's simple, Millicent," Ramona says, her voice not exactly quiet. We all want to be stars.

I'm not a star yet, but I'm close. I've been hoping to use my position in *Live, Love* to move up. Maybe do a film with no singing.

But I can't afford to leave Sunset. Kenneth has me under his thumb, and I can't afford to buy myself out of my contract. It's impossible.

I focus on what success will do for me and my family. If I can succeed here, I can make sure my family is taken care of. I think about them at every turn. I do it all for them.

"Let's go again," Kenneth says. My makeup artist, Jean, rushes to reapply my face powder. There's a moment where everyone shuffles into spot on set, right before the cameras start rolling again. The moment is a sharp inhale before everything becomes big and bright. Ramona's lips are still near my ear. I note the cameras, Kenneth in his director's chair with his left leg over his right. His beady brown eyes are on me and Ramona. "Miss Penderghast, I hope I'm not interrupting your tea party."

She doesn't move. I can feel my stomach flip. "I don't care what you do or how you do it, but next time, *I'm* going to be the star," she says. Then she turns and flounces to her mark.

Kenneth exhales, as if we're all taking years off his life. He glares at me, and I know he is hoping for my downfall. Anything to keep me near him longer. "From the top of the scene again, ladies, *please*. Miss Davies, if you could attempt to do your job properly this time . . ."

He calls action, and the scene begins again. I hit my cues and say my lines, but my mind is on Ramona. I titter and laugh, but all I can think about is how I can stop her.

Maybe I have to give her what she wants.

~

I'm skulking outside Ramona's dressing room. We broke for lunch, and she went directly there. I'm lurking. I hear two voices coming from her dressing room. One is Ramona, and the other is Cheryl Lawrence.

We've talked once or twice, but Cheryl's voice is distinct, and I can hear it, loud and raspy. She's smart, this woman. She practically runs circles around the *Courier* staff. She knows what she wants and is willing to pay for the best gossip.

Knowing that the biggest gossip hound in Hollywood is in Ramona's dressing room makes me uncomfortable. I strain to hear what Ramona is saying to her. I know that Ramona will stop at nothing to be the queen of Sunset Studios.

As if anyone could dethrone Francesca Weston.

I pace back and forth. My heels sink into the carpet outside her door, **RAMONA PENDERGHAST** in bold letters, the carpet mossy green and thick and soft. We used to have dressing rooms right next to each other. When we started at Sunset, doe-eyed, excited young girls, we'd have sleepovers in each other's dressing rooms.

The name on the dressing room door that used to be mine is **MAREN SAUNDERS**. I don't know her. This Maren could open her door and see me, but I keep pacing, too many awake pills in my system. I threw them up earlier, then overcompensated by taking more. I can't tell if Ramona is talking about me, but I think she is. She has to be.

My mind races, imagining what Ramona could be saying. I hear Cheryl laugh. Ramona is charming.

I'm squeezing my pages so hard that they're beginning to crumple. Another laugh, both of them this time. I should be anywhere but here.

But I want to finish this thing between Ramona and me.

The door swings open. Cheryl Lawrence, in an impeccable navy suit and dramatic matching hat and heels, steps outside. Her dark eyes scrape over me like I'm nothing. "Miss Davies. I didn't think I'd get to see you today."

"Miss Lawrence," I say, smiling softly. "It really is a lovely day when you cross my path."

"I'm working on a story," Cheryl continues. "Do you have anything to say about Tommy and Sophia Ross? Miss Penderghast had glowing things to say about the pair."

"I, uh . . ." I can't think of one simple, polite thing to say. "I need to talk to Miss Penderghast." It's not classy of me—a little rude, actually—but I turn away from Cheryl and knock. I open the door before Ramona can tell me to enter. I close the door. We face each other in her dressing room, decorated in soft greens that she chose to complement her eyes.

"Millicent," Ramona says warmly. "Have you come to your senses?"

I ease into a smile as fake as hers. She sits down at her vanity. It's hard to believe that we used to have sleepovers in this tiny room. My old one wasn't much bigger.

It's harder to believe that we were ever friends. I bite my tongue. "I'm not giving you anything you want just because you *think* you know something," I say. I try to keep myself calm and collected.

"Should I call Miss Lawrence back here? I think I have a great new angle for her story about Tommy and his wife," Ramona says. She's not even looking at me anymore; she's drinking in her own reflection. She loves how she looks more than anything else. I imagine running my nails right over her cheek, drawing blood.

"Do whatever you want," I say. "No one is going to believe you."

She turns to me now, pouts in her pretty way. "You're going to regret that, you know."

"I don't care," I say. "I'm not going to play your little game, Ramona. You lose. Move on."

With that, I step out from her dressing room, slamming the door shut behind me.

CHAPTER 16

1934

We're in my dressing room, and Tommy won't look at me. He's been off all day and trying to hide it. I can tell, but I don't think anyone else can. Today was all acting, no singing or dancing, and Tommy delivered his lines with all his usual bravado.

"Tommy."

He's sitting on my couch. I sit next to him. It's eleven thirty. We're done for the day. "Tommy . . ." I don't know what else to say.

He leans back. "Sophie lost the baby. She told me she felt it at the party."

I didn't even know Sophie had a baby to lose. I know they've been trying to no avail. I know they desperately want a family.

The first rule of our affair is to not talk about Sophie.

He lies down, his head on my lap. I run my hands through his hair. Alone, in the dressing room, it feels like we're miles away from reality. "She was only a few weeks along, I guess. She didn't tell me. She wanted it to be a surprise. I just keep thinking . . ."

I have never met a man who wants to be a father as much as Tommy does. Every other man I know is rather apathetic about children. But not Tommy. It's the one thing Tommy wants.

"I am so sorry." That's all I can think of to say.

"It's her fourth. Loss. Her fourth loss. In as many years. We're not a couple anymore. We're . . . people who live in the same house. We're people who sleep in the same bed. She doesn't even want to look at me."

I close my eyes. I don't know what to say. It's another stark reminder of how different our lives are. I'm twenty years old. I can't imagine bringing a child into the world. I couldn't do it. I'd be a horrible mother. I wouldn't know *how* to be a mother. And who would she be? Lorelei Davies? Millicent Dawson? I don't even know who I am.

But Tommy? He'd be a wonderful father.

He pulls himself up. His eyes are red rimmed, but he's smiling. It's forced. He kneels down in front of me.

He takes my hands in his. He presses his lips to my fingers, working his way up my arm. "Tommy," I say. He cuts me off, kissing me. I know what he wants, and I'm not about to give it to him.

With all the strength I can summon, I push him away. My lips are buzzing. "You should go home to your wife." I try to say it as firmly as I can. Everything in me wants to give up, to let him in. I can see the hurt in his eyes. He just wants to have me.

The knock on the door stops my train of thought. He pulls away from me, old habits. We can't get caught.

We won't get caught.

"Come in," I say. We're both dressed. Tommy rises to his feet. Nothing is happening, and yet my heart is pounding.

Harrison King opens my door. "Tommy." He doesn't look at me. I don't think he ever has. He wears a stiff black suit, and he's smoking a cigarette. "We need to go."

Tommy waves him off. "Give me a minute."

"Now."

I think most of Harrison's job is herding stars like cats. I don't know where he and Tommy are going, and they don't invite me.

"One minute," Tommy repeats, sounding like a petulant child. I wonder if he's ever been told no in his life. He looks at me.

He doesn't care that Harrison is watching. He leans in and kisses me, long and slow, like he would on the soundstage, in front of the cameras.

Romantic.

My heart stops, and I don't have the willpower to push him away. I know Harrison is watching us, but I can't find it in me to care.

"I'll see you tomorrow," he whispers as he pulls away. His voice is soft, just between us.

~

Tommy and Sophie are dancing.

The dance floor is cleared out. Everyone watches the beautiful couple with rapt attention. It's a smooth foxtrot, and he's guiding her across the floor. Her blue eyes don't leave his face.

I can see the implicit trust between them written on her face, even from my vantage point, hidden in the shadows. She would follow him even if he led her off the edge of the world. I realize that's what I look like when I dance with Tommy. Lovesick and doped up on the possibility of what could or should be.

"The most marketable couple in the pictures," I hear a man near me say.

"Sophie Ross isn't in the pictures," I can't help snapping. I'm a little jealous.

"That's her mistake," the man replies. I feel something crawl over my skin. I wish, oddly, that Ramona was next to me. She'd say something awful about Sophie.

But Ramona is nowhere to be seen, something that makes me happy and nervous in equal measure.

So I'm alone, watching Tommy whisk Sophie around on the dance floor. His lips move, but I know he isn't singing along with the band. Tommy detests that. I did it once while dancing in his arms, and he nearly left me when I did.

No, I can only assume he's telling Sophie how much he loves her. My heart is in my throat. I can remember all the times Tommy looked at me like that, under the stage lights and in private. I have to wonder if it's all acting, if he feels nothing for me or for Sophie.

And how would I tell?

His movements are all precise and deliberate. Sophie follows seamlessly, and I imagine they do this daily in their kitchen. I feel my stomach twist, something sharp running through me.

As the band does a perfect segue into the next song, the crowd applauds. I do, too, although I think I'd rather pull my own teeth out than watch any more of Tommy and Sophie dancing.

The room is small, suffocating. The heat is tangible on my skin, visible in the air, and I can't breathe. I can't take another moment of watching them, together, in love.

I turn away, ducking toward the entrance of the ballroom. This is someone's house, but I'm not sure whose, and I'm not wholly sure I'm supposed to be here. I'm trying to be seen. Trying to make everyone realize that Lorelei Davies is a force to be reckoned with.

It's when I'm outside that my hands stop shaking. My stomach untwists, and I light a cigarette. Pulling the items from my purse, lighting the match and then the cigarette, is the small ritual I need to pull myself back together. I exhale acrid smoke and close my eyes.

It backfires; all I see is Tommy looking at Sophie so softly that I want to curl up and die.

CHAPTER 17

1934

A copy of *The Courier* is staring at me, on the floor in front of my dressing room door. I know that someone, probably Ramona, has put it there. It's the first thing I see after my quick nap. The headline, in big bold letters, taunts me.

I LOVE MY WIFE.

I'm due on set for another million grueling hours, and I can't bear to see the full-page photograph of Tommy and Sophie. She looks incredible, beautiful in her cold, blond way. Her smile always suggests that she knows something you don't. And the way Tommy looks at her, like she hung the moon. It's a publicity photo; the two are out for dinner. They're sitting at a small table, Tommy leaning over to light Sophie's cigarette. They're laughing together. I can see Sophie's obscene engagement ring on her finger. It's ostentatious, a sapphire surrounded by diamonds in a silver band. Looking at it in the paper makes me want to hurl.

I have to wonder who took this photo, if someone followed them around for the best shot, if there are one hundred others on the cutting room floor that aren't as posed and perfect.

And the quote. Tommy proclaiming that he and Sophie are blissful, happy, stronger than ever. I see it, and my body revolts.

But I have a job to do.

"Enraging, isn't it?" Julian has emerged from his dressing room. He's wearing a soft knit sweater over a white button-down, looking as if he just stepped out of a magazine.

"Didn't you do some of these with your wife too?" I ask.

"I have never met a man who so publicly loves his wife like Tommy does Sophie," Julian continues. He lights a cigarette, offers me one. I shake my head. Julian pockets his book of matches. "Makes you think, doesn't it?"

"Does it?" I ask.

"It should." Julian looks at me. "Have you read the article?"

"I don't think I want to," I said.

"Good choice."

"What about Francesca?" I ask.

"Are you asking if I love her?"

"Yes."

Julian doesn't respond for a moment. He doesn't look at me. "Yes." His answer feels so forced that I don't believe it.

Julian takes the paper from my hands. I watch as he balls it up, throws it aside. He doesn't even think about the people who will have to clean up after him. "I need to get to set."

I know that under the casual demeanor, he's seething.

~

I have a theory that you can tell a man's whole personality by how he dances. If not his whole personality, then the way he fucks. When Tommy dances, he's self-assured, strong. A real leader. He dances like he walks on air, and he gives me no choice but to follow.

We're in Tommy's dressing room. He sits on the edge of his couch. Neither of us has said anything about Cheryl's article, and I don't think either of us will.

It's in the back of my mind, hovering. We both have a rare spare moment, and I know how I want to spend it.

"Undress." His voice is low. It's early, or it's late, and neither of us should still be here. His dressing room is right next to Julian's and a tiny bit bigger. I rarely visit him in his dressing room. We always meet in mine. He's watching me, his eyes not leaving my face, my body.

I do what he wants, slowly. My day dress ties around my waist, dark red. I release the bow at my waist, letting the fabric fall to the floor. My slip comes off next, and I stand there in my brassiere and tap pants, silky soft, peach pink. He looks me up and down.

I'm incapable of refusing him.

"Take it all off," Tommy says.

I do it, the hairs on my arms and legs rising when I'm completely naked in front of him. His face is completely unreadable. "Come here," he says. I straddle him. His eyes graze my body, like they do every time. His fingers graze my skin, his hands at my waist and hips. He unfastens his shirt buttons but leaves it on. He unbuckles his belt and lets me unzip his fly. I know what he wants; I know that it's me. I know he's flawed, and I am, too, but I can never control myself when we're this close. My mind is racing. When he kisses me—

He's forceful today, and I wonder if Cheryl's article has anything to do with it. He kisses my lips, my neck, my breasts, rough and strong, like he's trying to prove something. He uses his teeth, and I wonder if he'll leave a mark. He keeps me on his lap, holding me close.

"Good girl," he whispers in my ear as he fits himself into me. It's all about his pleasure. I'm happy to oblige. He's not thinking about Sophie. He can't be thinking about Sophie. "Good girl." He draws the words out as we move together. He's gazing up at me with hungry eyes. I want his approval; I need his approval.

He kisses me, keeps me close. He's desperate today. I can read all his moods. We're that close on screen and off.

I don't know how he feels about me. Not in his head or his heart. I understand how he feels about me physically, but that's different. This affair was his idea, and I went along with it. Every day, I wonder what would have happened if I said no.

The truth is we're both complicit. We're both betraying his wife.

When he finishes, we lie down. He curls into me, his head on my chest. I don't say anything. He's not in a talking mood. He kisses me again, and before I dress and leave, I pull a blanket over him. He's asleep.

CHAPTER 18

1954

Thea took the day off from teaching classes. She had to see what her other life could be. She got dressed, feeling as if everything she had in her closet was too juvenile. She ended up in a white button-down, a slim skirt that traced her hips and fell to midcalf, and low heels, an outfit that worked for both sitting and standing. She put her hair in a bun, feeling less in charge than ever.

Ingrid was waiting for her in the parking lot, a soft smile on her face. "Thea!" The moment Thea got out of her car, Ingrid wrapped her in a hug. "Jake told me that you were coming today. I'm glad I was here to greet you." Ingrid pulled away. "I know working here would be a big change, but Jake and I are both here for you. And Tommy would be so proud of you. You look so grown up." Ingrid linked her arm through Thea's. It was a brilliant day, the sun already shining down on them. The lot was big, soundstages and the commissary and rehearsal rooms and dressing rooms hidden within. Thea had parked as close to the office as she could, and Ingrid walked her inside. "If you're uncomfortable," Ingrid said as they moved toward the elevators, "I can change offices with you. I want to make this as easy as possible for you."

"I think I'll be okay," Thea said. Tommy's office was on the top floor of the building, next to Ingrid's and Jake's. As a child, Thea had loved to stand at the window and admire the goings-on below. It was the first thing she did whenever she visited. The name on the door still said **THOMAS ROSS**, each silver letter an inch apart. She nodded at Lauren, her father's secretary, and stepped inside. The office—with the big oak desk and leather chair, open windows, and big yellow couch Thea used to nap on—seemed cold. Different.

Ingrid watched but didn't say anything. "This is all mine?" Thea asked.

"Just as my office will be Max's someday and Jake's will be Willa's," Ingrid said. "We want to make sure you three have a stable foundation. You're why we built all of this." Thea turned to her. Ingrid stood by the door, watching her with a smile. In her own heyday, Ingrid was a redheaded siren who excelled at playing the femme fatale. "Jake will be in to say hello, I'm sure. And you can take things as slowly as you want, if you want to at all. I know it's a big deal, and you have your own life already." Ingrid crossed over and kissed Thea's cheek. "Whatever you choose to do, we will both support you."

"Will you tell me what happened that day?" Thea asked. Ingrid's lips pursed. They sat across from each other at the desk, Thea sitting at her father's place for the first time.

Ingrid leaned forward. "Normal morning. We had our meeting; Jake and your dad fought."

"Why did they hate each other?" Thea asked. "Why would they go into business together?"

Ingrid laughed. "They started hating each other after we built this place. Anyway, your mother came in the afternoon. I think they had lunch together. They were in here for a while. And then . . . Jake found him. I think he went to yell at Tommy a bit more." She inhaled. "And Jake found him, and he was dead. Thea, I'm so sorry. I can't believe he would take his life."

"You're right," Thea said. "It is completely unbelievable." As in, Thea didn't believe it. She suspected it wasn't the whole story.

"I have a phone call," Ingrid said, checking the time on her little wristwatch. "Get comfortable. Look around."

"I'm planning to go back to ballet," Thea said.

Ingrid nodded. "I thought so. Jake and I will be fine. But . . . make sure it's really what you want, okay?"

Once Ingrid left, Thea looked down at the desk. The desktop was neat, the way her father preferred it. She opened the lowest desk drawer and found a bottle of rye and a glass. She poured herself a drink and then looked around the office. She raised the glass. "To you, Dad."

She took a sip and leaned back in her chair. She knew the basics of the studio—that they produced, in a good year, twenty films and that the majority of those were romances. Thea knew their top stars, their top-grossing films.

But did she want any of this?

She began to go through the desk drawers. Right on top, in the first drawer to her left, she found a script.

AS LONG AS YOU'RE MINE

Thea pulled it out. She leaned over the typewritten pages, marked with notes in ink in the margins. The film was a romance—two characters, Tony and Lucy, meeting each other over and over again. The script wasn't finished, but it was clear her father had written it. It was his handwriting in the margins. This was his work.

She took the pages from the desk, careful to keep them in order. Another piece of him that she would keep.

~

The first thing Thea did when she got home was slip into her walk-in closet and close the door behind her.

The closet was where she felt the calmest. She sat facing the closed door, cross-legged, wrapped in one of her father's shirts. She closed her eyes. Her head ached from her bun. She shook her hair out. Maybe she did need to eat dinner.

Her closet was where she would move the magazines Julian gave her and hide *As Long as You're Mine*. She had taken care to keep the pages still as she had driven home. Thea wanted to read the script over and over again so she could understand her father.

She sat down, finding the envelope Tommy had given her for her birthday. When he had given it to her, she had assumed it was a check, but now? She had to open it.

Thea picked up the envelope, putting her finger on the wax seal, embossed with her father's initials. Her initials. She used a nail to rip open the envelope and pulled the paper out.

> My dearest,
> Thea, the first thing I want to tell you is that I love you so much. There was a part of me that always wanted a son. But I got you instead. You're better than any son I could have had.
>
> I haven't always been the man you think I am, and I'm ashamed to admit it.
>
> I loved Lorelei Davies for about two years before you were born. I loved her desperately, like I had never loved anyone before. I love your mother, of course, but what Lorelei and I had was different. Magic.
>
> In 1934, Lorelei became pregnant.
>
> I considered running away with Lorelei, proposing marriage. I wanted to be her husband more than anything in the world.
>
> By the end of the year, she would be dead, and your mother and I would have a child.
>
> I wish I could sit you down now and tell you everything. But you're too young to understand. I'm writing this on your tenth birthday. We've come home from a ballet recital. I've put you to bed, and I am so overwhelmed with love for you.

Lorelei Davies is your mother. I am your father. She died just after you were born, and I've barely spoken about her since. When she died, your mother and I adopted you.

I see more of Lorelei in you than I see myself. You have her sharp wit and quick smile. There's a part of you that comes from her, her intelligence and humor.

She killed herself because she was troubled.

She was so much more. And I see so many of her good traits in you.

I wish things could have been different, but your mother loves you too. We love you so much, and even though you're hers, you're also ours. It's complicated. I know Lorelei would have wanted you with us. The best life possible.

That's what we are trying to give you. We love you so much, and I know she would have loved you too.

With love,

Your father, Thomas Ross

CHAPTER 19

1954

Thea slipped into the back of Julian's freshman drama class. He had discarded his sweater and rolled his sleeves up, and he was reading from pages of a script. Julian was an engaging teacher. All his students were on the edge of their seats, watching him.

Thea had almost attended the college, Gershwin, a small arts college in the center of Los Angeles. But she was devoted to ballet, and Sophie thought college was only necessary to obtain her Mrs. Degree.

Julian was captivating. It was the way he spoke, putting meaning behind the words. He was so expressive, his face changing with every word he was saying.

"If I am wrong, then tell me, Katerina, please, tell me. If it weren't for you, I'd still be down there. I'd still be waiting. I'd be hopeless, if not for you." He looked up from the pages, making eye contact with each and every student. "You are my everything. The air I breathe. The life I long to live. And you . . . you have to believe me." Julian paused. "And here, I would subject you to a song and dance number." He waved an arm. His students applauded. He gestured to one student in the front. "Yes, July?"

Thea couldn't see the girl, but her voice was loud and clear in the small classroom. "You'd sing 'Totally Terrified,' right?"

"Extra credit." Julian pointed. The class laughed. He looked over his students. "James, I want you to give this a try." He held the script out, and a nervous boy stepped forward to take it. His voice cracked on the first line. The class laughed again. Julian cleared his throat, effectively silencing them. Thea had seen him teach before, in her ballet classes, but this was different.

He was in his element, totally focused on the students in front of him. Thea watched as Julian nodded to the student. James cleared his throat and continued, looking down at the script. "Eyes up. Who are you talking to?" Julian asked.

James's eyes widened in fear. Julian exhaled. He allowed the student to move on.

When he called for the end of class, Thea stayed in her seat as the students packed up their things, chattering away. Thea waited until just she and a few stragglers remained. "Julian."

He smiled as he looked toward her. "Miss Ross. I didn't know you enrolled in college."

"You saw me, huh?"

"Of course." Julian put his cardigan on again. "I know all my students, Thea."

"I was curious."

"Uh-huh."

Thea cleared her throat.

"Do you have some time?" Julian asked. "Let's go get some coffee."

~

Julian took Thea to a diner close to campus. The Stardust Diner, he told her as he opened the door for her, had been around forever. He escorted her to the last booth, then settled down across from her. She liked to watch him move. He moved with such grace, even though he didn't act or dance anymore. It was ingrained in him, just like ballet was ingrained in her. He carried himself so confidently. Just like Tommy had.

"Julian." A waitress in a blue-and-white uniform crossed over immediately. He kissed her on both cheeks.

"Thea, Joanna. Joanna, Thea."

Joanna was grinning. "He never brings girls around." She was taller than Thea, dark skinned with big brown eyes in a round face. She had a dimple on her right cheek and straight white teeth.

Thea blushed. Julian rolled his eyes. "Joanna is the best singer in the city."

"And sometimes I wait tables too," Joanna added, giggling at her own joke. Julian looked at her with such warmth and care.

"Coffee for two, Jo, please," Julian said.

Thea waited for her to depart before she turned to Julian. His eyes landed on her. "I want to know more about Lorelei Davies," Thea said. "Stuff I can't get from the papers and the magazines."

Julian couldn't fight his lovely boyish smile. "Okay," he said, tapping his cigarette on his ashtray.

Joanna returned with coffee and sat down next to Julian. He kissed her on the cheek. He looked at her with such affection. "This young woman is asking about Lorelei Davies." Julian picked up his coffee.

Joanna raised an eyebrow. "I met her once." Joanna smiled. She was beautiful, radiant. "She saved my life."

"Lorelei was a hero?" Thea asked.

"She would love to hear that," Julian said, fighting back a smile.

"She wasn't a hero," Joanna said. "She was brave."

Julian looked at Joanna with all the tenderness in the world. "She would love to hear that even more." He waited until Joanna excused herself and looked back to Thea. He cleared his throat. "She was complicated, but she was whip smart." He paused to light a cigarette. "Have you ever seen a film of hers?"

Thea shook her head. It felt rude to admit that she wasn't much of a film girl, despite her pedigree. She hated sitting in silence for a couple of hours, time better spent in her dance studio.

"Well, we have to fix that. I have all of them. You have to come see one."

Thea paused. Joanna brought them a plate of pastries, placing them between Julian and Thea. She sat back down next to Julian. "Are you still talking about Lorelei?"

"She's never seen a Lorelei film," Julian said.

"You have to. You have to see *Mrs. Donahue*," Joanna said. She looked at Julian, a small smile on her face. "She's amazing in it, so funny and charming. She plays the sister to a bachelorette set on marrying someone rich, but she really is the star of that film."

"Thank you, Jo," Julian said.

"Julian was in it too!" Joanna laughed and got back up again.

Once she was gone, the mood shifted back to somber. Julian watched as Joanna ducked back behind the counter and wiped it down. Then he looked at Thea, his dark eyes worried. "I never once thought she would end her own life. It had to be murder." Hearing him say it made her believe it. But the one other person she *could* ask, the one who knew everything about everything, was dead.

"My dad confessed to killing her," Thea said. The words were raw and sour on her tongue. She couldn't and wouldn't believe it. It all felt so unfinished. Sophie didn't want an autopsy. "It was in his suicide note. I met a reporter who thinks my dad's death was murder, as was Lorelei's."

Julian sipped his coffee. Thea focused on the chip in his cup as time stretched outward. "He didn't kill her. I *know* that. I was never a great fan of your father, but he loved her."

Thea's eyes were still on Julian. She was leaning forward, trying to capture every word that he said. "If they were both murdered, and Tommy didn't kill Lorelei, who did?" Thea asked. "Do you think it was the same person?"

Julian's eyes found Joanna behind the counter, talking to a coworker. Joanna laughed at something, her head tossed back and mouth wide open. "If I were a betting man," Julian said eventually, "I would say yes."

CHAPTER 20

1954

"I thought I'd find you here."

The voice broke Thea's concentration. She was in her at-home dance studio, thinking about her father. She was thinking about Lorelei Davies. Willa was convinced that every married man in Hollywood was sleeping with other women. It was just how men behaved. There was a part of Thea, a small part, that had thought that Tommy had affairs. She didn't want to know about them.

She was the result of one.

She thought, for a moment, that the voice was her father's. She looked up, seeing Harry in the floor-to-ceiling mirror in front of her.

Uncle Harry waited for Thea to invite him in. "How are you doing? These last few days have been hard for you, haven't they?" Harry asked. It was the first time anyone had asked her that, and Thea knew he wanted a real answer. She let go of the barre, turning toward Uncle Harry. "I'm tired. I'm back to work just because I can't stand being in the house without him, and I . . ." She trailed off. She looked up at him. "I'm tired."

"I know, Addie," Harry said. He was the only one who ever called her Addie. He looked around the studio. There were photographs on the wall, tracking Thea's progress in ballet. From her first recital at five years old to her latest headshots. Her first-ever pair of pointe shoes framed, suspended in a box, where she could see them and know how much progress she had made. "It was really sudden. But he'd want me to look out for you both. If there's anything you need, anything your mother needs, please let me know."

"I inherited Dad's shares of the studio," Thea said.

Harry relaxed into a smile. He smiled so rarely; it was like a comet when he did. He had never married, didn't have any family. She had heard of the fabulous parties he had held when he and her parents were all twenty years younger. "I thought you would," Harry said.

"I don't know what to do," Thea said.

"Well, he didn't think you'd be twenty years old when he died," Harry said. He was always thoughtful, quiet, and reflective.

"I don't know what I need."

They sat down on the floor of the studio, facing each other. Thea's music crackled from the record player, but she didn't get up to turn it off. She stretched her arms over her head, every movement intentional. Harry copied her, trying to make her laugh. She indulged him. Then they both looked up at all the portraits of Thea that lined the wall. She had seen them a thousand times, and so had he, but she was always staggered by her growth.

"It's okay that you don't know what you need right now," Harry said.

"Did you talk to him? Before it happened?" Thea asked.

Harry frowned. He shook his head. "He had wanted to talk to me, but I didn't know about what." Thea was under the impression that Tommy and Harry had talked every day. They were close, closer than Tommy and his actual brother were. "Then he died."

"Did he give you any indication?" Thea asked.

Harry was quiet. "No," he said. "I don't know why he would kill himself. He never wanted to leave you, Addie. He loved you so much." Thea felt tears prick her eyes. They were coming at the most inopportune moments. Thea would be in the middle of something, and a wave of grief would wash over her. Tommy would never sit front row for her, see her take center stage again. He would never be there to talk about books and music and the gossip from her company mates. He would never be there to support and help her.

How was she supposed to live like that?

"How many affairs did he have?" Thea asked.

Harry sputtered. "Why do you want to know that?"

Thea kept his gaze. "If anyone would know, you would."

"Just one," Harry said. His answer came after moments of silence, Harry's eyes landing anywhere but on Thea's face. "Girls tried. You have to remember that your father was one of the most famous men in the world. That's intoxicating. But he had one affair."

"Lorelei Davies," Thea said.

"Lorelei Davies." Harry nodded. "Truthfully, it may have started as an affair, but their feelings for each other, or Tommy's feelings, ran deeper than they knew. I saw them together, and the way he looked at her . . . he cared for her a lot. I don't know why their affair started, but by the end of it, he was in love with her."

"How did Sophie feel about that?"

Harry stifled a laugh. "She wasn't pleased. He told me once that he wanted to divorce Sophie. I was going to try to talk him out of it; then he told me Lorelei was pregnant."

Tommy would have left Sophie to marry Lorelei. He would have wanted to make things right.

And Sophie knew about it.

"I should probably leave you alone, get back to it. I just wanted to see you. Tell you that he loved you. He was so proud of you."

"Thank you," Thea said.

"Come see me anytime," Harry told her. "I mean it. He'd want me to look after you."

"I will," Thea said. "Thank you so much." He left her alone to go back to her exercises, her mind on her father.

~

On Thea's second visit to the Stardust Diner, she sat at the counter. Billie Holiday crooned from the jukebox, and there were a couple of tables full. The counter itself was empty, and Thea chose a stool in the center.

Joanna was there, leaning over a table full of customers. She lit up when she saw Thea.

"I was hoping you'd come back." Joanna slipped behind the bar, putting a menu in front of her. Thea checked the time on her watch. It was right after the breakfast rush. "Anything you want, it's on the house. Any friend of Julian's is a friend of mine."

"Oh," Thea said. "I don't . . ."

"You're still curious about Lorelei, aren't you?" Joanna asked. She smiled brightly and began cleaning extra menus.

"I had never heard of her until a few days ago," Thea said. "Now . . ." She trailed off, unsure what to say.

Joanna reached into her apron pocket and pulled out a clipping from a newspaper. "I didn't get the chance to show you this." She handed it to Thea. It was a press photograph of Lorelei Davies, with her smile breaking her face in two. She was kneeling, her arms wrapped around a little girl wearing a polka-dot dress with her light-colored hair in ponytails. The little girl was smiling, too, basking in Lorelei's embrace.

"When was this?" Thea asked.

"1933, I think. It was before I met her. I remember seeing this photograph run in the papers and being hit with how beautiful she seemed," Joanna said. She leaned on the counter, so Thea could smell her floral perfume. "When she died, all the stories were about how crazy she was."

Thea decided she hated that word. She hated hearing it leveraged against a woman who probably needed, more than anything, compassion.

She took in the picture, Lorelei's bright smile. It was a far cry from the seductive, come-hither expression Thea had seen in most of the other photographs.

"I couldn't get this image out of my mind," Joanna said. "This is how I chose to remember her. I guess it sounds silly, but . . ."

"She saved your life," Thea said. She wanted to ask what happened but didn't want to be rude. Instead, she said, "Black coffee, please."

Joanna nodded, pouring Thea's cup. "The woman I was lucky to meet wasn't who the papers described." She blinked twice, her thoughts far away from the present. Thea added sugar to her coffee, then took a sip.

Who was Lorelei Davies?

A mess of contradictions, it seemed. Joanna and Julian remembered her as a fierce, funny woman.

Newspapers recounted her as crazy.

"My dad just died," Thea said. "Tommy Ross."

Joanna's eyes fell on Thea's face. "I'm so sorry for your loss," Joanna said. "I know what that's like." She was about to continue when a customer waved her over. Joanna left her alone with the photograph. Thea inspected it closely, noting signs of wear over the crease, the faded ink. She looked at Lorelei's face, her perfect straight teeth, the dimples in her smile. Thea looked up at the mirror behind the counter, smiling just as widely as Lorelei.

She stared at herself for a moment, not seeing the similarity.

She stopped smiling, realizing how she must've looked, turning back to her coffee cup. The bell over the door jingled, announcing the arrival of a new customer.

What would it be like to be forgotten?

"Thea," Joanna said. She pushed a stray hair back, her smile still on her face. She stepped behind the counter again. Thea handed the clipping back. Joanna folded it up, then slipped it back into her apron pocket. "I am sorry about your father. I read the stories. I couldn't believe it. He was a marvel on screen. He and Lorelei were always wonderful together."

"Thank you," Thea said. She was coming to terms with a lot of things. Her dad's death. His letter and finding out that he was her father. Learning that Lorelei was her mother. Meeting Julian.

And none of it made any sense.

She missed Tommy so acutely that she felt it with every heartbeat.

And what did that leave Thea?

More questions than answers.

Joanna was concentrating on pouring cups of coffee. The more Thea thought about the day of her father's death, the same day Lorelei Davies died twenty years ago, the less anything made sense.

But there was Tommy's suicide note. And that, apparently, meant case closed.

CHAPTER 21

1954

Thea thought that Julian had been exaggerating about having a theater in his house. But it turned out that he lived in a bona fide mansion. Biggest house she had ever been in, including even hers, and the theater was the size of an actual cinema.

"Do you live alone?" Thea asked when he opened the door.

Julian evaded the question by giving her a quick tour.

And now, they sat side by side in the center seats of the center row. *Joe and Meg* played on the screen in front of them. It was Lorelei's first production with Sunset Studios in 1932.

Thea had heard of Sunset Studios in passing. Tommy starred in this film with Francesca Weston.

"She was my wife at the time," Julian said. Thea could tell that he was trying not to talk through the whole film. He was as excited as a boy on Christmas morning.

Tommy played the titular Joe, a down-on-his-luck dancer who dreamed of stardom. Francesca starred as Meg, Joe's love interest.

She couldn't remove her eyes from her father. He looked so young, without age marking his face. He was talented. And he was funny. Thea wished she could have seen this side of him before he died. She didn't realize she was crying until Julian handed her a handkerchief monogrammed with *JJW*. She could barely make the letters out in the dim lights from the screen, but she could feel the fine threads under her fingers.

"I'm sorry," Julian whispered. "I should have realized . . ."

"It's okay," Thea said. She squeezed the linen square in her hand, keeping her focus on the screen.

"This is the relevant part," Julian said. He pointed at the screen as Lorelei Davies began a rather complicated dance number. "She lit up the screen," Julian said. Thea watched Lorelei, her dark hair, her long legs. The way she made everything seem effortless and easy. At the very last moments, she and Tommy danced together. He took her in his arms, and they moved together in an effortless and wonderful way. Thea leaned forward. Her heart thrummed in her chest. He twirled Lorelei around, over and over.

The scene ended, and that was it.

Thea turned; Julian was watching her watch the screen. Lorelei Davies was in that one scene, and then she was gone. It was a daydream of Tommy's character and easily the best part of the film. Thea leaned back. She felt herself relax. She released her grip on the handkerchief. She hadn't known she was still clenching it. The tears had stopped, and for that, Thea was grateful.

Lorelei was so compelling on screen. She had a way of drawing the viewer in with just her eyes; her smile was slight, her face so expressive. Lorelei was both bold and demure, moving as if the choreography came naturally to her. It was impossible to look away.

Lorelei glowed. Some of that had to be lighting, but there seemed to be a source from within her. She radiated something Thea couldn't put her finger on, playful and coquettish. That was her *mother*. Thea's heart had sunk when Lorelei had disappeared from the screen.

The credits rolled. Thea and Julian watched the screen until it went black.

"I haven't watched that one in a long time." Julian broke the silence and lit a cigarette. His lighter was also engraved with his monogram, *JJW*. "I think my memory of her is different than how she really was."

"Can we watch one with you in it?" Thea asked, surprising herself.

Julian slid her a look. She had lied to her mother about where she was. "Are you sure?" Julian asked.

"Yes." Thea blinked back toward the screen. "What happened to your wife?"

Julian didn't answer. Too big of a question too soon. He got up, placing his cigarette between his lips. He disappeared for a moment, and when he returned, a new film was starting. "This one stars Francesca and me." He sat back down next to her. Thea pulled her feet under her. It was a little chilly in the low lights of the home theater, and her cardigan wasn't cutting it.

The opening credits rolled for *Mrs. Donahue*. "Sunset specialized in musicals," Julian said.

"What happened to them?" Thea asked without removing her eyes from the screen. Julian looked almost exactly like he did now, but he wore nicer clothes, and there was no gray hair along his temples and hairline.

"They folded after your father left," Julian said. His voice was still hushed, and Thea could feel his eyes on her. She looked toward him. "I'd left by then too," Julian added.

"Do you miss it?" Thea asked.

Julian tore his eyes away from hers. "No. It was grueling. Fifteen-hour days, in front of the camera all the time. People watching you, waiting for you to fuck up." On screen, Julian was tap-dancing with a line of beautiful young women. His smile was wide. He made it look so easy. He made it look like he was having the time of his life. Thea wondered what she looked like when she was dancing. She had never been filmed in all her years of ballet. She hoped she looked as radiant as Julian did. She remembered her first time rising en pointe, her first pirouette and fouetté.

It had felt like magic. Acting had to be the same way.

"I much prefer teaching," Julian said. "I was thinking of quitting for a long time, but when Lorelei passed . . ." He trailed off, not finishing his sentence. They were both staring at the screen, not feeling the need to talk anymore.

Thea understood, or she thought she did.

~

It was seeing Lorelei Davies on screen, how captivating she was, that drove Thea to call the number on Amy's business card. It was also reading her father's letter, his final words to her. She'd read it multiple times. She had some answers, but she also had more questions.

He was her father. He had been there her whole life. Thea wished he had told her in person, instead of in a letter. It was one-half of the answer she had always wanted.

Amy agreed to meet at the Stardust. The diner was nearly empty when she arrived. A prissy Elvis song played on the radio. Thea was early. She looked around. Joanna wasn't there, a different waitress in her place. Thea sat at the counter and ordered two black coffees.

The bell above the door chimed every time it opened, and the third time it did, it ushered Amy in. She wore a slick black skirt suit with the jacket removed, revealing a red button-down that matched the color of her lips. Thea couldn't stop staring as Amy made her way to the counter.

"I'm glad you called," Amy said as she sat down next to Thea.

"You overstepped," Thea said. "You came to my place of work. You ambushed me."

Amy paused. She lit a cigarette. From the jukebox, the Elvis song changed, sliding easily into another tune, Eartha Kitt growling her way through verses. "You're right. I'm sorry. I shouldn't have done it like that." She closed her eyes for a moment. The waitress came by with menus, and before Thea could say she didn't want anything, Amy ordered. "Two orders of pancakes, please, lots of syrup."

"Oh, I don't . . ." Thea couldn't remember the last time she had pancakes. They weren't on her strict diet. But her mother wasn't there to stop her.

And the idea of pancakes made her mouth water.

"Live a little." Amy winked. She waited until the waitress had left to continue. "I do want to talk about Lorelei Davies. I'm interested in her, really, more than your father. I think your father is a featured player in her story, not the costar. But your father knew her, and now that he's dead too . . ." She trailed off. Her brown eyes remained on Thea's face as she gave quite the impassioned speech. Thea sipped from her coffee cup, considering it all.

"Have you seen any of her films?" Thea asked.

"Just one. Called *About Last Night*. It came out the year after her death, and it was produced under her own company. She started it with Julian John Weston," Amy said. She paused. "I want to know more about her. I want to know *everything* about her. Don't you? I really want to write about her. I want to tell the stories of more forgotten actresses, and she is my first." She paused as the waitress set down two plates of thick and fluffy pancakes and a glass jar of real maple syrup. Thea picked up her knife and fork. The food granted her a reprieve so she could consider what Amy had said.

"Why do you think Lorelei Davies was murdered?" Thea asked. "Your notes were illegible."

Amy inhaled. She sipped from her coffee cup, putting out her cigarette. She took a moment before she responded. "I just . . . from what I've read, her death was sudden. Not right. Maybe I'm wrong. But I want to believe that she wouldn't just take her own life."

"My father didn't do it," Thea said. His name had been irrevocably tarnished since his death.

"What do you say? Look into this with me. Help me." Amy was leaning forward. Thea could smell her perfume.

She put her fork down. If Lorelei Davies was actually her mother, didn't she want to know everything about her?

Of course she did.

Thea finished her coffee, dabbed her mouth with a napkin. "I'm in."

CHAPTER 22

1934

When I walk into the commissary, everything stops, and everyone stares at me. I'm in my slip and a dressing gown, pins and curlers in my hair. But there are several other women dressed that way, so I know it's not my attire.

I pretend I don't notice. I have an hour to not eat before I'm needed on set again.

I take a tray and scan the tables. I spot Julian John Weston and Francesca at a nearby table.

There's a hierarchy here, and I don't know how, but I'm back on the bottom. It could be my imagination. I could be making it up.

But I'm sure something's changed.

Harrison King gets up. He moves, wordlessly, toward my table, where I have a cup of coffee and my pills in a little line, ready to take. He places a paper in front of me and walks away. It's the gossip column from *The Courier*, the only one anyone ever pays attention to. Cheryl Lawrence. Everyone knows that Cheryl Lawrence is the woman to please.

And the top item is about me.

It reports that I attended one of Kenneth's parties. And apparently, I was passed around like Cuban cigars. It's not true, but that doesn't matter. What Cheryl says goes.

Now I'm the studio slut.

I'm not imagining it.

Everyone *is* staring at me.

I don't read the column. I can't. I crumple it into a ball. I take my pills and then walk out of the commissary as fast as I can.

My mind is racing. Ramona must have done this. Of course she did; of course she would. She's confirming the rumors that already fly around about me.

"Lorelei."

Out of everyone in the commissary, it's Julian who follows me out. He's the person I least expect. Even though our dressing rooms are across from each other and we exchange polite words, I don't think he even knows who I am.

I rarely get to see the sun, brilliant in the sky. I'm usually on the set all through the day and night. I squint. "What do you want?" I ask. It comes out harsher than I intended.

Julian pauses, sliding on a pair of sunglasses. "I read the column. I know . . ."

"You know nothing," I say. He steps back from me, holding his hands up. I feel bad. I shouldn't take everything out on Julian. That's not kind of me. I inhale. "I'm sorry. It's been a rough day."

That's saying the least. The reason why I'm not on set right now is because I couldn't get the scene the way Kenneth wanted it, and the assistant thought it best if I take a break. I can't take it when Kenneth yells at me. There's no place in this world where he actually respects me and what I have to say. He'll never see me as anything but a plaything.

And knowing that is the worst part.

"Have you eaten today?" Julian asks. "You look like you're about to fall over."

I miscalculated. I thought I could go back to work and be okay, but maybe I was wrong. "I just need water," I say. Julian frowns. He doesn't believe me. "I have to get back to set," I add. That's not true, but I can't take the way he's looking at me. With pity. Like he wants to save me.

"They'll move on," he says as I'm already turning away, moving down the path. I pause but don't look back.

~

When I return to my dressing room, after hours more of filming, Julian is waiting. He has greasy food from the commissary.

But it's better than nothing.

CHAPTER 23

1954

When Julian invited Thea to dinner, she didn't know what to expect. Julian opened the door, then took the bottle of wine Thea brought from her father's collection. He was casually dressed. The radio was playing, and it sounded like it was coming from the kitchen. "How are you?" Julian asked.

"I'm okay." Truthfully, Thea felt a little awkward about having dinner with Julian. "You didn't have to do all of this."

"Nonsense!" Julian waved her into a dining room with a table fit for eight. He pulled a seat out for her. "I want you to meet someone."

"I think that's my cue," came a voice.

They weren't alone. The man who walked into the dining room was tall and brown, with dancing black eyes and a mischievous smile. "Walter Dawson, this is . . ."

"Thea Ross." Thea rose, extending a hand.

Walter's hand was warm and big. "It's lovely to meet you. I've heard a lot about you."

"I have heard nothing about you," Thea said.

Walter laughed, a divine, low sound. "JJ is like that. Overly cautious about our lives."

"For you, not for me," Julian added. Walter looked at him as if he had individually put all the stars in the sky. Julian seemed to glow in Walter's gaze. "I want to keep you safe."

"For you too," Walter teased. He winked. "I'm making dinner; you can't trust JJ in the kitchen. Please, sit. Drink something. Dinner will be ready in a moment."

Julian and Thea did as they were told. "JJ, huh?" Thea asked. She thought Julian was blushing.

"We've known each other for a long time," Julian said. He was wearing a little lovesick smile. And now, Thea understood why Julian had never remarried. "Before you get any ideas, he's the only one who gets to call me JJ."

"I would never dream of it," Thea said. "What about Julie? Does anyone call you Julie?"

Julian didn't grace her with a response. Walter entered the dining room. His hands were full, juggling three plates. Thea rose to help him. "What are you talking about?" Walter asked.

"Tell Thea who your sister is." Julian rose to pour three glasses of wine.

"Oh, well, she's Lorelei Davies."

"What?" Thea asked.

"Well, I always called her Millie. I'm two years older."

"But you're . . ." Thea trailed off, unsure how to handle this correctly.

Walter's smile crinkled the corners of his eyes. "She was too."

"She was?"

"We were siblings, so yes. JJ, I thought you said she was smart."

"Give her a second." Julian sipped from his glass of wine. "It's a lot to process."

"Not for me," Walter said with a wink. Facing them both was a little intense. Walter and Julian, sitting next to each other, were the picture of simple masculine beauty. "It's true. Lorelei Davies was a full-blooded colored woman who was light enough to pass."

"But . . ." Thea said.

"She did it for her family," Julian added.

"I'm sorry for your loss," Thea said.

"I'm sorry for yours," Walter said. "I heard your dad just passed."

"Thank you," Thea said. "Did you ever meet him?"

"No. Thomas Ross never came to visit us. She barely even told us about him." Walter looked away. "We only met one person Lorelei worked with."

"Me," Julian added, in case it wasn't obvious. He was trying to break the mood, which had turned somber.

Walter looked around the table. "She was brilliant. Seeing her on screen was different than knowing her." Walter looked at Thea, his dark eyes resting on her face. "It's uncanny, but I'd say you look just like her."

"Millie?" Julian asked.

"Joanna," Walter said. "Or what I can remember of her. Joanna was our oldest sister. She looks like Millie, too, but . . ." He trailed off. Both men watched her closely, assessing her face, her hair, her posture. She had been scrutinized like this before, at every modeling job and dance audition. But this was different, even if Thea couldn't place why.

Thea looked at both men. "My dad gave me a letter before he died. He said she was my mom."

Walter's jaw dropped. "Of course she was."

Julian leaned over, kissing Walter softly. "Next time I say something, just agree. It'll be easier."

"JJ thinks he's always right," Walter said. "That's something you're going to have to get used to if you spend time with him."

"I am always right. I can't help it," Julian said. His eyes were still on Thea. "When she concentrates, she squints just like Millie did."

"I don't see it," Thea said. "I've read the magazines; I've seen the photographs. I don't see it."

Walter was in the middle of lighting a cigarette. "Because you never met her. But I promise. You're exactly her."

~

"How do you think she died?" There was no dancing around the question. She and Walter Dawson sat across from each other, and while Thea was filled with so many questions, this was the one she desperately wanted to ask first.

Walter took his time replying. He leaned back in his chair, eyeing her. Julian had retreated to the kitchen, giving them some time alone. The man in front of her was her *uncle*. She had an aunt, two other uncles, and several more cousins. Walter had spent the majority of dinner telling her about her family, and Thea got a thrill with every new detail she learned.

"I held you the day you were born," Walter said. "I didn't know she was having a baby. She named you after our sister, and I held you and bounced you around her living room. You were so small . . ." He trailed off. "Then a week later, she was dead, and I didn't know where you went." He sipped from his glass of wine. His voice was soft. "I never thought she'd do that to herself or to you. You should have seen her look at you."

Thea leaned forward. "What do you think happened?"

Walter frowned. He was choosing his words carefully, not wanting to say the wrong thing. "I don't know. I remember her as Millie. She was my sister. We teased each other; we joked. She's the reason why I met the love of my life. I never saw the woman the world saw."

Julian came back in, wearing an apron and juggling two small cake plates. He set them down in front of Thea and Walter. They had had a large dinner, and Thea wasn't sure she had room for dessert too. She picked up her small fork. Julian sat next to Walter and kissed his cheek.

"What was she like?" Thea asked.

Julian and Walter shared a look. "She was thoughtful," Walter said. "She supported us for years. It's why she went into acting. She didn't want to be on the screen. But she wanted our youngest sister to have a better world than she or Joanna did."

"To be fair, not many people liked working under Kenneth Webster," Julian added. "She liked acting a lot more once we were in charge."

Walter nodded. "Nobody asked her to help the family. I think she saw what happened to Joanna and . . ." He trailed off, picking up his dessert fork. "She thought a lot. She was always imagining the worst things that could happen. She was always thinking up all these scenarios. She was nervous. I think she didn't like being seen."

"But she was luminous on screen," Julian said.

"For what it's worth," Walter said after a small pause, "I always thought that she was murdered."

CHAPTER 24

1954

It was Amy who saved a copy of the paper with Tommy's suicide note in it. Thea still hadn't seen it, despite trying her best.

Amy met her in her dance studio. Thea was conditioning, stretching, getting herself back into fighting shape. Her foot no longer ached; she could stand to put pressure on it.

Amy sat with her back against the wall, across from the floor-to-ceiling mirrors. The paper's pages were spread in front of her, but Amy's eyes were on Thea.

"Thea," Amy said. Her voice was soft. "You don't have to do this."

"I do have to do this." Thea stopped dancing and let her whole body release and relax. She hadn't realized how anxious she was, how tense, until she had started dancing, and then she'd felt it, the anxiety coursing through her body. She grabbed her glass of water and turned off the record player. She sat in front of Amy and turned the pages toward her.

It was three lines, written on a typewriter.

> 11/07/1954
>
> I confess to the murder of Lorelei Davies.

Sophia, Theodosia: I am sorry.

It was signed. She knew her father's signature just like her own.

They had both overdosed: Lorelei, it was said, with barbiturates, and Tommy with chloroform.

Thea couldn't fathom that her father could be capable of something so awful.

"I don't love doing this," Amy said. "I know my stories hurt people. I am so sorry. I am so, so sorry."

"My dad hated typing. He always wrote by hand," Thea said. The letter he had given her was written in his sharp cursive. Thea didn't know if Tommy knew how to type.

There wasn't a typewriter in his office. Lauren did all his typing for him.

She read it again. She knew there was no way Tommy had written that note.

The more Thea thought about it, the more she realized none of that day made sense. She was teaching. Julian was playing the piano. And then, one phone call, and she learned her father had died.

And she couldn't focus on anything else until it all made sense to her.

Did she believe Amy when she said that the deaths of Lorelei and her father were intertwined? She didn't know.

Did she want to find out?

Thea stood, using the barre to pull herself up.

"I should go," Amy said. "I've taken up too much of your time already."

"No," Thea said. "Don't go. I just can't think while I'm sitting." She extended a hand, and Amy took it. Thea used all her strength to pull Amy up, and they almost bumped into each other. "Thank you for showing me the note." Her words came out as a breath. "My mother coddles me."

"It was my pleasure. Not pleasure. You're welcome." Amy's lips were so close to hers. If Thea leaned in, just a little, they'd be kissing. "I really should go. I have a deadline."

"Go meet your deadline," Thea said.

Amy stayed there for a moment; they were still awkwardly holding hands. Then she let go, and Thea turned back to her barre.

Amy left the paper with her. Thea read the note again, feeling a rock in her stomach.

There was no way this note was written by her father.

~

Thea and Amy began in the archives of *The Courier*. They had come in on a Sunday morning, when it was guaranteed to be quiet.

Amy was dressed in a pair of trousers and a button-down shirt. Her glossy dark hair was tied in an intricate bun. She sat on the floor of her office, cross-legged with bare feet.

Thea had to assume that Amy was the only woman at *The Courier* with an office, and that was because she was the gossip columnist. Above her desk hung a black-and-white glamour portrait of a white woman with a serene smile and a knowing look behind her eyes. "That's Cheryl Lawrence," Amy said. "I'm not allowed to take it down."

It was unsettling working under the portrait. Cheryl watched their every move, intent on judging them. "She was the first gossip columnist here," Amy explained, looking up at Cheryl's imperious gaze. "She put it in her contract that her portrait can never be taken down. She trained me before she retired. I was handpicked." Amy brimmed with pride.

Amy smoked as they pawed through the boxes. "I'm not finding anything of importance." They had decided to split up the work, Amy searching for stories about Lorelei, and Thea looking for stories about Tommy.

Thea sat across from her, in the center of a circle of brown boxes with labels dated from 1929 right up until the present. She'd started with the earlier boxes. Tommy had started in Hollywood as talking films got popular. There was, according to one article, something about the cadence of his voice, soft and easy, that made every woman in America fall in love with him.

He was lucky, striking it big. There were actors who couldn't hack talking films, and Tommy was at the right place at the right time. She found photos of her mother and father, grinning at the cameras.

"Are you finding anything?" Amy asked, bringing Thea back to the present.

"Nothing helpful." She flicked through more articles. I LOVE MY WIFE, one proclaimed, over a smiling photo of Tommy and Sophie. Scanning the article, Thea read about how her parents were happier than ever and any rumors of Tommy having an affair were just that. Rumors.

Amy leaned over her shoulder. Thea was enveloped in her bright, sweet scent. "Whoa."

It was hard to marry this image of her father with the man Thea had known. He seemed like a different person. Sophie was laughing. Tommy looked besotted with her. They were at a dinner table, and Thea could see a large ring on her mother's ring finger, one darker stone surrounded by diamonds.

"I can't believe Cheryl has nothing about Lorelei Davies. I've read her pieces. About Ramona Penderghast and Francesca Weston and Mary Hough," Amy said. "She wrote about every influential woman in Hollywood. So why isn't there anything on Lorelei?" Amy squeezed her dark eyes shut. She did that when she was thinking, as if she had to block the world out to hear her thoughts.

"You know," Thea said slowly, "there is someone I can ask." She bit her tongue. "I know Julian John Weston."

Amy pulled away from her in surprise. "You do?"

"He brought his students to take one of my classes."

Amy's eyebrows flicked up. Her reactions to everything were quick: Blink and you'd miss it. "Interesting." Her tone betrayed none of her thoughts.

"I can ask him. He doesn't think Lorelei committed suicide either."

"What about your father's death?" Amy watched her, eyes not blinking.

"I think he agrees with you," Thea said.

Amy raised an eyebrow. "Smart man." She reached into a box, early 1935. She pulled out a paper with a spread of Thea's father, her mother, and herself. AT HOME WITH BABY THEODOSIA. "I remember seeing this," Amy said. "They talk about adopting you, keeping you. It was *great* press." She laughed. Thea had never seen this article before. There were photographs: Tommy holding her, Sophie leaning over a baby bassinet.

Amy held her gaze for a moment longer, then turned back to the boxes. "I was adopted too. Two years old, I was brought over from China. Mark and Elizabeth Evans."

"I've never met another person who was adopted," Thea said.

"Me neither," Amy said. She looked up at Thea and then blushed slightly. "I'm honored to be your first."

"Me too," Thea said, returning Amy's shy smile.

They went through boxes, pulling out relevant stories about Tommy and Sophie.

Amy lit a cigarette. Thea found a photograph of her father, in a tux, beaming. Sophie was beside him, dressed in white, looking up at Tommy with clear adoration. Could she and Amy do this? Build a story based on twenty-year-old rumors and come up with an answer different to the story everyone knew?

They were going to try.

CHAPTER 25

1954

Thea drove both herself and Amy to the location Julian had given her. Thea knew that she'd eventually have to introduce Julian and Amy, that Julian would be a huge key to Amy's story about Lorelei.

But there was a greedy part of her that wanted to keep them separate. She was scared they would like each other better and leave her out of it. If Thea introduced Amy to Julian, Amy would have no need for her.

"*Julian John Weston?*" Amy asked. "I've seen every Julian John Weston film. Every. One. I'm a big fan." She was sitting in the passenger seat of Thea's car, Tommy's Corvette. She leaned into the mirror to reapply her makeup. "You really know Julian John Weston?"

"You didn't believe me? He's just a person," Thea said. The sparkle of film stars, even mostly forgotten ones like Julian, didn't faze her. She had grown up around them. It was different for Amy, even though her job was reporting on them. "You'll be fine. Let's go."

Julian was waiting on the porch of the small house. Amy trailed behind Thea, looking uncharacteristically nervous. "Julian, this is Amy. Amy Evans, Julian John Weston."

"I love *The Heart of It*," Amy said. "I love it so much. I've seen it so many times. You're radiant in it."

Julian's smile was slight, almost invisible. He shook Amy's hand. "Thank you. And you . . . you're at *The Courier*, aren't you?"

"I took over for Cheryl Lawrence," Amy said proudly.

"She's working on the story about Lorelei Davies," Thea said.

"The real story, not whatever Cheryl wrote when she died," Amy said. "What are we doing here?"

"I haven't been in this house in twenty years." Julian pulled a set of keys from his pocket. "When Lorelei died, I bought it, but . . . I haven't come here since then."

The house was a shrine to Lorelei Davies. Her film posters on the walls, lined up in chronological order: *Joe and Meg*, *Her and I*, *Maybe Someday*, *Mrs. Donahue*, and *Allergic to Love*.

Thea knew that Lorelei's final Sunset film, *Live, Love*, was never finished.

"Sometimes kids break in here; they just see an empty house . . ." Julian stood at the threshold, his arms behind his back. There were things obviously missing, taken from shelves and cabinets, empty dust spots in their places.

"We don't have to do this," Thea said. Julian had gone a little pale, frozen in one spot.

"I just . . . I miss her all the time. Around this time of year, every year, I think about the last time I saw her, and she had . . ." Julian trailed off, looking at Thea. He cleared his throat, inhaling, calming himself down. "It doesn't matter. Go inside."

The house stood empty and eerie, like someone was watching their every move. The sunlight shone in from the windows, dust dancing in the beams. Julian looked around, still a few steps from the open door.

"Why did you buy the house?" Amy asked.

"I thought she would want me to," Julian said. "I knew she'd want me to keep it."

"For me?" Thea asked.

"I suppose so," Julian said. "I guess I was saving it for you."

They made their way through the house, starting in the bedroom. The closet was full, all organized by garment type. Thea stopped at a black-and-white dress, still soft and diaphanous after all these years. Above the clothes were hatboxes, and that was where Amy lingered.

Thea went through to the bedroom. It was, like the rest of the house, well preserved. The mattress was stripped of sheets. The vanity mirror was cracked, and Thea wondered who had done it. On the nightstand were three pens all lined up. Thea opened the drawers to the nightstand and then the vanity. They were empty except for dust. Even the mattress had a thick layer of dust.

"Hey," Amy said from the closet. "Come here." Thea did as she was told. Amy sat on the floor of the closet. She had a hatbox in front of her.

And it was filled to the brim with paper.

Thea sat across from Amy, the box between them. Envelopes, all of them different sizes and faded with age. Thea picked one up. None of them had a mailing or return address. But each bore the same name in slanted cursive.

Lorelei. Lorelei. Lorelei. Lorelei.

The same handwriting Thea had seen every day of her life. Her father's. She opened a couple of the envelopes. They were empty, but Lorelei had saved them all.

~

Thea went to check on Julian. He hadn't moved from the small living room. It was like he couldn't bear to look through the house. "It's probably time to sell some of this stuff," Julian said.

"You don't have to do it," Thea said. She was thrilled to discover more about Lorelei. See where she lived, see her clothes and her home. But the woman herself was missing. Thea would never get to know Lorelei. And now she'd have to rely on the memories of others to fill in the gaps.

Julian reached into his pocket, then handed her the keys. "It's up to you." Something else that would require a decision. Something else that she wasn't ready for. Thea took the keys and slid them into her purse.

"Thea!" Amy called from a distant bedroom. Thea and Julian found Amy in the smallest bedroom. It had no furniture. Amy sat in front of the empty closet, in front of a pile of journals.

Julian exhaled. "She was always writing."

Each journal was embossed with the year. From 1920 right up until 1934. There were sometimes multiple books for a year. Thea sat next to Amy, picking one up. It had been burned and was unreadable. "I wonder what happened here." Thea looked up at Julian. He was hovering by the door, unable to step inside. Thea looked around the room again.

"Can we take them?" Thea asked. Julian's eyes were closed. When he opened them, he focused on Thea. "It's your house. You can do whatever you want."

CHAPTER 26

1954

Cheryl Lawrence was still alive, and Julian took Thea to see her. The overpowering stench of cigarette smoke hit Thea in the face as Julian opened the door, letting her in.

The house was small and immaculate. It was dressed in girlish shades of pink, the curtains drawn over the window, casting the living room in shadows. It was a modest little place, and Julian pointed her up the stairs.

Nerves rolled over Thea's arms and legs. Julian had assured her twenty times over that she'd be fine, but she hated the unknown.

"This one," Julian said, stopping at a closed door. He looked Thea up and down, observing her casual trousers and button-down shirt that had been her father's. "She's an awful woman," Julian said. "Don't let her intimidate you."

Ominous final words. Thea nodded, swallowing hard. He opened the door, going in first. "Cheryl."

Thea trailed after him. He stood in front of a frail woman propped up in a giant bed. She glared at Julian through wide glasses. Her bedroom, too, was dressed in shades of pink and smelled like cigarette smoke. "You never visit anymore." Cheryl's voice was low and raspy.

Julian raised an eyebrow. "I'm sorry. I've been busy." Cheryl lifted her chin, not accepting the apology. Unfazed, Julian continued. "This is Theodosia Ross."

Thea stepped forward, her heart in her throat. "Lovely to meet you, Mrs. Lawrence."

"It's Cheryl, love. Men were never of use to me." Cheryl's cloudy brown eyes landed on Thea, and it was as if she saw right through her.

"Does she look familiar?" Julian asked. He concentrated on lighting a cigarette.

Cheryl took a look at Thea. "Turn around." Thea did what she was told, turning in a slow circle. When she was facing Cheryl again, the older woman looked toward Julian. "Should she remind me of anyone?"

Thea looked back to Julian in time to catch his frown. "Never mind." He cleared his throat and nodded to Thea. "Cheryl was the first gossip columnist at *The Courier*. She was the one who started the rivalry between your father and I."

"I was bored," Cheryl said dryly.

"Yes, thank you for that," Julian said.

"Bring that chair over, and let the girl sit. Then you can go make us some tea and let us talk." Julian did as he was told, placing the padded chair from the vanity near the bed.

The older woman waited until Julian left before turning her gaze back to Thea. "He told me your father is Tommy Ross. I'm sorry for your loss."

"Thank you," Thea said. "And I want to ask about him, but I also want to talk about Lorelei Davies."

"Now there's a name. You know she was Millicent Dawson? Terrible. No one wants to see a movie star named Constance or Millicent. Those names are for frigid girls who won't let a man feel them up. But Theodosia. That's beautiful."

"My grandmother, on my father's side, I think," Thea said.

Cheryl looked at her, her eyes boring into Thea's face. "Help me up." Thea obeyed. Out of the bed, Cheryl was a tiny bit shorter than

Thea and quite frail. "To the other bedroom," she directed. They crossed the hall, and Cheryl opened the door to a bedroom, painted blue and very cold. Thea turned the lights on, and they shuddered to life. Cheryl sat on the bare mattress. "The closet." Thea opened the door to the closet to see boxes and boxes of files. "I decided that some things should stay with me when I left *The Courier*. If you're looking for my work and notes on Lorelei Davies, it'll all be here."

"Why?" Thea asked.

Cheryl's look was distant. Thea didn't know if the older woman had heard her. Then Cheryl answered, "I wanted to keep it. This is some of my favorite work."

"Can I take them?" Thea asked. "I'd love to read more of your pieces."

"Whatever you wish. But . . ." At this, Thea turned back toward her. "You have to promise to visit. And tell me what you find out. An old lady needs some companionship." Cheryl's eyes seemed huge behind her glasses. She was older now, and Thea couldn't see a resemblance to the glamour shot in Amy's office. "Now that I look at you, properly, you do seem a little bit like her. It's the nose, I think. Lorelei had a distinctive nose."

"She's my mother," Thea said.

Cheryl looked at her, a long moment, and then sighed. "Of course she is."

CHAPTER 27

1934

Tommy is undone. His tie, his shirt, all unbuttoned. He's leaning on my doorjamb and watching me with his dark eyes.

I'm wearing a dressing gown with nothing underneath. I know that he can see the curve of my breasts, the long lines of my legs. I'm sitting at my vanity, spraying perfume on my neck. I tilt my head to the side, and I feel his lips press to my skin.

"Tommy." I do all this for his benefit, drawing it out, trying to torture him every way I know how. His arms are around me.

"I'm going to tear this off of you." His voice is a whisper by my ear, and I can't resist him any longer. I rise from my chair, allowing him to pull me close. His lips are on my skin, and he fusses with the tie on my gown.

But instead of pulling it off, he surprises me by lifting me up. I wrap my legs around his waist as he presses me against the wall, our lips desperately searching for each other. He's supporting me; I can feel the muscles in his arms flex as he holds me up. My body is pressed to his, and I think I can feel his heartbeat synchronize with mine. His body is hard and warm and strong.

"Bed," I gasp. "Bed, now."

He's compliant. He usually doesn't do what I say, what I want, but tonight is different. He all but throws me on the bed, following in an instant.

When he pulls off my dressing gown, he stops and takes in my naked body.

It's the look in his eyes as he does it. I see it all the time while filming, but with me it feels *real*. The look of adoration, as if *I* hung the moon, as if I'm everything he's ever wanted. He leans down, running his fingers across my stomach. I buck at his touch. His hand, heating my thigh.

"Say it," Tommy says.

"I want you," I say. He removes his shirt, pulling it off and dropping it on the floor.

"Say it," Tommy says again.

"I need you."

And when he presses into me, his lips against mine, his hands on my breasts, my body, I can't catch my breath.

~

"What do you write in those?"

I don't notice that Tommy has woken, watching me from the bed. He sleeps like the dead. I've moved to the vanity, where I'm writing in my journal.

"Dear diary," I say, looking up. "I only ever think about Thomas Ross."

"As it should be," Tommy says. "But really. What are you writing about?"

I close my journal, feeling rather protective of it. "Nothing." He pulls himself from my bed, beginning to dress. It's early enough that the clubs are still open, and I have no doubt he's headed to one of those to charm and dazzle everyone around him.

I've pulled my robe on over my nightgown. The one thing I want to do is go back to bed. "Notes."

"Let me see." His tone is teasing. I swallow hard. In these pages, I've dissected everything Tommy has ever said to me, everything Kenneth has ever done to me. I can't let him see it. I have no intention of letting Tommy know what Kenneth does to me.

I close the book. "Kiss me."

"No." He's teasing me. "Tell me what you write." He buttons his shirt so slowly it may as well be foreplay. He knows my eyes are on him. As a final touch, he rolls his sleeves to his elbows. He wants what he wants. I'm not going to give it to him.

I turn around, facing him. I put my pen down. "I'm writing about what I want you to do to me." I'm hoping to catch him off guard.

Tommy smiles, pleased with himself. He kneels down in front of me. "Open your legs."

I do as I'm told. Tommy's fingers trail over my bare thighs. My heart is pulsing, and he takes his time, teasing me like I do him. "What is it?" Tommy's voice is soft, and I know what he's trying to do.

I pull away from him. "Leave."

He rises, still smiling. This is a game to him, and he wants to win. He's used to getting everything he wants.

He won't let this go.

I pick up the journal, grabbing it before he can. I strike a match and light it on fire. Tommy steps back. "You're crazy," he spits.

"Get out." I hold the burning book up. I can feel the flames licking my hands.

"Lorelei!" Tommy yells. He picks up an atomizer of perfume and throws it at my vanity, breaking the mirror.

"Out!"

I wait until I hear the door close, and I hope Tommy's gone. I run to the bathroom, dousing the flames in the sink.

Not all of it is gone, but the damage is done.

I start a new journal.

CHAPTER 28

1934

There's a big press soiree that's centered around us.

I don't want to go.

I'm wearing a black-and-white color-blocked bias-cut halter dress that clings to my body. The halter neck crosses over my front. The belt is wrapped tightly around my waist. My hair is in a braided crown, revealing my neck. I feel beautiful, but I can't fight the frown on my face. I see Julian and Francesca, in close discussion. They're dancing to the band, and I'm on the outskirts watching.

DAVIES AND ROSS. DAVIES AND ROSS. They're promoting us as the next Astaire and Rogers. And Tommy is across the ballroom with his wife.

Sophie wears a white gown, this one with transparent fluttering sleeves and a neckline that kisses her throat. She always wears white when she makes appearances. It gives her an angelic quality. I'm her opposite tonight. I can see Tommy, black tie and tails, looking as devastating as he did the first day we met, sneaking looks at me. Ramona is in the corner, holding court as she usually does.

These parties always seem too lavish. I think about the money spent on the band and champagne and venue, and then I think of my family. There are people out there who have nothing, and these events are barely remembered the day after. The champagne will be vomited up; the memories will be hazy. And my family is struggling to put food on the table.

The band starts up another song, and I'm surprised to see Tommy taking the microphone from the singer. Sophie is watching him. And when he starts singing "Isn't It Romantic?" I feel myself choke up and turn on my heel.

I'm thinking about how he called me crazy. It cut me to the quick, even though I know he said it because he was angry at me. But I'm not crazy. And if that's what he says when he's angry, what will he say when he is furious? Everyone already thinks I'm crazy, and that I can't help. But I didn't think he saw me that way too.

This dress is suffocating. I think my dresses are made too small, inspiring me to lose more weight. I make my way to the foyer of the hotel, breathing hard. I step outside, into the night, trying to catch my breath. If I concentrate, I can hear Tommy still crooning. My heart is in my throat. It was a couple of weeks ago, at an affair much like this, that I resolved to end our tryst. And my confidence in that has shaken every time I've seen him.

A round of applause. I can hear Tommy very kindly thanking everyone. The band starts up again, and I listen, but I don't hear Tommy singing along.

I look into the night sky. I can't stand seeing him and Sophie. My chest is still tight. "Lorelei," Tommy says softly. He's removed his suit jacket, and he looks just as good, if not better, without it. He pulls a pack of cigarettes from his pocket. He hands it to me.

"What?" I eye it warily.

"I think I was an ass." He gives me a nervous little smile. He's really putting himself on the line.

"So you want me to light you a cigarette?" I ask.

Tommy winks. "Please."

I go to tap out a cigarette, but a delicate chain falls out into my palm. I hold it up. It twinkles in the moonlight. I look to Tommy, and he's pulling out a cigarette from his silver case. "I'm sorry I was such an ass," Tommy said. The chain has a little pendant, a silver art deco star with an emerald on it. It's stunning. Tommy places his cigarette between his lips and clasps the necklace around my neck. It falls under the hollow of my throat. It's cold against my skin. I'm still holding the empty cigarette box.

"We can't do this anymore." I turn to him just in time to see his face fall. "I can't do this anymore. Seeing you with her . . ." I let my sentence trail off because if I keep talking, I'll take it back. I raise my fingers to the pendant. "I can't accept this."

"No, keep it." Tommy takes a step away from me.

"I want to go home." I'm supposed to make a speech tonight, and we're supposed to be seen together. Kenneth and the higher-ups will want to see us together in photographs.

"Lorelei."

"Thomas."

A flicker of a smile at his lips. I want to lean over and kiss him. I clear my throat. "Thank you."

~

And after an hour and two glasses of wine, I excuse myself to the bathroom. Anything to get away from the dining room for a moment. The attendants are both colored women. They are in stiff black uniforms, the same kind I remember my mother wearing. I don't look them in the eye. I'm always nervous that they'll be able to tell, no matter how light my skin is or how flat my hair is. The truth is that I feel guilty. I lean into the mirror, refreshing my lipstick.

The stall behind me opens, and Sophie steps out. She's adjusting the skirt of her dress, and I see her before she sees me. She looks up, her ice-blue eyes meeting mine in the mirror. I realize that I've worked with Tommy for two years and I'm not sure I've ever spoken to Sophie.

"Lorelei." She leans over the sink, washing her hands. "How nice to see you."

"Nice to see you, too, Sophie."

She leans into the mirror, searching for flaws in her perfect face. Next to her, I feel awkward. Next to her, I'm nothing. Her engagement ring glints in the lights of the bathroom. Sophie turns toward me, statuesque. "You know, Tommy's told me all about you. You're crazy."

I try not to let my feelings show. That word again. Following me around wherever I go, no matter what I do. Sometimes I want to do something really crazy, and then I'll show them all. I keep my eyes locked on my reflection in the mirror. She thinks she has the upper hand, and I'm going to let her keep thinking that.

"Excuse me, miss, but there's another woman waiting for the mirror." The attendant speaks directly to me. It's like she can tell, like the veneer that is Lorelei Davies is completely see through to other colored women.

"Of course, sorry," I say, reaching into my purse. I hand the woman two ten-dollar bills, guilt manifesting in monetary ways. Sophie is at my side as we leave the bathroom. "Lorelei, if you could do me one favor." She's smiling, and I know Tommy can see us from his vantage point. "Stay away from my husband. I never want to hear your name again." Her eyes drop to the necklace at my throat.

"Likewise." She's shaken me, but I don't let it show.

I ignore Sophie and, by extension, Tommy all night. And I can feel his eyes on me.

CHAPTER 29

1954

"First, we need to make a list of the people who would have wanted to kill Lorelei," Amy said. She sat across from Thea at her father's desk. No matter how much time passed, Thea would never think of the office as hers.

Amy leaned over the desk. She wrote something down and then turned her paper toward Thea. "How many murders have you solved?" Thea asked.

Amy exhaled, sharply, almost a laugh. "I didn't join *The Courier* to take over for Cheryl. I did it because I love the news. Gossip, I like less. I want to tell stories, not spread unfounded rumors."

"Why Lorelei?" Thea asked.

Amy's warm brown eyes met hers. "Did you know that a woman killed herself by jumping off the *H* in the Hollywood sign? Peg Entwistle. I just can't help but feel that there are so many women who deserve to have their story told. And Lorelei. She was so magnetic on screen. *About Last Night* was her sixth film released. Who could she have been had she not died? She was on the brink of something great. There's something there." She nodded firmly. "Now we're going to make a list of who would want Lorelei dead and why." Amy turned the paper back to her. Thea leaned forward, watching as Amy wrote. Kenneth Webster, Tommy Ross.

They didn't have many suspects.

Thea said, "All I have are her journals, and those are her thoughts, nothing concrete. I wish I knew more about her." Amy crossed her arms over her chest, taking in what Thea said. It was nice to have someone to talk to about this. She couldn't talk to anyone else. Willa would be her first choice, but Thea hadn't talked to her since Tommy's memorial. Their relationship was over. Who would understand?

"But at least you can see her on film," Amy said.

"It's something, I guess. But I want to know the real her. Not the actress version. Not the public person."

They were quiet for a moment. "Do you think she had someone who was obsessed with her?" Amy asked.

"I don't think she got that famous," Thea said. "She would have written about it."

Amy considered this. "This was twenty years ago. Trying to build a suspect list will be hard."

Thea leaned back in her chair. "My mother was invited to a party for Ramona Penderghast. Maybe I could try to talk to her there."

"Oh, Ramona Penderghast is back," Amy said. "She'd know something." Thea was eager to see how Ramona compared to how Lorelei had written about her. Lorelei had written about a woman who was committed to being on screen, dedicated to getting what she wanted. Thea wanted to know how the real woman compared. "That's your mission, then," Amy said. "Get Ramona to talk to us. *On* the record."

~

One thing Sophie was insistent she and Thea do was go through Tommy's clothes together. The master bedroom closet was big, but most of it was filled with Sophie's things, dresses and skirts and blouses, matching accessories, all organized by color. The Ross house had twelve rooms, five of which were bedrooms. Tommy commandeered the closet of the closest bedroom.

He had as many clothes as Sophie. The room was empty except for the closet, which was full, about to burst.

"I made him some of these," Sophie said. "I was rather handy with a Singer." She was folding his button-downs, some stark white, some soft plaids. Thea had already taken one, a midnight blue check with lines of yellow gold in it, put it on, and wrapped it tight around her body. She could still smell his aftershave, strong and spicy.

"You were? What else did you make?" Thea asked.

Sophie was standing, pulling clothes from shelves. "Some dresses. A pair of blue jeans, if you can believe it. Your grandmother hated those. Your father always wanted me to make him a suit, but I thought . . . he was always in amazing clothing. My skills would never have compared."

"I think he would have loved it," Thea said.

Sophie frowned. "Me too. I wish I'd done it." It was late afternoon, the sunlight filtering into the bedroom. Sophie sat down next to Thea. "I made the gown you were baptized in." She began to fold shirts, stacking them according to color.

"I was baptized?" Thea asked.

"Of course you were. Your grandmother insisted on it." Sophie smiled softly.

For the past few days, Thea had been trying to find the best moment to bring up Lorelei Davies. She wanted to know what her mother knew.

And this was *a* time. Maybe not the perfect time.

The perfect time would never come, and Thea would put it off forever waiting for it.

"The envelope Dad gave me," Thea said. She pulled the syllable of each word out so that by the time she was done talking, Sophie's cold blue eyes were on her, expecting something. "On my birthday? It was a letter." Thea reached up and touched the star that sat at the hollow of her throat. She hadn't taken it off since the moment her mother put it on her. "He said that Lorelei Davies was my mother."

"Of course he wrote you a letter," Sophie said.

"Why did he give it to me?" Thea asked.

"I don't know," Sophie said softly. Thea thought about the interview Sophie had done, how at ease her mother had seemed sitting with Colin and talking about Tommy's death. "I thought it would be a check."

"What happened?" Thea asked.

"Right before your birthday, he told me everything." Sophie said. They were sitting across from each other. Her mother wasn't looking at her, folding and refolding the same shirt. She stopped. "He told me that the night of her death, he went to see her, to convince her to give him his daughter. When she refused, he killed her and called Harrison in to stage her death. He killed her for you. To take you." Sophie inhaled. She was looking around for a cigarette. She stopped fidgeting, looking Thea right in the eye.

"Mom," Thea said. She didn't know how she was going to finish that sentence.

Sophie exhaled. "It doesn't matter. It never mattered to me. You have his eyes. You have his laugh. You have the same look when something upsets you. You are him. And I'm glad to raise a part of him." Sophie finally put the shirt on top of the pile. They were still surrounded by Tommy's clothes, and Thea didn't know what they were going to do with all of it. There were some things she wanted to keep, as if tactile things would keep the memory of her father with her. As if he was wrapped up in these shirts, so many beautiful shirts, and pants and jackets.

"Why did he kill himself now?" Thea asked. "Why wait?" This was the most candid Sophie had ever been with her.

"Thea." Sophie closed her eyes. "I think I want to go to bed."

"Wait, Mom," Thea said. "I just want to know."

Thea had always been closer to Tommy. They'd talked about everything and nothing at all. She knew how he had felt about everyone at Ballet Los Angeles. She knew how he had felt about everyone at

Constellation. Thea and Tommy had had the same feelings about television and music.

It was easy with him.

Sophie controlled everything around her. Thea struggled to get Sophie to see her as an adult, not a little kid who had to be herded and watched and coddled and directed.

"I guess he couldn't deal with the pressure anymore. I guess he thought it was the only way out."

Sophie exhaled. They were both silent for a moment. It was a lot to reckon with, and for the first time, Thea was furious with her father.

He had left them both to deal with his aftermath and hadn't told her everything.

"I am so sorry, sweetheart. But what matters is that you had a good life. The type of life I would have killed for. You'd have to ask him anything else," Sophie said.

Thea couldn't ask her dad.

And she didn't trust her mom either.

CHAPTER 30

1954

Ramona Penderghast's party was held at a bookstore that had a wealth of classics and new books. Thea had arrived thirty minutes before the party specifically to wander through the stacks and had come away with two Christies and a Jackson.

Thea kept to the sidelines, watching her mother. Sophie wore a black cocktail dress, her hair tumbling over her shoulders. Sophie held a glass of champagne and was sparkling, surrounded by a small group of men and women. She made a quip, inaudible from Thea's vantage point, and everyone around her laughed.

Thea wore a black dress that was almost a miniature version of her mother's. She was a little uncomfortable. Her low black heels pinched her feet.

Thea, with a glass of water, watched as her mother stepped to a makeshift stage with a microphone and cleared her throat. "Good turnout tonight," Sophie said. Her low, throaty voice caught the attention of everyone. "I know, you're not here to listen to me talk. You're here for the woman of the hour. And may I present the woman of the hour, the actress, the *duchess*, my old friend, Ramona Penderghast."

The woman who stepped up beside her mother looked younger than Sophie but also seemed timeless. She wore a dark-red evening gown that cinched an impossibly tiny waist. Her hair was black and long, her skin was white, her eyes mossy green.

She was the most beautiful woman Thea had ever seen. This Ramona gave her mother a tight hug, whispering something that the microphone didn't pick up. When she began to talk, her voice was melodic. "Thank you so much, everyone. I didn't know if Hollywood would remember me. I've been away so long, all my films forgotten."

"*TAMING OF THE SHREW*," someone yelled from near Thea.

"*MRS. DONAHUE*," another added.

A chortle rippled through the crowd. Ramona's lips, drenched in red to match her dress, turned upward. "Not totally forgotten, and I am grateful. I want to take a moment to acknowledge my dear friend Tommy Ross. He was a wonderful friend and a perfect dance partner. He walked me down the aisle at my wedding. He was always there to talk to, always there with a joke." She led a round of applause, gesturing to Sophie on her right.

Ramona cleared her throat, turning the attention back to her. "This book is a love letter to Hollywood, to my life as a duchess, everything. It's called *First Act* because I believe that I'm on my second act. And with that, I would love to announce that I have signed a two-picture contract with Constellation Pictures. I will be back."

A ripple of applause. Sophie stepped back up to the microphone. "Ramona will be available to sign books all night. Please remember to purchase your copy. And, everyone, please, drink more."

More applause. Thea sipped from her glass. She tried to remain as invisible as possible. She should, as a new shareholder of Constellation Pictures, go introduce herself. The idea of talking to the raven-haired beauty made her tongue tied.

"Thea." She'd recognize her mother's voice anywhere, even in a crowd full of low, tangled conversations. Ramona Penderghast stood right next to her mother. Both were holding glasses of champagne. "Here she is," Sophie said. "My daughter."

Thea extended her hand. "It's nice to meet you."

Ramona's smile was soft. "You too. I wish I could have seen you with your father. I'm so sorry for your loss."

"Thank you," Thea said.

"He really was a wonderful man," Ramona continued. "I've heard you inherited the Ross work ethic."

"He forced it into me," Thea said.

Ramona laughed. "You do remind me of him."

"She does, doesn't she?" Sophie asked.

"You were a duchess?" Thea asked.

Ramona nodded. "For a while. We're . . . separating."

"Ramona, you didn't tell me that," Sophie said. "I thought he was here."

"No, I'm staying at a hotel. It's all aboveboard, but he realized that he liked the idea of me more than anything. I thought . . . you know what? It doesn't matter. This is a party, and we're here to celebrate." Ramona shook her hair from her eyes, looking to Thea. She extended an arm toward her. Thea looped her arm through Ramona's. "You are going to stay right by my side. I'll tell you every embarrassing story about your father that I can think of."

"No drinks. Someone is still underage," Sophie said.

"Of course not," Ramona said with a wink.

"Ramona."

"Sophia."

"I love you."

"I'm sorry for your loss."

Sophie looked Ramona up and down. "You're staying with Thea and me. For as long as you need."

"I'm not going to impose," Ramona said.

Sophie frowned. "I'm offering."

Ramona considered this. Thea had never seen anyone win in a battle against her mother. "Fine, Mrs. Ross, but I'm not staying forever." With that, Thea and Ramona were off. "It's been so long since I've attended a Hollywood soiree; I'm woefully out of touch. I need you to guide me."

"I'm not sure what I can do. I've only attended parties for Constellation Pictures," Thea said.

Ramona laughed. "Even better. We'll take the world on together."

~

Spending time with Ramona was very much like spending time with her father. She had this pull that attracted everyone in the general vicinity. They made a beeline right to the bar, where Ramona ordered glasses of champagne and club soda and handed the champagne to Thea.

"Back in the day, these nights were endless. Sunset soirees were legendary." Thea could hear a soft lilt in Ramona's voice, an accent that didn't exactly sound American. "And, of course, as a duchess, I attended parties every night. But nothing compares to a Hollywood soiree."

"My dad walked you down the aisle?" Thea asked.

"Oh, yes. It was very kind of Sophie to let me borrow him for the day. My own daddy had died just a couple weeks earlier, and I wanted to call everything off. But Tommy . . . he had a way, you know? Of course you do. He took an ocean liner and was with me every moment of the day. Tommy was more incredible than anyone ever really knew."

"Yeah," Thea said. Her throat was tight. "I'm sorry you're separating."

"Ah, love comes and goes. You'll learn that soon enough. You, my darling, are the absolute picture of beauty." Ramona turned to her, cool green eyes meeting Thea's. "I swear, you have his eyes."

"Everyone says that," Thea said.

"I miss him every day," Ramona said.

"Miss Penderghast."

Ramona turned to a man behind them with a smile. "Kenneth, you angel." Ramona greeted him with a kiss to the cheek. The man was big, bald, in a tux with a bow tie, a little overdressed. Thea wondered how Ramona knew the name of everyone there. "Ramona," Kenneth said. He kissed her cheek, a little too close to her red lips.

"May I introduce Thea Ross?" Ramona asked. "She's Sophie's daughter. This is Kenneth Webster, a legendary director."

Kenneth looked her over, his eyes narrowing. "Thomas Ross's daughter?" he asked. "I'm sorry for your loss."

"Lovely to meet you," Thea said. He extended a hand. Thea shook and found he was sweating. When he released her, it took all Thea's will to not wipe her hand on the skirt of her dress. "Thank you."

She took a step away from Ramona, who was still in tense conversation with Kenneth. If this was a Constellation party, she and Willa and Max would be at a table, making snide remarks while drinking glasses of champagne. She could see her mother across the crowd, laughing almost a little too loudly. She wondered if her mother was in the same type of dull pain she was. If Sophie was, she was good at hiding it.

Ramona returned, and they took another loop around the room. "Did you know Lorelei Davies?" Thea asked.

Ramona laughed. "We started at Sunset at the same time. She was . . . an interesting girl."

"Interesting?" Thea asked.

"Complicated. I remember her as being very talented but quite troubled." Ramona took a sip of her club soda. "There would be days where she couldn't film because she couldn't get up off the floor of her dressing room. She'd be crying, or she'd be totally comatose. It always seemed like a lot of effort to turn herself on. You know, we had to split ourselves in parts to survive back then." Ramona spoke so thoughtfully, so introspectively. "I would love to discuss her more, but this isn't the place. I will say that she was ambitious. And I always liked that about her."

"She was?" Thea asked. She took a sip of her champagne, the bubbles going right to her head.

"We had to be, darling. It's how you survived in Hollywood."

"And splitting yourself in pieces," Thea said.

"Very good," Ramona said with a wink.

Thea stayed by Ramona's side all night. It turned out to be fun.

CHAPTER 31

1954

When Thea woke up, late and still in her longline bra and petticoat, Ramona Penderghast was sitting at the kitchen table, drinking coffee, reading the papers. The previous night had seemed almost dreamlike to Thea, circling the room a half step behind the film star, being privy to her little comments and jokes.

Thea had even managed to make her laugh a couple of times.

"Good morning," Ramona said. "Your housekeeper makes stunning coffee. It's been years since I've had coffee like this."

Thea sat down across from the woman. "Ilsa has been with my family for years." She looked around. "My mom out?"

"Left before I could even comprehend where I am," Ramona said. She put the papers away, looking at Thea again.

"How come my dad never talked about you?" Thea asked.

"He never talked about his past, did he?"

Thea shook her head. She craved coffee, but she didn't want to get up to get it. She and Amy planned to meet later, but until then, Thea was going to lie around. "I've seen a couple of his films, but he was intent on me seeing him as a real man. That didn't stop him from taking me to every Constellation Pictures event since I was ten."

Ramona's mouth turned down. "That's a pity. There was a time when he was the most famous man in America. Luminous on screen, beautiful. He was a great friend, even after I moved to Europe. He's the one who got me the Constellation contract. But I guess you knew that already."

"Why are you returning to the screen?" Thea asked. She didn't want to admit that she had no idea what was going on with the business. Every time she thought about it, it felt like she was drowning. When she went to the office to try to get her bearings, understand what she was doing, she ended up feeling more foolish.

"Simple." Ramona's smile was soft and sad. Even now, in the harsh light of morning, she was one of the most beautiful women Thea had ever seen. She had a trim, perfect hourglass figure, her hair clipped low and falling over her shoulder. Her skin was pure and flawless as porcelain. Without makeup, her lips and cheeks were pink. "Film is my first love. I think it's the only thing I'll ever love." Thea opened her mouth again, but Ramona continued. "You're going to ask about Lorelei again."

"Is now better?" Thea asked.

"You are nothing if not persistent." Ramona looked around. "You don't have cigarettes in this place, do you? Mine are upstairs."

"One moment." With all the strength she could muster, Thea pulled herself from the table and made her way to the kitchen. There she found an unopened pack of cigarettes and a lighter. She poured herself a large cup of coffee, then added a little bit of sugar and cream. Ilsa was in the kitchen, intently watching the small television. Thea planted a kiss on the older woman's head.

Thea returned to the table. She gave Ramona the cigarettes and lighter. "Perfect," Ramona said. Her voice was a purr. She lit a cigarette and then looked at Thea. "Everyone thought Lorelei and I were friends. I suppose we were, in a way. When I first met her, we were auditioning for the same featured dancer role."

"In *Joe and Meg*?" Thea asked.

"That's the one," Ramona said with a sigh. "I was so jealous. When I saw her on screen, I knew she was better—a better dancer, at least. She put the work in, but . . ." She paused, sipping from her coffee. "She was troubled. She was . . . intimate with a high-up director. She was messy."

"What director?" Thea asked.

"Kenneth Webster. One of the men I introduced you to last night. She was intimate with him, and yes, she was intimate with your father, and I don't doubt she was intimate with Julian John Weston as well. She slept with anyone who could advance her career."

Thea's skin crawled. The idea of Lorelei with all these men. There was something predatory about it.

Maybe Tommy wasn't really her father.

Ramona removed the cigarette from her lips, exhaling smoke. "I tried to get by on talent, actual talent. And when I married my husband, he was my first. Lorelei was passed around like Cuban cigars." Thea frowned. "I'm sorry it's not what you want to hear. Lorelei Davies was an idea. She's a cautionary tale." Ramona locked eyes with Thea. Something, somewhere, in the house creaked. "Why are you so curious?"

Thea's mouth went dry. She sipped from her coffee cup, trying to formulate a coherent sentence. Ramona's green eyes were cold and impassive, daring Thea to say anything. "I suppose I want to know more about her and my father."

Ramona stubbed out her cigarette. She drained her coffee cup. "There isn't much to know. Your father, God rest his soul, fell for a slut."

~

Lorelei Davies was discovered at Cloud Nine. Thea had never thought that this search would bring her to a club, in a slinky black dress, sitting next to Amy.

They sat in the back of the club, watching the woman on stage. She was singing what seemed to be an Irving Berlin standard, but it was hard to tell. Amy was drinking a bright-pink cocktail. Thea didn't dare order anything stronger than a Coke. She wondered what her mother would say if she could see Thea sitting here, next to a woman she barely knew, listening to a singer croon about love. When she looked around, she recognized some Hollywood bigwigs, including Ramona. She sat in front, at one of the most visible tables, wearing a red dress with a plunging neckline. Her hair was swooped into an intricate bun. She caught Thea's eye and winked. Thea blushed in response.

Honestly, Thea was surprised the club was still open. It felt like a relic of a different time, a seedy, clandestine meeting place. The club was dark, the lights lowered, so patrons could barely see each other.

"I think that the owners are in the mob and this place is a money-laundering front," Amy said. She was smoking, her eyes darting around the club. She was taking in every detail of the place.

"Your next exposé," Thea joked.

Amy laughed. "We'll see how my story on Lorelei goes."

"Why did we come here?" Thea asked. She wanted to be reckless. She'd borrowed the black dress from Amy. It had a slim skirt and a square neckline with deep, sultry pleats in the corners, emphasizing her bust. It was more mature than she really was. Amy had decided that none of the clothes Thea owned were right for this excursion. All Thea's dresses were girlish, childish. She owned nothing that represented the adult that she had become.

Amy was older than Thea: Amy had two roommates, a job, and a steady beau. She was daring. She wore a shade of red lipstick Thea could only dream of wearing. Thea lived with her mother and always did exactly what she was told. She and Amy couldn't be more different.

And yet here they were *together*.

Her thoughts bounced around her head. She couldn't keep them straight. All she knew, really, for sure, was that every nerve in her body seemed to be lit on fire when she was near Amy.

Amy was new. Thrilling.

"Don't you want to see the place where Lorelei Davies was discovered?" Amy exhaled cigarette smoke. They blended in here.

"She was Millicent Dawson back then," Thea said. It was the most important part of Lorelei's story. How did Millicent Dawson, a colored girl from Watts, become Lorelei Davies, a white Hollywood starlet?

Thea assumed that becoming Lorelei Davies wasn't her choice, that Lorelei went along with it.

Amy took a sip from her drink. It was a seedy little place, but Thea thought she could see the appeal. On that stage, Lorelei would be in charge.

"One night Kenneth Webster sat right where Ramona is, and he saw her," Amy added.

Thea tried to picture it. Sixteen-year-old Millicent Dawson, on the verge of something new. Her slightly oval face, the smile that lit up a room. Her hair in curls over her shoulders. She'd be wearing a bias-cut dress. She'd grip the microphone with perfectly varnished nails, crooning. She'd play coy in the way a sixteen-year-old could, batting her eyelashes at men in the front row.

And she'd be *noticed*. Maybe that's what she wanted. Maybe that's what a sixteen-year-old thought would provide security. She wanted whatever Kenneth Webster might offer her. She was going to take it.

Maybe Lorelei was there to provide background noise, to muffle private conversations. But Thea saw being on stage as power. Lorelei was there to entertain. Entice the audience to have fun.

Thea thought about Lorelei constantly. Julian was the one person who seemed to think of Lorelei as a friend. Ramona called her a slut. The papers weren't kinder. In the articles Cheryl Lawrence had given her, Lorelei was picked on constantly. The obituary, written by Cheryl, called her a little too heavy. How was Lorelei supposed to function with that amount of pressure? And Thea thought about how terrifying it must have been to be a young woman with no one on her side. Of course Lorelei was scared. Thea would have been too. Thea *was* scared, constantly, but she didn't know about what. People who stared at her, watched her, expected something she couldn't or didn't want to give. Anxiety pulsed through her constantly, her best friend and worst enemy.

Thea had been making her way through Lorelei's journals. Lorelei saw everyone as out to get her.

Thea understood how she felt.

When the song ended, the audience applauded, and Thea heard Ramona's laugh above the murmuring crowd.

It seemed as if Ramona wasn't scared at all, of anything. Amy wasn't either. Thea wished she could be a little bolder.

But here she was, sitting in a bar, in a borrowed dress, at night without her mother's permission. That had to count for something.

CHAPTER 32

1954

Ramona Penderghast agreed to an interview, on the record. Doing it at Constellation Pictures made sense. It was where they would have the most privacy.

Ramona arrived at the office at 2:00 p.m., wearing a neat pair of trousers and a shirt tucked in, a silk scarf wrapped in her hair. She seemed so sophisticated, so at ease. She even took her heels off, allowing her feet to sink into the carpeting. The first thing she did was cross over to the window to watch the main street of the studio lot.

"It was in this very room I told Tommy I was getting married," Ramona said. She crossed her arms. Thea was afraid to say anything. Ramona turned. "He told me I was making a mistake. If he were here . . . he'd tell me he was right." Ramona's laugh was cold.

"That's not true," Thea said.

"You know it is." Ramona sat on the couch, ankles crossed like a lady. Amy sat across from her. With no other choice, Thea pulled one of the desk chairs over, then settled next to Amy. Amy sat the tape recorder between them. She tilted her chin up, giving Ramona a serious look. "For this to work, I'm going to need the truth. I want to tell the real story."

Ramona raised an eyebrow, her face unreadable. "You have my word."

"This is Amy Evans, speaking with . . ."

"Ramona Penderghast." Ramona supplied her name.

Amy nodded. "How well did you know Lorelei Davies?"

"We started at Sunset around the same time," Ramona said. "We usually were put up for the same roles. We started out as friends, but I did some horrible things to her when I thought that she was in my way." Ramona closed her eyes. Along with recording the interview, Amy was writing down every minute detail, everything she would need to build the story of Lorelei Davies.

"Did you know she was having an affair?" Thea asked.

"That is the voice of Theodosia Ross," Amy added for the recording.

"I caught them kissing once, and I was . . . it's silly to say now, but I was jealous. I wanted Tommy's attention so badly. If you had it, you were set at Sunset. And everyone knew he had a wife. Everyone just thought he didn't care." Ramona swallowed hard, her big green eyes dropping to the ugly yellow corduroy of the couch. "There were a few ways a woman could really get ahead, and that meant, more often than not, being attached to a man. I was jealous of her, but she was more troubled than anyone knew."

"How else could you get ahead?" Thea asked. There was a quality to Ramona's voice, soft and supple, that made Thea want to listen to her all the time. She was no different than she had been at the book party, the same woman in more casual clothes.

"Well, Lorelei was also sleeping with her director and anyone else who could help her get ahead. Can I smoke?" Ramona asked. Thea nodded. Ramona lit a cigarette. "I never thought that sleeping with anyone could help *me* get ahead. I thought that pure work and talent would get me there."

"It did, didn't it?"

Ramona nodded, considering the question. Her green eyes landed on Thea. "You remind me of her. Your voice is the same. Isn't that funny? I'm back here for a week, and I think I'm seeing her everywhere." Thea could tell her, but she didn't. It was her secret, her story. And she didn't want to tell just anyone. "You have the same little chin too. I always thought that Lorelei was just beautiful."

"Did you know she was a colored woman?" Amy asked.

Ramona nodded. "She told me at the very beginning of our careers."

"What was she like?" Thea asked.

Ramona remained silent for a moment. "She was always overthinking. Obsessed with how people saw her. And when she was okay, she was fun. But she was always thinking of herself and what she could do. In a panicked way. I don't think we ever really got to be friends."

For a moment, the only sound in the office was Amy's pen against paper. "When was the last time you saw her?"

Ramona exhaled. "During the *Live, Love* filming, I think. When she left, I thought I was going to get everything I wanted." She trailed off, not finishing her thought. "I wish I treated her better. I wish I could tell her that. But I was cruel to her, and I never got to apologize."

"Do you think she killed herself?" Thea asked. Ramona's eyes settled on her, boring straight through her.

"Of course she did," Ramona said. "Of that, I've never had any doubt."

~

"The second most important thing is a timeline." Thea and Amy were sitting on the floor of her father's office, eating takeout from the boxes, towels spread out over the carpet.

"We should start with the day of my birth," Thea said.

"I was thinking the same thing." Amy wrote something down on a piece of paper. Around them was their small collection of things from Lorelei's life.

"October thirty-first. She died November seventh," Thea said.

"In those seven days, she either decided to kill herself or she was murdered," Amy said.

"My mom—Sophie—said that my dad killed her because she wouldn't let him see me," Thea said. Amy frowned. She wrote this down.

"He told you he loved her," Amy said.

"Maybe he did kill her," Thea said. "Maybe she killed herself because of me." The thoughts were rolling through her head. "She had me, and then she died. How could it not be because of me? She wrote about it. How she thought everyone saw her. What if she was scared that I would see her the same way? What if she thought this was the best thing for me?"

She hated to think about it, but the more she read Lorelei's words, and the more Thea immersed herself into Lorelei's thoughts, the more she thought it was plausible.

CHAPTER 33

1954

"I am the only reason why Lorelei Davies got famous."

Thea listened to Kenneth Webster, the hulking brute of a man she had met at Ramona's book party. She and Amy were sitting by his Malibu pool, reclining in chairs directly facing the sun. Amy's tape recorder sat right next to them, picking up everything he said. He was an older man, older than Julian or her father. He had a couple of women Thea's age hanging around the house. Kenneth had said to ignore them, but Thea didn't know how that was possible.

He hadn't done much since Sunset folded a decade and a half ago. He'd spent that time cavorting and philandering, promising young women he could make them famous. He had made a fortune directing films and was so rich he didn't have to work anymore.

"I made her." A lot of this interview had been Kenneth talking about himself, his family, his business, as if the story was about him. Amy was patient, letting him talk. Thea sat up, her feet touching the pool deck.

"At Cloud Nine?" Thea asked.

"I saw her on stage one night and just knew she would be a star." Kenneth lit a cigarette, blowing smoke into the midday air.

The way he spoke about Lorelei and every woman like they were just objects, playthings for his entertainment, horrified Thea.

"I always thought she would make it. She was willing to do whatever it took," Kenneth said.

Thea had read about it in the journals as well, the surprise when Lorelei had gone to his office for the first time and he had forced himself on her.

"Don't believe anyone who says she didn't want me. Of course she did. We had an understanding."

Kenneth had already waxed poetic about Lorelei's body: Her breasts were the perfect size, her legs were long, her waist was small. Thea hated hearing it and wished she was anywhere else. "Why her?" Thea asked. She and Amy were taking turns asking questions. He looked at her, beady brown eyes hidden behind sunglasses.

"I wanted to fuck her." His answer was honest. Thea wouldn't believe anything else he said. "She could have made it. She could have been so great." He wistfully looked out over the pool. He and Lorelei saw their sexual encounters so differently. He saw it as helping her. Lorelei saw it as a debt she had to pay. Even though they were sitting in the sun, a chill ran down Thea's spine.

What else would he do to keep her?

"What did you think when she left?" Amy asked.

"I was the one who fired her," Kenneth said. "She made her own bed, and then she had to lie in it. She went right from me to Julian John Weston. He's the one who paid her debt. I assumed he was fucking her too."

"You don't respect her at all." When Thea said it, it came as a surprise. She had been raised to never say her real thoughts. "You're talking about her like she was your property, not another human being. You just wanted to control her all the time and then got mad when she didn't want that. Did you ever think about what *she* wanted? Or did you just see her as some prize?" Thea kept her voice calm, like Sophie did when she was furious. She glared at Kenneth, hoping to intimidate him.

Kenneth looked at her, taking his sunglasses off for the first time. "She was mine. I found her. I created her. I gave her everything. And what did she give me in return? Nothing. I wasn't surprised when she killed herself. She was a trainwreck headed nowhere." He looked at them both, then turned back to the pool. "Ladies, if you'll excuse me, I have business to attend to."

Thea had never been more grateful to get a dismissal in her life.

~

There was someone Walter wanted her to meet. Thea was still getting used to having an extended family.

They were silent as he drove. Thea didn't know what to say to him; everything felt wrong. So they played the radio. Thea wished Julian was with them. It would make the whole thing so much easier.

The dress store, called Millie's, was located in Burbank. Thea had never heard of it before. Walter parked and opened the door for Thea. She slid out and followed him inside. The small store was filled with customers. Dresses hung everywhere along with racks of other garments. "You brought me to a dress store," Thea said. She wanted to linger, run her fingers over every dress, choose one and try it on.

"For a reason," Walter said. "And not to buy dresses."

He led her to the back of the store to a woman standing behind the counter. She was wearing slacks and a peasant blouse, elasticized neckline pulled down to her shoulders, a measuring tape wound around her neck. She looked enough like Walter for Thea to realize this was his sister. This was her aunt. She looked up and grinned when she saw Walter. "Walter Dawson! You never come visit anymore. Why? What has you so busy? It can't be the books or anything. You didn't . . . Who is this?"

"Phyllis Dawson," Walter said, wrapping an arm around the woman and pulling her close. "This is Thea Ross."

Phyllis took a step closer to her. She wasn't listening to her older brother. "You look like Joanna. Millie." The women's genes in the Dawson family had to be strong, despite Thea's lighter skin color. They had the same heart-shaped face, dimples, full lips. Phyllis's face was longer, and she was beaming at Walter.

"This is Millie's daughter," Walter said.

Phyllis pulled her into a hug. She smelled warm, sweet. Thea hugged her back. "I have so many questions," Phyllis said.

"Me too," Thea said.

"I'm looking at a ghost." Phyllis let her go, holding Thea an arm's length away to get a good look at her. Phyllis inspected her carefully, taking in every one of Thea's features. "I want to know everything about you."

"Let the girl breathe, Phyllis," Walter said. He was watching it all with an amused smile.

"Do you want a dress? I'm making you a dress," Phyllis said, asking and deciding in one breath.

"She's the best seamstress in Burbank," Walter added.

"I can't accept that," Thea said.

"You don't have a choice. Come in the back with me."

Thea did as she was told, stripping her day dress off and standing on a little stool in her undergarments. "Where have you been?" Phyllis asked. It seemed she was still trying to get used to the idea of Thea's existence. That was fair. Thea was still getting used to Phyllis's.

"I was adopted when I was a baby. A week old. I just found out myself, and then I just met Walt and . . ." Thea trailed off. Phyllis was deftly wrapping the measuring tape around her body.

"I was sixteen when Millie died. I thought I would have her forever, and then she was dead. She always made sure to visit. The money she sent allowed me to learn how to sew, so I named this place after her. But I miss her every day." Phyllis knelt down to get an accurate hem measurement. "Who raised you?"

"Tommy Ross," Thea said. "He's my dad; he and Lorelei had an affair." Phyllis leaned back on her heels, looking up at Thea. She was the sum of her parents' parts. It was just a shame that she had never really got to know her mother. Or, Thea considered, her father.

"Oh," Phyllis said. She had to be in her late thirties, but she still looked around Thea's age, her face unlined and unblemished. Her smile lit her face up. "You have to meet everyone else. I didn't even know she was having a baby."

"She hid it." Thea's voice stuck in her throat. She blinked back tears, not wanting Phyllis, her aunt, to see her cry.

"I was just her kid sister. She didn't want me hanging around. But I adored her. When she died, I cried for a month straight. I couldn't believe I'd never see her again. She was in the pictures, sure, but that was never the same as sitting down at the table with her, cooking with her. I'd always ask her to tell me stories about set." Phyllis exhaled, trying to keep her voice steady. "What about you? What do you do? Who are you?"

"I'm a ballerina," Thea said.

Could she find pieces of herself in this strange woman? Phyllis stood up. With Thea on the pedestal, they were the same height. "She would love that." Thea had to take her word for it. "I can't wait to get to know you," Phyllis said. "I hope you want to get to know me too."

CHAPTER 34

1934

It's taken a fortnight to film the most intensive dance sequence of *Live, Love*. A fortnight of sleeping in my dressing room, for convenience, and getting up at three in the morning for hair and makeup, my muscles still sore from the night before.

I try to tell myself it's a marathon, not a sprint. Tommy and I dance most of it together, which calms some of my fears. Kenneth watches from every angle. The gold gown I wear drops to a deep V in the front and back, exposing the skin between my breasts and shoulder blades. Before I dress, I stand in my underwear, and a makeup artist dusts glittery powder all over to make my skin sparkle. I'll glow on screen.

It's my favorite part of the film. We had two months of rehearsal focusing on this scene.

We're in the thick of it, and with every passing day, Kenneth's mood gets worse.

It's six in the morning, and I'm not sure what day it even is.

When I catch sight of Tommy, looking the everyman in a sweater and slacks, his dark hair pushed from his eyes, my heart soars. He smiles. Winks at me. We start at opposite sides of the stage. I'm supposed to twirl my way to him, and I hope I don't get dizzy.

I can see Ramona from the corner of my eye. She's in the middle of a discussion with a tiny brunette I don't recognize.

I inhale. I focus. I know what I'm doing; I have to let my body guide my mind. Kenneth sits in his director's chair, commanding our attention. We aren't here playing a game; this is our job.

I think about the girls who would kill to be in my place.

"Good morning, everyone," Kenneth says. He lights a cigarette, eyeing all of us suspiciously. "We have a lot of work to do today. Let's try to get through it with some panache, okay?" His eyes find me. I exhale. I'm ready. Kenneth leans back into his seat. We're behind, and I know it's because of me. "Action."

And I'm off. I'm twirling, the skirt of my dress flaring out as I do. I can feel it propelling me forward. I can see Tommy; he's ready to catch me, ready to be right by my side.

I'm about a foot from his arms, maybe less, when the sole of my left foot hits something slick. Then I spin out of control, twisting my ankle.

Before I realize it, I'm on my ass, on the floor of the soundstage.

"Cut!"

My ankle throbs. It's the one thing I can focus on. That and the fact that I just fell, and everyone saw me do it. I think I hear Ramona laughing. Tommy is by my side, helping me to my feet.

It's my left foot; the ankle is twisted. I can't put any pressure on it.

I squeeze my eyes closed, fighting back tears. The entire soundstage has come to a complete stop. I'm thinking about how magical I looked, turning, right before I fell. "FUCK!" It's Kenneth, voicing displeasure better than I can.

"I think it's broken," Tommy says, quiet and in command. He's feeling my ankle, and his touch is barely enough to distract me from the pain. "We'll have to call a doctor."

"I can dance," I say.

"No," Tommy says. He looks up at me, his brown eyes cutting off any protestation I may have.

I didn't expect this setback. I don't know how I fell, but I do know that Ramona will take my place and I'll be out. Tommy picks me up like I weigh nothing. I wrap my arms around him, burying my face in his neck and closing my eyes. "It's not the end of the world, but you need to rest it." Tommy's voice is soft. He's taking me to my dressing room. He opens the door one handed and deposits me on my couch. He sits next to me, placing my head in his lap. "Close your eyes; you'll be okay."

"Kenneth will be furious."

"You let me handle that," Tommy says. "Accidents happen." He says it so sweetly that I almost believe him.

"You don't have to stay with me," I say.

"Yes, I do," Tommy says. His fingers dance over my skin, and I feel the hairs on the back of my neck rise. He kisses me, quickly and leaving me needing more.

"I'm staying with you until the doctor comes. I can't leave you alone." It's in moments like this I forget what we're doing. I forget about his wife and her miscarriages. I think that we could really be something, on screen and off.

I exhale, trying to get myself to relax. My mind is racing; my heart is thrumming. Relaxing is not what I do. I don't know how. Tommy seems to sense that. He pulls me closer, reaching over to turn on my radio. He sings along, and I close my eyes.

Whatever happens will happen.

CHAPTER 35

1934

My sprain means I'm out for eight weeks. Kenneth wanted six, but the doctor insisted on eight. I can barely put weight on my foot, and I'm stuck at home, with the radio and books to keep me company.

It's better that I'm at home. I don't want to be at Sunset, with people staring at me. I have script pages brought to me. Eva comes to check on me every once in a while.

Three days after my ankle sprain, I welcome a photographer and reporter from *Life* magazine into my home. Kenneth set up the interview before my injury, and he didn't cancel. I'm just lucky Kenneth can't be bothered to be here. He'll contribute to the article, sure, but this is about me.

A studio publicist chooses a light-pink day dress for me from my closet. It hits the middle of my calf, and I wear a pair of matching heels. I practice smiling in the mirror, trying to find an expression that looks natural.

When the doorbell rings, I turn her on. I *become* Lorelei Davies. The reporters, both men, both a little older than me, arrive with a whole crew: makeup and hair for me, lighting for them. "Miss Davies," one of them says. He sounds excited. Except for their different hair colors, and the fact that one has a camera and the other has a notebook, they look nearly identical. Colin and David. David and Colin. "We're so excited for this."

"I am too," I say, in my signature Lorelei Davies voice. She could not be more different to who Millicent is. "Why don't you come in? I have coffee for you."

David, the one with the camera, stakes out my house and decides to start me on the couch. The lights are set, and Colin drags a chair from my kitchen table and sits in front of me.

"How are you today?" He opens with an easy question. I pull my legs underneath me and lean over the arm of my chair, closer to him. Colin's eyes are dark, and when I move, they light up. I know he's probably bragged to his friends about interviewing me, that he's been counting down the days.

"I'm excited," I say. I smile, easily disarming him. I know what he wants to see. I've spent years shaping Lorelei Davies. She's charming. She's witty. She's flirty enough to make every man think he has a chance with her. She is everything, and she is nothing.

As much as I hate it, Lorelei Davies has become a vital part of me.

Colin's writing a puff piece. He asks me about my films, my work, admires the cinematic posters I have up on my wall. All the films I've been in. I've left a space for *Live, Love*, right after *Allergic to Love*. He asks about my family, and I tell the story I always do: that I was orphaned at a young age and that the Sunset family is my family. He nods, scribbling in his notebook. He writes down everything I say, filling pages and pages. He leans forward.

"You're only twenty years old, and you've managed to achieve so much already. What do you think is in store for you next?" he asks.

I'm twenty. I'm older than Joanna will ever be, but not by much. It feels like ages but also like no time at all since she passed away. "I hope to continue acting," I say. It's a silly nonanswer, but it's what I think he wants to hear. "I love it. I love being an actress. It's one of the most special things in the world." I pause, then add, "I simply want to be wonderful."

He frowns; I think he's practiced that face in the mirror. He reminds me of the boys on the train who tried to get me to go to the Trocadero with them. I still think about those four. They still make my hairs stand up on end. "I think that's a good goal."

We spend hours talking, and I forget that it's an interview. David is taking photographs. Every so often, wordlessly, he reaches over to adjust my head and body position. He sometimes stops to watch me intensely. I try to ignore him unless he has an actual request. My hands are numb, and I squeeze my fingers together.

We move through my little house. Photographs of me making coffee, photographs of me in my bathroom, at my vanity. "What's one thing no one knows about Lorelei Davies?" Colin asks. He's following us around my house, an amused little smile on his face. I know he wants a good answer to this, a real confession, but something lighthearted and fun. I think about the real answer, think about telling him that I'm a colored woman, my whole family sans one member is alive, and they live in Watts.

I imagine how fast I'd be blackballed.

I wonder what it would be like, telling anyone. It's my closest-guarded secret. So instead, I smile. "I write everything down. I keep journals."

"You do?" Colin asks.

"I save them all too."

"Can I read one?"

"I'd let you, but then I'd have to kill you." I wink, and I get the laugh I want. I'm charming. I'm delighting them all.

~

The photographs take longer than the questions do. We eventually move on to the bench on my front porch. I put my feet up on the railing, and I hope I look relaxed. "One more question," Colin asks. "I want to know about Thomas Ross." He's been dancing around him all day. The subject of Tommy. I knew it was coming; I watched him talk himself out of asking the question several times.

"Tommy is my dance partner and costar. He's a wonderful man to work with, and I hope he and his wife are happy," I say.

Colin narrows his eyes. He doesn't believe me; I know he doesn't believe me. Tommy and I are careful, but rumors fly fast and hard, and there's nothing I can do to stop them. Colin thinks he has a story, one that's not about my cozy life at home. He thinks he can upend Cheryl Lawrence with this interview. "Is there anything else?" he asks.

"About Tommy?" I laugh. "He's a coworker, and I keep it strictly professional with my costars at all times."

CHAPTER 36

1934

I'm truly alone. I know I live alone, but I'm so often at the studio, or at a party or nightclub, that the ringing silence of my empty house is rather foreign to me.

I spend mornings on my couch, my leg propped up on pillows. I transition to the bed in the afternoon, moving as slowly as possible to not aggravate my ankle more.

Today, the moment my ass hits the bed, I hear my door open. It's Kenneth. I know it's him from his heavy footsteps. "Lorelei."

"Bedroom." I pull myself up so I'm sitting. I realize, a moment too late, that I'm undone, in a soft and simple brassiere, tap pants, and a dressing gown on top. I'm not wearing makeup. My hair is tied up, away from my face, in a silk scarf. I'm not ready to see anyone.

He stops at the doorframe, pausing. I look up at him. I realize it's Wednesday, and he expects to have me. He's already loosening his tie. "Wait," I say. Kenneth steps toward my bed. He helped me buy this house, when I signed my contract for *Live, Love* and following films. He said if I'm going to be a real film star, I need a good place to live.

I never considered that meant he'd have a key, that he'd have access to me all the time. I wonder if he's been in my house when I'm not here. I wonder if I have anything in this world that just belongs to me.

"What, Lorelei?"

"I'm not feeling up to it." I know he won't care.

"Come on," Kenneth says. He checks his watch. "I only have a couple of hours." As if anything with him has taken more than a couple of minutes, but I guess he'll fall asleep afterward. He steps toward my bed; he's already unbuttoning his shirt. He looks me over; I can see the lust in his eyes.

Does it matter what I say? Does it matter what I want?

It doesn't.

"No," I say.

"If you don't, I'll terminate your contract and fine you for the remainder of *Live, Love*." His voice is cold. He's in charge. He's used to getting what he wants. And what he wants right now is me. "Don't forget, Millicent Dawson. I created you, and I can destroy you."

My contract.

The $200,000 I can't afford. It's what keeps me under his thumb, so to speak. He's furious. His voice is low, and he doesn't yell like he does on set. He doesn't need to perform for anyone. It's just the two of us here. "I'll have Eva draw up the paperwork this afternoon."

He's right. I can afford to pay back about a quarter of it. I think he has me on such a low salary to keep me close. He uses my real name as a weapon against me. "I want out." I say it before I've thought it through. I can't do this anymore. I can't keep letting him take advantage of me. I can't let him keep using me.

And if that means I'm in debt to him and Sunset and I have to go back to singing at clubs? I would take that in a moment before letting him fuck me again. "Get out." I'm aware I may lose my house. I'll lose everything I have.

But in that moment, I make a decision. Lorelei Davies will never be someone's plaything again.

~

When Tommy finds me, still in bed, hours after Kenneth has left, I'm sobbing. The reality of what I've done has hit me. Kenneth has won. Ramona has won.

And all I am, all Lorelei Davies is, is nothing.

"Whoa, whoa, whoa," Tommy says. He appears like something out of a dream and kneels next to my bed. I don't know what the next months will bring. I don't know what the next hours will bring. "What's wrong?"

"I just . . ." I trail off. Was I fired? Did I quit? No matter what, I'm not a Sunset star anymore.

I'm no one.

He wipes my tears with his thumb, kissing me gently. "Why don't we get out of here?" he asks. I want to say no. I think about how he called me crazy. I think about his wife. He's the one thing I want right now. No matter how much I try to fight it, my feelings for him run deep. "I'll pack you a bag. We're going away for the weekend." He makes the decision unilaterally. I'm in no position to disagree.

And there's no other place I'd rather be than away from here.

CHAPTER 37

1934

While Tommy drives, I look at the sky, wishing I had brought my pills with me. I don't know if I'm coming off them, but my hands shake.

We stop at a San Francisco inn. Tommy gives me the money, and we check in separately. I sign in as Millicent Dawson. The clerk seems to recognize me but doesn't say anything.

My room is on the main floor. His is up one. I settle in, climbing into the bed, not bothering to unpack. For the first time in days, I feel like I can breathe. I'm away from the studio, away from my life. Now I'm in a yellow room that's about the size of my bedroom at home. The windows are open, letting in a soft breeze. I sit up straight, my legs stretched out in front of me. The more time I spend away from Los Angeles, the more relaxed I am.

Tommy knocks on the door and comes in. He's wearing a button-down and slacks, his shirtsleeves rolled to the elbow. He closes the door behind him, then smiles at me. His hair is falling into his eyes. "Should we go to dinner?" I ask.

"Why do you think we'd leave this inn?" Tommy asks. He's already unbuttoning his shirt. I watch him, entranced by his fingers and his wrists. He walks toward the bed, shedding his shirt, letting it fall to the floor. "Why do you think we'd get dinner?" His voice is husky. "Lorelei, the only thing I want is you."

He kisses me, hard and desperate. His tongue slips between my lips, and his hands are on my waist, pulling me on top of him. "Careful." I can't bring myself to do anything but whisper.

I straddle him, ignoring the pain shooting through my ankle, and run my fingers over his bare chest. I can feel his arousal underneath me, how much he wants me.

And he does want me. That's the one thing I'm certain of.

The bed is soft, softer than mine at home, and I feel like we're sinking together. He's looking up at me, his dark eyes limitless. His hair has fallen into his face, and I reach over to push it back. Then I take my time with his belt before throwing it aside.

"You're a marvel—you know that, right? You and everything you are." His voice is so quiet, but he may as well be yelling. He's not often like this, acquiescing to what I want. "I liked you so much the first time we met."

I try not to think about him saying these things to his wife. I think about his hands, on my bottom, strong and warm.

I think about the fact that I have the most desirable man in the world underneath me.

He sits up, catching me before I fall back, pulling me toward him. It's not love. It's not love. I have to remember that.

It's physical.

He wouldn't want me if he knew the truth. I'm committed to living a lie, at least for another weekend.

"And you're wearing too many clothes." He strips my plain button-down, revealing my soft brassiere. He brings me to him, kissing me between my breasts. His lips are soft against my skin. He looks up at me with a wolfish grin.

We take our time, teasing each other. Letting him so slowly undress me. For the first time ever, we aren't rushing or hiding. We're free to take our time, exploring each other in ways we've never done before. He's obsessed with a scar on my kneecap, a mole on my left hip. His fingers trace my body, leaving a trail of heat as he does.

When he has me down to my tap pants, he takes his time with the little zipper. Every hair on my body stands at attention, and I'm drinking in his brown eyes like we've been dancing for hours.

His fingers slide in first. He has me on my back. The air from the window is giving me goose bumps. We get messier, our kisses sloppy. He presses himself into me. I gasp. And as he kisses my neck, I don't want to be anywhere else.

~

True to his word, Tommy and I stay in the yellow bedroom all weekend. We don't leave for meals. We don't leave for anything. We have everything we could possibly need in the room.

I wake tangled in his grasp. It's the dewy early-morning hours, when the sun has just risen. I try to pull away, and he brings me back into him. He kisses my temple; I run my fingers over his stomach.

We're *together*.

I wonder if this is what I've always wanted. To be next to Tommy in this way. He rarely sleeps at my house. I pull myself up so I'm sitting. It's our last morning at the inn, and even though he packed me a bag, I didn't open it once. Tommy is barely awake. I kiss the cleft in his chin and then his temple. He doesn't stir. I kiss the corner of his mouth. He doesn't move. I watch him, totally at peace. It's the only time Tommy isn't moving. I wish he could see himself the way I see him. He's beautiful, simply and heartachingly so.

I know that every moment I spend with him is a mistake, but there's no way I can stop myself.

CHAPTER 38

1954

To Sophie's utter delight, and her very high expectations, Thea booked the Coca-Cola campaign. Modeling, on the surface, looked easy, but Thea knew that it was much harder than it seemed. The stage lights shone down on her; she posed for photos and filmed commercial spots, repeating the tagline over and over. It was much like being in the corps de ballet, holding the same positions while the soloists danced, fighting the urge to move when her muscle cramped.

That day, she had to hold positions while photographers snapped photos of her surrounded by other fresh-faced young adults pretending to be her friends. It was sterile. Her mother watched every move she made. She was underneath pounds of makeup, wearing a red-and-white polka-dot dress with a wide smile plastered on her face.

It was a national campaign; Thea would be seen everywhere. Sophie hovered near the cameraman, constantly reminding Thea to smile. Her mother had behaved like this during shoots for as long as she could remember. Sophie was never more alive than when she was managing Thea's career. Thea always suspected that Sophie used Tommy's connections to build Thea's portfolio.

Her fingers were stiff from holding the bottle, pretending to pour it into glasses. Beside her, her fellow models changed positions. It was a long afternoon in the middle of a long day. The bulbs flashed.

Thea wanted to scream. Her skin itched. The more she modeled, no matter how often her mother told her she was so good at it, the more she hated it. Thea had hated it from the first moment she was set in front of a camera and told to smile.

"Wonderful," the photographer said. They had been at this for hours. Thea put the bottle down. After a costume change, they'd be back at it again. Sophie waved her over.

"Brilliant, Thea," Sophie said. She fussed with Thea's hair, although Thea was sure her hair hadn't moved since it was set. She exhaled. "Go change."

"No." She thought she thought it. She didn't know she *said* it until her mother frowned.

"Theodosia, go change."

She recognized the tone in her mother's voice. She heard it, the cool undertone and her full name. Sophie expected her to do exactly as she was told. Thea shook her head.

"Theodosia," Sophie said.

The air on set seemed to still. Thea knew that everyone—all the higher-ups, the ad men, the photographers, the creatives—was watching her. She looked around, toward the cheery picnic set where she had been posing all day.

Thea had all the choices in the world, and she was going to make one. "I don't want to do this. I don't want to be a model. I never did."

"Theodosia Adeline Ross." Her mother's voice was soft, a hiss. She was also aware that everyone was looking at them.

Thea couldn't leave everyone else in the lurch. She straightened her back. "I'll go change, but we need to talk about this soon," Thea said. "I'm never doing this again."

Sophie frowned. She was furious but trying not to show it. Thea didn't know what had just broken in her, but something had.

And it felt good.

~

For twenty years, Thea had done everything her mother and father required of her. She decided to throw herself into what she wanted: conditioning and teaching and solving a twenty-year-old murder.

When they returned home from the photo shoot, Sophie had whisked herself from the car to the kitchen to talk to Ilsa. Thea had shut herself in her dance studio and spent hours in there. The Ross women were currently not speaking to each other. That was fine with Thea.

Amy thought they needed to let off some steam.

Thea decided she was right.

Amy took Thea to a club in the Topanga Canyon. It was a private place, and Amy had a membership. Amy drove, and Thea played with the lipstick-red pencil skirt of her dress. "You look amazing," Amy said.

"I hope so," Thea said. Thea had taken a red boatneck dress with a plunging back from Sophie's closet, another black mark on her behavior. It was ill fitting. Sophie was several inches taller than Thea. She knew she looked childish, like she was playing dress-up.

She wanted to be anyone else. She was eager to go somewhere she'd never been and be someone she wasn't.

Although, who really knew what that meant?

The place was nice. They entered through a vestibule and were buzzed in. "I love this place," Amy said as she guided Thea in. "I hope you do too."

Thea looked around, taking in the two dance floors and a closed-off pool. The best part was that there were women dancing with other women. Men with other men. It was discreet, intimate, and unlike anything Thea had ever seen before.

Her whole dancing life had been in studios, *en pointe*, in front of audiences, or with her father. She'd never had the chance to visit a place like this.

"Do you want to dance?" Amy asked. She wore a black dress with a full tulle skirt. Something that should have seemed girlish but looked sophisticated on her in a way Thea could never hope to pull off.

Of course she wanted to dance.

She'd danced with Willa, but slow dancing with Willa in the Turner kitchen was different from dancing in a club to a band playing a slow song, Willa's arms wrapped around her, letting Willa lead her to the song on the radio. Different from Thea and Amy on a dance floor with other women doing the same thing. She held on to Amy, not dancing so much as swaying to the music. There was something so thrilling about this. Thea had always done what was expected of her, no questions, no complaints.

When did Thea get to do what she wanted?

She was eighteen when Willa had kissed her for the first time. Thea had barely understood what was happening, just realized that Willa's perfect clavicle, her neck, her long arms made something tighten in her stomach. The way talking to Willa made her feel like the only woman in the world. How it felt like they could laugh forever. She and Willa had been alone, in the Turner house, always the Turner house, and they were sitting on Willa's bed. Thea was talking about something, when Willa kissed her.

It took Thea months to realize what it meant. But she did, eventually, understand.

"I need you to do me a favor," Thea said. "I need you to read the journals from 1934. I don't think I can bear to read about Lorelei and my father."

"I thought we weren't talking about work tonight," Amy said.

They had agreed on that, but it was the only thing Thea could think to say. All her other words, thoughts, feelings were bold enough to bring a blush to her cheeks. "I just need you to say yes; then I won't talk about work at all again tonight."

"Then yes."

With her mind whirring, Thea reached up and kissed Amy. Amy kissed her back. No fear, no instinct to hide who she was. It was the first time Thea was this open about her affection with anyone.

Amy was the second woman she had ever kissed, and she was kissing Thea back. Her heart leaped. Her stomach flipped.

"We shouldn't do this," Amy said, pulling away. She pressed her forehead to Thea's.

"I want to be reckless just once," Thea said. She knew it was a bad idea. She wanted to make a mistake, mess up. She wanted to be anyone but Theodosia Adeline Ross. "Just once. Kiss me again."

When Amy kissed her again, Thea let herself melt into it.

CHAPTER 39

1954

One of the most important things, at least for Amy, who was building a brilliant story on Lorelei's life, required a road trip. Julian wanted to drive, but Thea wanted to take Tommy's Corvette.

Julian and Walter didn't tell them where they were going. They wanted it to be a surprise, assuring both women that they would love it.

They went in two cars, Julian and Walter leading and Thea and Amy following. Thea lied to her mother, saying she was spending the day at the dance studio, in training for teachers. She no longer cared what her mother thought about her. She and Sophie weren't speaking to each other, not really. Thea sort of preferred that, at least, to Sophie micromanaging her every move, her clothes and hair and daily schedule. The Ross house was big enough that they never had to see each other.

Thea drove, keeping Julian's black car in her sight as she did. Amy had her notebook open in her lap, going over the notes from the Kenneth Webster interview. "I read about him in her journals," Amy said. She rolled down the window to light a cigarette. "She recorded everything he did to her."

"He saw her as a toy," Thea said.

"And still has the audacity to say he created her," Amy said. Maybe that was truer than they thought it was. Kenneth Webster chose Lorelei's name, her look, her image as the girl who fell in love at Sunset.

"He controlled her like my mother controls me," Thea said. She meant it as a joke, said it with a little laugh, but when she looked over, pulling her eyes from the road, Amy was looking at her with concern. "My mother is . . ." She trailed off. She didn't know how to finish that sentence. "She loves me."

"And maybe Kenneth loved Lorelei," Amy said. "That doesn't make it right."

Thea exhaled. Amy had a point.

Thea didn't think what Kenneth felt was love. It was power. He preyed on Lorelei, the same way he collected the girls who were hanging around his mansion. Sex and power were interlinked for that man. Lorelei was an insect trapped in his web.

The drive wasn't long, and it ended at a little yellow house with a porch and a swing. Thea parked behind Julian's car. Phyllis leaned out a window. "WALTER!" she yelled. "You've not been home in ages. But you grace us with your presence today because you know I'm cooking."

"And because I brought you someone," Walter called back. Thea climbed out of the car, and Phyllis's smile broke her face in two.

"My goodness!" Phyllis said. She disappeared from the window and, in a moment, was on the porch. She ran to hug Thea first, and Thea could smell her perfume. "How have you been? You look so lovely." She kissed Walter and Julian, and Amy was introduced last.

Walter escorted Thea up the few steps to the house. "Don't let them intimidate you, okay?" It was the same sort of thing Julian had told her when she had met Cheryl for the first time.

"Momma," Walter called. There was a record player on in the distance. The table was small, set for eight. There would be no room with eight people crowded around the table.

A woman came down the stairs, wiping her hands on the skirt of her dress. She was little, her hair curly and gray. Her eyes were big and bright, and in her face, Thea could see herself. The woman stopped.

"May Dawson, this is your granddaughter," Walter said.

Thea hadn't known that *this* was where Julian and Walter were taking her.

But now she was there, it felt right.

May Dawson stared back at her, and for a moment time stopped. Then the older woman crossed the few steps to the door and wrapped Thea in a tight hug.

Thea was right: With her grandmother, three uncles, and aunt, plus Julian and Amy, the table was a tight squeeze.

It was also the most natural thing in the world. It took a second for Thea to adjust to the rhythm of the table, passing dishes around and over each other. The conversation mixed and mingled, but everyone wanted to know about Thea.

She was used to being in the spotlight, but not like this. She gave them her story, with Julian and Walter filling in the finer points. Ralph and Calvin peppered her with questions, and she answered them as best she could. Thea found she just wanted to watch. She wanted to see where and how she fit in with this group of people. She watched Julian and Walter and the immense love they had for each other. Ralph and Calvin, both in their late thirties, traded jokes and insults over the table. And Phyllis talked a lot.

Thea wanted to be able to capture this and keep it forever.

~

After dinner, she and May, who insisted Thea call her Granny, sat on the porch. Julian and Walter were washing the dishes. She could hear the piano being played from inside the house.

Amy stayed at the table, interviewing Calvin for her story. Dinner had been loud and boisterous—the opposite of what Thea was used to at home. The Ross family politely discussed their day. The Dawson family told jokes and teased each other.

Even after a couple of hours, Thea knew that this was where she was supposed to be. This was her family. And her father, or someone, had taken that from her.

Thea had been raised as a white woman, but Lorelei was colored, and that meant that she was too. She'd been denied her culture and her family.

She couldn't help but be angry. There was a whole life she could have had.

"You look exactly like her," May said.

"Like Joanna? I've heard. I wish I could have met her," Thea said.

"Like Millie," May corrected gently. "You're her spitting image." Thea wondered if she was seeing what she wanted to see. "All the Dawson women look alike. You got the good looks." May laughed, loud and wheezing. "You don't act, too, do you?"

She shook her head. "I'm a ballerina. I dance with the Ballet Los Angeles." May blinked at her, taking this in. It was surreal. Thea felt the same way.

May pressed a hand to Thea's cheek. "I want to get to know you all," Thea said. "If you'll let me." She wanted to ask about Lorelei—Millie—but now it felt inappropriate. Thea had learned that her grandfather had died a couple of years ago. She'd learned that she was, in age order, at the older end of her cousins. She was learning about herself as much as she was learning about Lorelei. This was what she wanted. And she wanted more.

"My girl," May said, after a moment's pause. "That's all we want."

They sat in silence for a moment. Then Thea cleared her throat. "What do you think happened to her?"

May exhaled. "I knew she was pregnant. I knew she was going to have the baby. She would have given the baby to us." She stopped for a moment. Her eyes were turned to the night sky. Thea leaned into her, and May wrapped an arm around her. The gesture was so maternal. Thea wasn't sure Sophie had ever held her like that. "I have never been sure what happened to her," May said. "But she would want you to be loved."

Thea frowned, closing her eyes. It wasn't much, but it was something.

CHAPTER 40

1934

Cheryl Lawrence has lunch at the same diner every day. It's where she holds court, where she gets her stories. It's a drive-in diner, Carpenter's on Sunset and Vine. She dines in her car, a big black thing, with the doors open. I've heard that she orders the same thing every day for lunch, that all the carhops know her, that it's the place to find her if you want to.

It's the first thing I do when Tommy and I return from our little weekend away.

I thought long and hard about this. This is my first step to coming clean, to making Lorelei Davies mine.

I want to be in control of what happens to me and to her.

Cheryl Lawrence eyes me as I slide into her car with her. Now, she's no beauty—she's a little too heavy—but that doesn't stop her from judging all of us. "Lorelei Davies." Cheryl's voice isn't warm. I know she has a child, somewhere, but I can't imagine her as a mother.

"Miss Lawrence," I say. "How lovely to see you again." I extend a hand. She shakes it.

"Funny, I was just thinking about you, Miss Davies. You look well," Cheryl says. She takes a moment to light a cigarette. She doesn't offer me one. I don't light one myself. I know I don't look *well*, that it's a backhanded compliment. "I heard something scandalous about you and Thomas Ross. After you lied to Colin Lowe at *Life*."

I lean in toward her. Her car is messy, papers and trash all over the floor. It's horrid. "If you drop that story, I can promise you a more interesting one." Now I have her attention. Cheryl could never resist a better story. I raise my eyebrows.

Cheryl leans forward. "Go ahead." She has a pen poised and ready, hovering over a piece of paper.

"First, I need your assurance that you will never, *ever* print a word about Tommy Ross and me. No photos, no innuendos, no hints, no references." I narrow my eyes. A carhop approaches to take my order. Without moving her eyes from me, Cheryl waves her away. I don't know why Cheryl likes this place; it's not subtle or private.

"Depends on what this other story is," Cheryl says. I wonder if a woman could be president. She would have to be just as ruthless as Cheryl is. I could see her leading a country. She never stops when something is in her way. She is feared and respected.

"No. I need your assurance, in writing, that you will never breathe or print or insinuate a word about Tommy Ross and I."

It's a strong opening move—I know that. I hope I've piqued her interest enough to go for it.

With eyebrows tightly knit, Cheryl takes a moment to write a statement and signs it with the date. March 5, 1934.

I sign it. My hands shake.

Once that's squared away, Cheryl leans forward, as if we're sharing a secret. Well, I guess we are. "It's about Kenneth Webster." I can't believe I'm doing this. My heart pounds. But I need to do this, for Tommy, for us.

"Go on," Cheryl says.

I inhale, trying to keep myself steady. I pretend she's a camera; I pretend that these are lines someone has written for me. "For the past four years, he's been using his position of power at Sunset to have sex with me." It haunts me more than I would care to admit. His mauling my body, his lips on my skin, the honest-to-God howl he makes when he ejaculates. His need for control over my body, monitoring my diet, my pills, everything.

And I want to be done with it. With Kenneth.

To my surprise, Cheryl sits back in her seat. She laughs. She laughs so hard tears appear in the corners of her eyes. She wipes them away. "Oh, sweetheart. I suppose you said no too. I suppose you didn't want to let one of the most powerful men in Hollywood fuck you senseless. And I assume you didn't get *Allergic to Love* or *Live, Love* because of that." Her tone is cutting. She has never minced her words. "Are you fucking serious? I'm supposed to lead my column with 'Kenneth Webster fucks actress'? Why do you think he got in this business to begin with? The money was just a bonus." Cheryl casts me a dark look, and I know I've made a mistake. "You've fucked me twice over. Now, get out of my sight." I get out of the car. I'm still shaking. People stare at me as I leave, my head down, trying not to attract more attention than I have already.

By the time I'm back in my own car, I'm sure that Cheryl has already reneged on her promise. Of course she will.

And there's nothing I can do to stop it.

~

Following our getaway, Tommy and I don't talk. I don't attempt to call him, because I know Sophie will answer.

All I do is write in my journal, sit in my house, and wait for Cheryl Lawrence to end me. Time moves slowly when I'm not on set. I get news that Kenneth has moved forward with *The Taming of the Shrew*, casting Ramona and Tommy as the leads. I read industry news as it comes, trying to plot my next move.

The things I know: I owe Sunset a lot of money.

The things I don't know: everything else.

The silence rings around my house at all hours, and I keep the radio on so that it feels less empty than it is. My house has four bedrooms, three bathrooms, and now it feels too big. I wonder if I can sell it. Maybe use the money to move on.

But where would I live?

The thoughts bounce around my head. Even though I'm not filming, I take my pills: awake pills in the morning, sleep pills in the afternoon. It helps, dulls my senses a little bit. With my pills, the world looks a little rosier.

I sometimes put on a dress and lounge around the Trocadero or the Cocoanut Grove. I let people see me. That's a big part of the game. Cheryl has written about how I've been fired; the rumors surrounding my release are because of my ankle.

Cheryl writes about how *Live, Love* was shut down because I couldn't act. How I wouldn't leave my trailer. How I'd cry or yell or go silent. How I couldn't remember my lines. It's all true. And when I do go out, people whisper and laugh about me. So I retreat into my house.

My *Life* spread comes out, but there's not much that can save me from the damage of Cheryl's column.

When the phone rings, two weeks into my self-imposed exile, I look at it like a feral animal. I almost forgot what it does. I sit at the table, then pick up the receiver and press it to my ear. "Hello."

"Lorelei." It's Julian John Weston. His voice is warm. I can picture him sitting in his dressing room. "I've been thinking about you."

"No, you haven't." The words pop from me before I can stop them.

He laughs softly. "Yes, I have. I miss having you across the hall from me."

"I thought you were doing *Shrew*."

"You know how it works." He continues: "There's a film premiere in a couple of weeks, and I want you to come with me."

"What about Francesca?"

He avoids the question. "Will you come with me?" I know he has ulterior motives. I know he does. I don't know what they are. "Come on, Lorelei. It's just a night with me and a film."

"And you want to be seen with a social pariah? More than with your wife?"

He exhales. For a moment, we're both silent. I can hear the distant murmur from my radio in my bedroom. "Francesca and I are no longer together." He doesn't say anything else, and I want to ask why. I want something to focus on besides my own misery. But that doesn't mean it has to be his misery.

And I don't know what drives me to do it, but the next words out of my mouth are "I'll go with you." I guess it will do me good. People love Julian. And if I'm on his arm, I hope that means they'll love me too.

"I'm glad to hear it. I'll arrange the dress and everything." He does sound genuinely pleased, but then again, he is an actor. I don't know if I actually believe him. "I'll call you with more details?"

"You can come over too," I say.

I can hear the smile in his voice. "Of course. I should have. See you soon, Lorelei."

I want to believe that this will be good for me, good for us. But the doubt settles heavily, deep in my stomach.

I go to bed early.

CHAPTER 41

1934

Julian does take care of the dress, and it's beautiful. It's inky-green satin that kisses my skin. The bodice crosses my chest, with a drape falling over my left shoulder. The skirt is long, and I'm zipped in. The back is low cut; I can't wear a bra. I feel magical in it. With my hair swept up and a dark-red lipstick, I'm ready to take on Hollywood. I'm in heels, even with an ankle that's not fully better. The one good thing about having no job or prospects is that I can focus on healing. I top the dress off with the necklace Tommy got me. It's too special to wear all the time. I clasp it around my neck. The star pendant sits at the hollow of my throat, and I feel like it's a good omen.

The rest of my body, however, doesn't agree. I woke up this morning feeling ill, my stomach turning, constantly on the verge of throwing up. It's nerves. It has to be nerves.

Julian picks me up, perfectly on time. He's wearing a tuxedo, his bow tie askew. His dark hair is untamable, falling into his dark eyes. He's excited. He walks me to the Cadillac limousine he's hired for the evening and hands me a single red rose. He puts it behind my ear. "There. Now you're perfect. Don't be scared," he says. "I'll be with you the whole time." I look at him. His brown eyes are on my face. He's talking in a calm, reassuring tone.

"Why me?" I ask.

"Honestly?" Julian asks me. I nod. "I miss seeing you every day. And I thought that maybe you needed to be around other people." He hands me a glass of champagne. We're sitting together in the back of the car, drinking champagne. It's unbelievable. I take the glass, but I don't drink. My stomach still feels off. "Are you all right?" Julian asks.

I nod, take a sip. When he's not looking, I spit it back into the glass. "I'm just nervous."

"You have no reason to be," Julian says. "All we're going to do is pose for pictures, and then we're going to sit in the dark and look at a big screen." He gives me a smile, quick and funny. I feel relaxed when I'm with him, more than I do with Tommy. I can't figure it out. Something about him is so reassuring. Even though my stomach feels like it's in knots. I want to ask about Tommy. It's the only thing on my lips, only thought in my head.

The drive from my house to Grauman's Chinese Theatre takes thirty minutes. It's thirty minutes of panic rising in my body. When we get there, the red carpet is rolled out. The press is waiting, cameras at the ready. Julian gets out first. I know my role. I wait for him to open the door and escort me out. I'm feeling lightheaded, tired, sick. But I paste a smile on my face. Lorelei Davies is who these people want to see, and that's who these people will get. I keep close to Julian. The press calls out questions. It's interesting to see how Julian handles everything, smiling and waving. A little way down the red carpet, I see Tommy. He's with his wife, and she wears a dress similar to mine but, of course, in white.

I ignore them. I face the press. They're yelling questions. Asking about the trajectory of my career, about Cheryl's article about me. "Lorelei," one reporter calls. He's at the front of the crowd, a prime spot, and I can see his smug grin. "What's it like being crazy?" My vision blurs.

Julian puts his arm around my waist. "We're here to celebrate Ingrid Belle's newest picture," he calls, smoothing it over so easily. "Let's all focus on that."

"Thank you, gentlemen," I call. Julian steps away so we can individually pose for photographs. I think about what will grace the covers of the papers tomorrow, what people will say about me. Bile rises in my throat, and I swallow it back down.

Julian is back, his arm around my waist. "I won't leave your side all night."

"Why are you being so nice to me?" I ask. We step into the lobby of the theater. It's a bona fide who's who. Tommy and Kenneth talking. Ramona on the arm of an actor I think I should recognize. Cheryl Lawrence is off to the side, watching the proceedings. I see everyone I know, everyone I've ever worked with. They all stop to look at Julian and then at me. My heart patters, and I can no longer hold it inside. I pull away from Julian and race, as fast as I can in heels and with an injured ankle, to the powder room.

I don't pause to see if it's empty. I find the nearest sink and vomit into it.

~

I can't leave the powder room. And this time it's not nerves; it's not paranoia—it's physical. Every time I step toward the door, my body revolts again, until I'm vomiting bile and not much else. I sink to the floor. I know the film has started by now; I would love to see Ingrid Belle on screen. She's not a Sunset actress, and I don't know how Julian knows her. But we've all come out to support this film.

After about thirty minutes of deep breathing and hoping, I sneak into the theater and into the seat next to Julian. On screen, Ingrid Belle, a redheaded beauty, is loading a gun. I don't know what's going on, but I like the look of Ingrid. She's decisive on screen, and I imagine she's like that in real life too. The film has more grit than any of mine do. Ingrid's character isn't just falling in love. She's driving the plot.

I'm envious.

Twenty minutes before the end, I excuse myself again. I end up back in the powder room in the downstairs lounge, hovering over the toilet, praying that I don't vomit again. My nerves are frayed, my stomach hurts, and I'm tired. I stay in the bathroom until I know my stomach is empty. I look at myself in the mirror. There's one attendant, a Black woman, and she looks away from me. My makeup is streaky; my lipstick is faded. My lips are cracked. I need a drink of water and to go to sleep. My entire body is humming.

When I step out of the bathroom, Julian is waiting for me. I thought he'd be angry, but he just looks concerned. He has his suit jacket folded over his arm. He looks me over and wordlessly leads me out of the theater.

"I'm sorry." I say it once we're back in the limousine.

"You don't have to apologize," Julian says.

"It was a great film, from what I saw," I say. "She's amazing."

Julian's leaning back in his seat. I don't think we're headed to my house. We're headed to his. "I'm not leaving you alone tonight."

I inhale. "Julian . . . I didn't say yes because I'll have sex with you." My cheeks are burning. I should have known that's what he wanted. It's what every man always wants from me.

He laughs, then gathers his composure. "I don't want to have sex with you. I don't like women like that. I want to make sure you don't choke on your vomit in the middle of the night. And I'm calling a doctor."

"It's midnight," I say. "No doctor will make a house call at this hour." Relief prickles my skin. I exhale again. I know I look a mess, and my breath must smell. But all I can focus on is that he must like me for me. Not like Kenneth, who sees me as a toy. Not like Tommy, who sees me as a woman who isn't his wife.

He doesn't want to take advantage of me.

Julian just smiles. "You're the first person I've told."

"What about Francesca?"

Julian doesn't answer.

His house is nice. Too big for one or two people. It overlooks the hills, and the Hollywoodland sign is visible in the distance. It's lovely. He walks me from the car to a spare bedroom. I get out of my dress, the emerald satin pooling at my feet. He turns away, a true gentleman, handing me one of his shirts so I'm not naked in his house. When I'm dressed, he brings me a glass of water, and it doesn't do much to settle my stomach. I don't know what's wrong with me. Maybe it was a reaction to seeing Tommy. I didn't exchange a word with him, and yet he sent me into a tailspin. Julian is waiting for the mysterious, magical doctor. I heard him on the phone while I was changing.

And I begin to cry again. I'm drinking water and sobbing when Julian leads a man in. The stranger is as tall as he is, with a lighter hair color. Other than that, they are identical. Same brown eyes, straight nose. Same long arms and strong hands. I look up at them, and the stranger frowns. He's carrying a small bag.

"Lorelei Davies, this is my brother, Jesse James Weston. He's a doctor," Julian says. Jesse James Weston. I didn't know he had any siblings. "She's been ill all night," Julian says to his brother.

Jesse kneels next to me. I wipe my eyes. I'm in no way presentable. He looks me up and down. "I'm okay," I say.

"She spent most of the night vomiting, Jess," Julian says.

Jesse Weston has his arms crossed over his chest. "Go get her another glass of water. We'll start with the most obvious test first, okay? Work our way from there." He has a slight drawl to his voice, one Julian worked hard to get rid of.

I drink two more glasses of water, then awkwardly pee in a cup while the Weston brothers hover outside the bathroom, waiting.

Two weeks later, Jesse Weston calls me with my results.

I'm pregnant.

CHAPTER 42

1954

Thea spent all day in her dance studio, dancing long-memorized variations in soft shoes. She started with the exercises she gave her students, bending her body into demi-plié, then down into grand plié, and then into arabesque.

She was terrified to go back. Thea was scared she would get another injury or wouldn't be able to get back in step with her coworkers. She had gotten too comfortable being off, and she didn't know how she'd return.

Amy came by, after work, to pick up Lorelei's journals. Thea introduced Amy to Sophie, saying that they were coworkers at the dance studio. Sophie had looked right past Amy, as if she knew Thea was lying.

As Thea danced, Amy sat, cross-legged underneath the barre, flipping through the pages.

Lorelei really did write down *every* thought. Like she was afraid of forgetting anything. Lorelei also tucked news clippings and photographs between her own thoughts and musings. Amy waved her over. "Look at this."

It was a newspaper clipping, pressed into the pages. Thea hadn't seen it on her own cursory look through, but that journal was particularly full. Thea stopped dancing. She sat next to Amy to see what she was pointing to. It was a photograph. Lorelei was dancing with someone, but Thea couldn't see her partner. Lorelei wore an evening gown, her hair up in a braided crown. Thea had to squint—the photograph was grainy—but Lorelei's face looked fuller . . . and so did her tummy.

"She's pregnant here," Amy said.

"She is." It was subtle but unmistakable.

"This journal has a lot of entries about her making a film called *Live, Love* and then not making it and then leaving Sunset. But there seems to be a lot of stuff about your dad too," Amy said. She looked up at Thea. "It's not *risqué*, but it's certainly something you don't want to read."

Thea exhaled. "You never want to think about your parents like that."

"Some of it is really sweet," Amy said. "She writes about him spending time with her after her injury. But she can't ever get a real read on him."

"He was married."

"Does she leave any clues about who might have killed her?" Thea asked.

Amy exhaled. The more they discussed, the more Thea was convinced that Lorelei's death was an accident. Maybe not suicide, but nothing malicious. She just couldn't see how anything else was possible. "She writes a lot about thinking everyone is out to get her. She blamed Ramona Penderghast for her injury." Amy looked up at Thea. "Who knew she was pregnant?" Amy asked. She looked up at the photographs that lined the wall of the dance studio. "Those are all you?"

"My dad and Julian John Weston knew," Thea said. She looked up too. "All me. My mom has a big box somewhere of all my modeling campaigns too."

"Goodness. Can I see them?"

"I'll try to find them," Thea said. She placed the newspaper clipping back within the pages. She took the journal from Amy.

Thea focused on trying not to mess up any of the pages, making sure everything was placed in the way that Lorelei had left it. As she did, two pages fell out, ones Thea hadn't seen before. She picked up the pages and unfolded them. They were typed and dated early October of 1934, brokering an adoption between Mr. and Mrs. Thomas Ross and Miss Lorelei Davies.

The document included a list of conditions, the first of which was that Lorelei would be given one million dollars to give her baby up. Amy leaned over, her hair falling over her shoulder. It was signed by Sophie but not by Lorelei.

It was nothing official. For a moment, neither woman said anything.

"What else do you think your mother knows?" Amy asked.

"We're going to find out," Thea said.

~

Sophie insisted they continue to have lunch at Sal's. It wasn't a Friday or the end of the month, but they were trying to capture the spirit of Tommy again.

"Mrs. Ross, Miss Thea." It was Dean. Always Dean. The last time they were here, Tommy's death was fresh, and Thea was a newly minted millionaire.

"We all miss seeing Mr. Ross around," Dean said. "Hasn't got easier for us. I can only imagine how you're feeling."

"Thank you, Dean," Sophie said.

"The usual?" Dean asked.

"Coke for her; mimosa for me," Sophie said. Dean nodded and turned away. The diner was mostly empty now. A couple of tables, far from their booth, were occupied. Thea could remember climbing into this booth every month with her father, her feet swinging as she decided what to have.

She loved skipping ballet to go out with her *film star father*. Everyone had been jealous.

"I don't think I can remember his laugh," Thea said. It was too soon, the memories of him starting to fade from her mind. And the more she tried to focus on him, the less tactile it all became. She could no longer feel his touch, his grip.

She thought about him constantly.

She closed her eyes, trying to remember being a child, standing on his feet when he taught her to waltz. His applause at every one of her ballet recitals and performances. Dinners in his office. Everything.

"It'll be hard for a while," Sophie said. "You've been doing so, so well."

Thea nodded, silent as Dean brought their drinks. Once he left, she looked over at her mother. "How did you end up with me?" Thea asked. "I mean, how did you adopt me?" Sophie lit a cigarette.

Dean came back to take their order. "Toasted cheese for Miss Thea?" he asked with a wink.

"Of course," Thea said.

"He loved you instantly," Sophie said after Dean left. "The minute he—we—saw you. It was love at first sight."

Thea nodded, taking this in. "Why did you write Lorelei Davies a contract offering her a million dollars for her baby?"

Sophie paled and leaned forward. "How do you know that?"

"Does it matter?" Thea asked. Sophie's lips pulled into a frown. Thea had spent her life studying her mother's moods and how, precisely, they were reflected in her face. She was careful, always so unreadable, old money manners and refined grace in a woman who was raised without wealth.

"It does to me, Theodosia." It was *how* Sophie said her name, just like she had at the Coca-Cola photo shoot. "It matters to me."

Thea swallowed hard. "Julian told me."

Sophie's eyes narrowed, like she could sense the lie Thea was telling her. "Well, I went to her right before you were born. I offered to buy you, yes. But she declined. Your father never knew that."

"Why do you think he did it?"

Sophie frowned. "I've thought about it a lot. I guess he didn't want anything to threaten our family. I guess, if she wouldn't take the money, he wanted to make sure she was out of the way."

"But he didn't know about the money," Thea said. "You just told me that."

Sophie wasn't looking at her, staring at the liquid in the glass in front of her. She exhaled sharply. "I don't know, Thea. I don't have any of the answers you want. You'd have to ask him." They were silent for a moment.

"But he loved her," Thea said, closing her eyes.

"Did he?" Sophie asked. A moment passed. "Thea," Sophie said. Thea opened her eyes, looked at her mother. "I love you so much. I wouldn't do anything differently."

CHAPTER 43

1954

It seemed, to Thea, that no matter what Lorelei tried to do, her life was dominated by men. They all wanted something from her. Parts, pieces of her.

The phone rang. Sophie was home, but Thea went to get it. "Hello." It was Amy. She had gone back to her office. Thea put the base of the phone on the ground and sat in her closet, closing the door.

"How are you?" Thea asked.

"She's pregnant now. She spent a film premiere throwing up. Her doctor was Julian's brother. She wrote about how she has to tell Tommy the truth. Do you think she did?" Amy asked.

Thea inhaled. She tipped her head back, against her circle skirts, all neatly hung up. The fabric whispered as she moved. "What if she was talking about her race? He knew about me. He wanted to marry her."

That was the real secret Lorelei had to keep. She wondered how Tommy would have reacted, learning Lorelei was Black. Thea hoped that he would have accepted her, loved her anyway.

But there was no way to know that now.

"How are you feeling?" Amy asked. "You've learned a lot about yourself in the past couple of weeks."

Thea nodded, even though Amy couldn't see her. She had to keep moving. If she stopped to think about everything, she worried she would curl up in her bed and sob. "I'm tired," Thea said. "And I don't know what any of this means for me."

"Does it have to mean anything for you right now?" Amy asked.

"How would you feel?" Thea asked.

There was silence on the line. Thea could hear the keys of Amy's typewriter. "I would be confused, I think."

"I am," Thea said. She closed her eyes, breathing deeply. It was too much for her to sort through.

"She wrote you a letter," Amy said. "It's dated November seventh."

"The day she died," Thea said.

"Do you want me to read it to you?" Amy asked.

"No . . ." Thea said. Her heart leaped into her throat. She couldn't explain it, but she didn't want to hear it over the phone. "I can't. Not like this."

"Okay," Amy said. "I understand. But you should read it. I think she'd want you to." It was hard to know what Lorelei would want. That was what they were working toward.

She would want to know how her daughter had grown up, what Thea had turned out to be. Thea hated that Lorelei would never see her, never be proud of her.

"I have to go," Thea said. She didn't wait for Amy to say anything. She hung up, climbed into bed, and began to cry.

~

"How well did you know my mom?" Thea asked. She, Julian, Amy, Walter, and Phyllis were all crowded around the Dawson-Weston dinner table. Walter had insisted on cooking for them all, and Amy was working on her story. Amy was more excited about the prospect of dining at Julian John Weston's house than she had been to meet Lorelei's family.

Amy had brought the journal with her, and Thea had read Lorelei's letter to her. She read it several times over, feeling acute heartbreak every time she did. She cried over the pages, careful not to get her tears on them, her mother's only words to her.

Thea and Amy had sat together, side by side through dinner. Now Amy was talking to Walter and Phyllis, learning all about Lorelei's childhood. Thea and Julian had moved to a small sitting room, giving them their privacy. Thea and Julian sat across from each other.

"Sophie?" Julian asked. He shook his head. "I met her twice, I think. But she was always a little intimidating. She was never without Tommy." He leaned back into his worn leather chair, his eyes still on Thea. "Why do you ask?"

Thea inhaled. "She tried to buy Lorelei's . . . me. She tried to buy me. She offered one million dollars for Lorelei's baby."

"Huh," Julian said. "Of course she did."

"Lorelei didn't tell you?" Thea asked.

Twenty years had elapsed between then and now, and that seemed to make the memories hard to recall. Julian lit a cigarette. It was those hours after dinner where everyone was full and tired. Walter had tried to push dessert on them, but everyone had declined. From the dining room, she could hear Phyllis's laugh, loud and contagious.

"I think she would have been embarrassed. I didn't know Tommy was your dad for months. Lorelei wouldn't tell me. She was so proud sometimes. I didn't know Sophie at all," Julian said. "We spent time in different circles, but from what I know of her, of course she would want Lorelei's baby." He tapped his cigarette on the ashtray nearest to him. He looked over his shoulder, finding Walter in deep discussion with Amy. Thea was a little in love with Julian and Walter. She had decided that she wanted that sort of romance.

Amy looked up and winked at her. Thea winked back, even though she felt silly doing it. She didn't know if she and Amy had that romantic potential either.

For the millionth time, she wished Tommy were there. She wanted to be able to ask him everything. She thought that would give her a straight answer. Thea pulled her legs to her chest, wrapping her arms around her knees.

"I think Sophie is lying to me," Thea said. She was thinking back to their talk at Sal's.

"Why?" Julian asked.

Thea didn't know how to answer that. They sat in silence for a moment. "When was the last time you saw her? Lorelei, I mean."

"It was right after you were born," Julian said. "She called me when she was in labor. Walt and I came right over. Walt didn't know she was having a baby. And you were there." He closed his eyes, then called for Walter. Walter crossed over, bracing his hands on Julian's headrest. "Didn't Millie say something to you, when she had the baby?"

Walter exhaled. Amy and Phyllis were still in conversation, of which Thea could hear snippets. "I think so," Walter said. "She wanted me to take care of you. I thought she was just tired. Didn't know what she was saying."

"Then she died," Julian said.

"She was supposed to take you to your grandparents," Walter added. "She wanted to go to Europe, but her dates were wrong, or something, and you came early. She spent a week with you, and then she was supposed to take you to Watts."

Thea pictured growing up in that house, small and dusty but with so much love it was bursting at the seams. She pictured who she might have been—not a ballerina, but maybe a seamstress to follow in her aunt's footsteps. She could have been anything, and that choice had been taken from her.

She was supposed to be Joanna Dawson, whatever that meant.

"I knew she was unhappy," Walter said. "She never talked about it—her life, her work. She always wanted to keep it all separate. I didn't think she was unhappy enough to end her own life, especially when I saw how she looked at you for the first time."

"She wanted to start a production company for you," Julian said. "It's something I realized later. That it wasn't just for her."

Tears pricked Thea's eyes. "I wish I could have known her."

> *11/07/1934*
> *You are lying on a blanket. You're asleep. It's the first time you've stopped screaming in the whole week you've been alive.*
>
> *I'm not ready. I'm not ready for any of this. But here you are, with a mind of your own. You know what you want. It's a good sign.*
>
> *I am going to give you to your grandparents, but I wanted some time with you first. Of course, Julian and Walt are both around, but they understand that we need some girl time.*
>
> *I want to watch you grow up. I want to watch you become your own woman and take the world head on. But I'll have to watch from afar. Maybe one day, I'll be able to tell you everything. But, for now, you'll be my niece, and I'll visit and bring you gifts and play with you.*
>
> *It's the best thing for both of us.*
>
> *You are the love of my life. I'll do anything to protect you, keep you safe. And your grandparents will love you so much. Your auntie will be so thrilled to see you. It'll be an adjustment, but it'll be good for all of us.*
>
> *Someday, I will tell you the truth. I want better for you. I want you to be the woman you will be wholly. Not a piece there and a part there. I want you to be yourself. It's a luxury I don't have.*
>
> *No matter what you choose, no matter who you turn out to be, I love you so much. What I've learned is that dividing yourself into parts to please other people hurts. I never want you to go through that pain.*
>
> *There are so many things I want to tell you. Be careful. Don't trust anyone. Love with your whole heart.*

Devote yourself to your schoolwork first, and your talent. Boys will come. These pages, and my love, will go with you. And when I see you, I hope you'll know how much I love you. You'll be coming of age in a different time. I hope it'll be better than mine.

I know I'm making the right decision because it's mine. It's not Julian's or Walt's or Tommy's. I'm your mother and I'm the one in charge. So, I have to trust myself. And I have to hope that you'll understand.

You'll grow up in a home full of love instead of with a woman who barely understands herself.

I love you so much. Take that with you every day.

-Your momma

CHAPTER 44

1954

The second time Thea visited Cheryl Lawrence, she was alone. She had asked Julian; he was teaching.

She didn't want to visit again. Thea had read every story Cheryl had written about Lorelei, and they were all mean. Scathing, calling her untalented, too heavy, dismissing her as a forgettable nobody. Cheryl wasn't this mean to everyone: She praised Ramona Penderghast, revered Francesca Weston.

It was just Lorelei.

Maybe Lorelei wasn't crazy.

Maybe she just had people watching her, expecting things from her, wanting her to fail. The pressure had to have been suffocating.

Thea understood. She had seen the pressure in ballet: The competition, the drive to be better than everyone around her. The sleepless nights, the hours in rehearsal, her constantly aching body.

All for something that was always just out of reach.

Thea found Cheryl Lawrence in the dining room, propped up at the table. In the distance, there was a radio playing. She was surrounded by dishes, some half empty. She wasn't wearing her glasses, and she seemed smaller, frailer, than when she and Thea first met.

"Theodosia Ross," Cheryl said. "Come. Sit down."

Thea did as she was told. "I'm sorry to drop in on you like this." She sat two places to the older woman's right, as if Cheryl would snap and bite her like a rabid dog. "I brought back your boxes."

"Did you read everything?" Cheryl asked above the noise from the radio. "Get everything you need?"

"Everything I could stomach," Thea said.

Cheryl's hands shook as she tried to light a cigarette. Thea did it for her. Cheryl exhaled before she responded. "I was quite harsh on her."

"Why?" Thea asked.

Silence. Cheryl waited as her housekeeper, a colored woman who had to be Thea's age, cleared the table. "Annie, turn off the radio," Cheryl said.

"Yes, Miss Lawrence." Annie disappeared without looking at Thea.

After another moment, the radio was cut off, and they could talk at a normal volume. Cheryl exhaled cigarette smoke. The kitchen was painted white, and the walls were stained brown. "The truth is that it was just the job. I held no ill feelings towards the girl."

"You were so mean," Thea said before she could stop herself. She was sitting straight in her chair, unable to let herself relax. "Did you know she was a colored woman?" she asked.

"I heard the rumors," Cheryl said. "But I didn't want to report it if I wasn't sure. I was never sure."

"But you reported her baby," Thea said. She was trying to make sense of it all. Cheryl's old job made little sense.

Cheryl exhaled cigarette smoke, then used the butt to light a new one. "Because I *knew* about the baby. Of course she was pregnant. I reported what I could verify. And maybe I was harsh on her. She needed to develop a thicker skin. She was never going to make it if she broke down every time I was a little mean to her." Thea didn't think calling a woman "generally twenty pounds too heavy" was just a *little* mean.

"You wrote a story about how Lorelei was 'passed around like Cuban cigars,'" Thea said.

Cheryl exhaled. "I was wrong about that. I went off intel from Ramona Penderghast."

"And that made it okay?" Thea asked.

Cheryl didn't respond. Cheryl's stories reminded Thea of the way Sophie talked to her. Insults and barbs, all given under the guise of making her stronger.

In Thea's case, it had worked.

In Lorelei's case, it hadn't.

In her time, Cheryl had been a powerful woman. Thea knew that. Her name had been everywhere, and she'd had the power to influence every star's career.

"I had a code, sweetheart," Cheryl said. She was staring past Thea, maybe waiting for Annie to return. "It was always the truth. I wasn't going to lie to sell papers. All those stars? They were enough. Maybe I am ashamed," Cheryl continued. She wasn't even talking to Thea. Her attention was somewhere else. "Maybe I was too hard on her. That's why I kept my stories about her." Cheryl's eyes found her again. Her gaze was bright and unrelenting, boring straight to Thea's soul. "She killed herself, and I had to be partially responsible." Her voice was soft, but she seemed more lucid than before. Cheryl seemed to be realizing this now, putting it all together.

"She didn't kill herself," Thea said.

"Even so," Cheryl said. She was frowning now, her cigarette on an ashtray in front of her. "I try to never think about her."

Was it possible that Cheryl had never thought about how her words could hurt her subjects? That now she was beginning to realize how she'd affected people?

"What about Julian? And my dad? You didn't have to pit them against each other," Thea said.

Cheryl looked at her again. "I didn't." Her reply was simple. There were so many things Thea didn't understand about her father's life. "They already hated each other. They were going for the same roles, singing the same songs, and dancing the same dances. I just reported on what I saw. And those two men . . ." Cheryl didn't finish her sentence. "I may have added fuel to the fire, but nothing I did made their little feud worse."

"The boxes are in my car," Thea said awkwardly. She didn't know how to segue away from this line of conversation.

"Ask Annie to help you bring them in. She knows where everything should go," Cheryl said. She was still glaring at the dishes around her.

Thea rose from the table, knowing that the stink of cigarette smoke would linger on her clothing.

~

Thea sat between Julian and Amy. They were watching *About Last Night*, the last film Lorelei ever completed.

Thea liked it; it was different from what she had done at Sunset. Julian had told her that Lorelei was inspired to start her own production company after seeing one of Ingrid's films. Thea wondered if Ingrid knew that.

Julian and Lorelei started the company together, but he had quit acting after Lorelei died. "Those few months taught me that I didn't want to do it without her," Julian had said. "After she passed, it didn't feel right." Julian had been affectionately obsessed with Lorelei, and it sounded like they'd brought the best out of each other.

And she was beautiful.

About Last Night was the one film Amy kept returning to time after time, and Thea understood why. Lorelei's turn as a wife determined to have her husband killed was enthralling.

Lorelei moved as if she were dancing, all grace and poise. She was cool, beautiful, and seductive, letting her costar fall into her trap.

Thea loved it. She loved being able to soak up as much Lorelei as she could. She still didn't see the similarity Julian swore they had. Amy's hand was on Thea's thigh, her fingers light. Her touch made it hard for

Thea to concentrate. Their relationship was nothing more than some kissing and two dreams that had woken Thea up hot and bothered.

She was trying to be clear, clearer than she had been with Willa. But it seemed Amy understood.

All Thea wanted was some *fun*.

She reached down, squeezing Amy's hand.

On screen, Lorelei was undressing, the camera tight on her upper body. She would have been pregnant, but it was hard to tell. Technically, Thea was in this movie too.

This was the one way she could get to know her mother, along with Lorelei's journals and the memories of people who actually knew her. Thea felt a wave of anger and resentment. She was supposed to be someone else. The opportunity to be someone else had been taken from her when she was a week old.

Who was she supposed to be angry at? Not Lorelei. Not her father. She wondered what it would have been like being raised by them together. The dancing, the films, the love Thea would have been surrounded by.

On screen, the credits rolled.

"I think she had so much potential," Amy said. She was staring at the screen. She had been silent almost the whole film, her fingers never leaving Thea's thigh. "This film is so good. The directing, her acting. She really shined in it."

"Thank you," Julian said. "I would have liked to do more directing."

"Why didn't you?" Thea asked.

"I moved to teaching the year after she died. I couldn't step onto a film lot without thinking about her," Julian said. "Everyone else just forgot about her, but I couldn't." He was frowning.

Thea turned to him. "Do you ever feel her?"

"I think she's watching me all the time," Julian said. "When I first saw you, it felt like she was right there in the room, telling me that you were baby Joanna. I felt her tell me that you needed me."

Thea had never believed in ghosts. Willa had gone through a phase where she was obsessed with the supernatural: wanting Thea and Max to have séances with her, convinced she could see the future in a mess of tea leaves. Thea had indulged Willa's whims but secretly thought Willa was silly for believing it.

But now?

Thea wasn't sure. She saw Lorelei every time she closed her eyes. Thea dreamed about her, thought about her constantly. Thea was being haunted by a ghost, one that needed justice. She thought about the woman Lorelei could have become—the actress, the businesswoman—and how that was all overshadowed by her murder.

Thea wanted to put things right. She didn't know what Lorelei would want.

The truth would have to be enough.

They had dinner, Chinese food, eating on the floor of the living room. Walter joined them, sitting next to Julian.

Thea wished Lorelei was there to join them. There were so many things she would never get to know from her mother.

Trying to be content with what she had was hard. She had gotten her wish, but in the most awful way possible.

CHAPTER 45

1934

Tommy turns up at two in the morning, and I've already been asleep for hours. He's wearing a suit, with his tie long discarded.

"Lorelei." It's the *way* he says my name. My breath catches in my throat.

"Come in," I say.

We sit on the couch, a few inches apart. He takes great care not to touch me. I'm still wearing my girdle, even though there's nothing to hide.

"Tommy." He's spent ten minutes smoking and not looking at me. I don't know how to say it. I decide to be blunt. "I'm pregnant. It's yours."

I have to believe this baby is Tommy's. I would rather die than carry Kenneth Webster's spawn.

He's silent. He lights another cigarette. My heart is in my throat. "Are you sure?"

I nod.

"You're not joking, are you? This isn't something to joke about."

"It's still early."

The way he kisses my tummy, right over my belly button, over the black silk of my nightgown. He's never kissed me like this.

"You're having my baby." He whispers it with such wonder, and I feel a stab in my heart. "You're not showing yet."

"It's too early."

"Marry me. I love you. Marry me." It's the first time he's ever said those words to me. Those words aren't allowed in our affair. It's not love. It's physical.

Tommy's breathless, forgetting that he's already married. "Sophie and I aren't working out. Lorelei, I love you. I love you. I want to raise this baby, our *son*, as a family."

I can't reply. I don't know what to say. His hand is still on my stomach, and his eyes are imploring. When he looks at me like this, it's hard for me to say no. I'm in Tommy's orbit, and I can't resist.

"I'm the third Thomas Anthony Ross," Tommy says. His gaze has dropped to my stomach. He's not talking to me, just my stomach. "If we have a son . . ."

"You want him to be the fourth Thomas Anthony Ross?" I ask.

"I want him to be anything other than the fourth Thomas Anthony Ross. What about your dad? What's his name? You never talk about your family. I want to be a part of it all."

I bite my tongue. I know Tommy would leave me in the dust if he knew about my background. He can never know I'm not white.

He wouldn't like me if he knew I wasn't.

"We should get you back to bed." Tommy's voice is husky, and he doesn't give me the chance to respond before he lifts me in his arms, taking me to the bedroom.

"I can walk," I tease as he sets me down.

"But why would I let you?" He removes his shirt and climbs into bed with me. He kisses my stomach and then my lips. I note the order.

"So what about your family?" Tommy asks again once his arms are around me.

"My sister died when I was young. Joanna. I'd like to name my daughter after her." It's the first thing in two years I've told him about my family.

And to my surprise, he laughs. "Sweetheart," he says. "If it's a girl, you're on your own."

~

When I was eight, my oldest sister died. I'm always scared that thinking about her too much will rip her from me altogether. I think of Joanna in an abstract way, her dancing dresses and lipstick and perfume. I think of her as someone I could have been, had I not become Lorelei Davies.

I don't remember much. My mother found her, and Walt tried to keep me from seeing her.

Joanna was the sister everyone wishes they had. She was patient with me, kind with me, and even though it's been twelve years, I sometimes wake up not remembering that she's gone.

Sometimes I confuse my memories with what really happened. I wake from a dream where I'm a child and I've hurt myself and Joanna is rocking me in her arms. I can still remember her touch, her arms around me. I can hear her singing in my ear, distracting me from my pain.

Tommy's fallen asleep. I can hear his breathing begin to regulate. His arm is draped over my body. This is a rare night that we don't have sex. We just talk, and only for a few brief moments before he falls asleep.

I smooth his hair from his face. Moonlight bounces off his cheeks, the cleft in his chin. I think about who our baby could be. I want to keep her from this world. I want him to grow up and be whatever he wants to be, not an actor or a hoofer if he doesn't want to.

I put a hand on my stomach, over Tommy's. I move quietly, gently, so I don't wake him. I close my eyes.

Everything else fades away as I think of our child. I think about his laugh, her curly hair. I hope he inherits my temperament and Tommy's angelic looks.

I don't know what I want, but maybe it isn't a life with Tommy.

"Tommy," I whisper. He won't wake; I know this from experience. Not even a fire could rouse him once he's out. "Tommy. I hope this won't change anything, but I'm a colored woman."

The words hang in the air, dissolving like sugar on my tongue. Next to me, Tommy's chest rises and falls, and he's given no indication that he's heard me.

He hasn't.

I lean over, pressing my lips to Tommy's cheek. It's been a day or so since he's shaved, and he's sporting some stubble.

Before Tommy and I got involved, I knew exactly what I wanted.

Stability.

This is anything but that. I put a hand on my tummy, wondering if I can feel the baby inside me, growing within me.

Tommy snores, a snort and a gasp. I wonder what he's dreaming about.

I kiss him again. He doesn't stir. It's the rise and fall of his chest that tells me he's alive.

And I lay in silence, planning for my future.

CHAPTER 46

1934

The bubble of what *could* be is popped a week later.

I'm on the couch when there's a knock on the door. It's a herculean effort to pull myself up, but I do, not sure what to expect.

I open the door to see Tommy and Sophie. Together.

"Lorelei." Tommy's voice is soft. He doesn't look directly at me. I'm in a brassiere and tap pants, a dressing gown open around my body. My hair is undone, and next to Sophie, who is pristine, I'm a monster.

I push my hair from my face. Frankly, I'm too tired to deal with all this. I barely manage to get myself to the kitchen table.

Tommy pours me a glass of water. Sophie sits across from me. I have two chairs at my table, so Tommy stands.

Sophie's ice-blue eyes are on me. She scans my face, then my body, tries to see if I'm showing yet.

I'm not. I check often.

She inhales and then exhales. I can't bear to look at Tommy. I try to keep my calm.

"You are so stupid," Sophie says. Her voice is low, full of anger. "When my husband told me . . ." She takes a deep breath, trying to calm herself down. "I don't want a divorce. I don't want to lose my husband. I think we can all agree that this should be dealt with as soon as possible." A flush has risen to her cheeks, making her look a little bit more beautiful. I'm not sure how this is going to go, but I'm sure she already has a plan. I take a sip from the glass of water. I have to keep my calm.

"I don't care. I'm keeping this baby," I say. It's the boldest stand I can make.

Sophie lights a cigarette. She makes every move slowly and methodically, drawing the moment out.

She doesn't look at Tommy.

Tommy doesn't look at her.

I try to keep my eyes on the ice princess in front of me.

"I think it would be to the detriment of us all if you were to keep the baby." She talks in such a polished way. She's used to getting what she wants. Tommy, for his part, looks properly cowed. "We want you to take care of it. And then you need to leave." She smiles softly, as if she's so proud of her little plan. "I understand that my husband has a wandering eye. I understand that he will have his little dalliances, but I told him that something like this is unacceptable."

I hold my breath. She's still talking, not letting me get a word in to defend myself. I sneak a look at Tommy, who is still leaning against the kitchen counter. "I don't think this town is big enough for the two of us." She raises an eyebrow.

I meet her eyes. "I'm not leaving."

"Oh, please," Sophie says. "You can find another man to support you." She exhales smoke in my face. I resist the urge to cough. I know how she sees me, as a common whore. Word had spread about Kenneth and me.

Things have a way of getting out.

I know I'm a laughingstock. "I'm not going. I'll take care of it, but I'm not going." I don't know if I'm in the position to negotiate. I don't care. Tommy looks at me now. I'm annoyed at how silent he's been through this. He was proposing marriage a week ago, elated at the thought of a small him running around.

But now . . .

I take a sip from my water glass and continue. "I won't contact you or *your husband* again, but I'm not leaving. I have too much at stake."

Sophie purses her lips, trying to decide whether that's a reasonable alternative. I won't back down. She nods.

"Thomas," she says. At this cue, Tommy steps forward. He removes an envelope from his inside breast pocket, then puts it on the table. "All the money you'll need and an address. Do it this weekend." When Sophie rises, Tommy offers his arm to her. Together, they are the most breathtaking couple.

And I wonder how I could have ever believed that Tommy and I could be together.

~

Screaming.

I'm sitting in a small living room that doubles as a waiting room. A woman across from me, wearing black and a pinched expression, keeps her brown eyes on my face. She's waiting for a reaction, and I'm not going to give her one.

"Shouldn't be too much longer," she says. She's reading a dime-store novel. She's the one who escorted me into this house and took half the money Tommy gave me as payment.

I've dressed as Millicent Dawson in a faded floral dress from the last dregs of the 1920s. I press a hand to my stomach; the dress is large, shapeless, so I don't need my girdle. I can't believe we ever wore these things.

With a brimmed hat over my hair, I hope she doesn't recognize me.

"I'm in no hurry," I say.

"I should think you are in a little bit of a hurry."

Another scream. I saw the girl go in, led by a burly man in a suit. The girl had been no older than sixteen, and, of course, I thought of Joanna.

Something in my stomach turns. Her screams are agonizing.

The woman watches me, her gaze unchanging and unmoving. I swallow hard.

This is for the best.

I think of Joanna again. No one ever told me how she died. I overheard my parents talking about it in hushed tones.

And even then, I don't think I fully understood what it meant.

Joanna had tried to do it herself. She was pregnant and couldn't be. She used a wire hanger in the bathroom.

The girl, sweaty and bleeding, is escorted back into the waiting area. The woman's eyes briefly slide to her. I wonder if she has anyone to go home to or if she's alone. I want to bundle her up in my arms and never let go. She's got skin a couple of shades darker than mine, a mole over her upper left lip. Her hair is coarse, tight, curly, weighed down with sweat. She's barely supporting herself.

The man stands behind her, wiping his hands off with a white towel that is covered in dried blood. He looks at me, a frown on his face. "You next?" The girl is still shivering.

I think of Joanna again.

I swallow hard.

I'm not going to let Sophie win. I rise from my chair on shaking, newborn-deer legs and wrap the girl in my arms. She resists for a moment and then folds into me. "This is a mistake," I say. I still have the rest of the money Tommy gave me. I lead her out, letting the door to the house slam behind me.

She watches me with big brown eyes as I tuck her into the passenger seat of my car. "I am so sorry," I say as I make sure the doors are locked. "What's your name?"

"Joanna."

My heart stops as I maneuver her to my car. It's a sign; it has to be. "I'm Millicent," I say, feeling more like my true self than ever. "I'm not going to hurt you, I promise."

I can't take her to a hospital. I don't want this girl getting in trouble. Instead, I end up driving her to Julian's house.

I run to the door, knocking as hard as I can. Julian opens the door, dressed in pajamas, his hair messed up. "Lorelei. What's goin' on?" When he's this tired, he begins to betray his southern roots. No one would know that Julian John Weston is a born and bred Texan, drawl and all. He worked hard to smooth the rough edges of his accent. It takes me by surprise, and I almost forget what I'm doing.

"I need your help."

Julian follows me outside, to where the scared girl waits. "This is Joanna. She needs medical help," I say. Julian opens the car door, then scoops her into his arms. He whispers something to her I can't really make out. I follow him into the house and close the door.

They're already halfway up the staircase. I hustle to follow and help Julian place Joanna in bed. She's still dressed, and it seems as if the blood has stopped. Her eyelids are at half-mast. I sit next to her. "I'll call Jesse," Julian says. He checks the time on his watch.

"Make sure he's . . ."

"Discreet. He is. Tea for you and Joanna," Julian says.

"Thank you," I say.

"What are friends for?"

I climb into bed next to Joanna. I think about all the times I've held Phyllis like this. Her eyes are shutting. "I'm so sorry," I say.

"Is that . . . Julian John Weston?" Her voice is soft.

I have to bite back a laugh. "Yes, you'll see him again after you see the doctor. Don't worry; it'll all be okay." I press a hand to my own stomach, wishing it could be true for me too.

Once I'm sure Joanna is asleep, I slip out of the room. Julian is sitting on the stairs, looking disheveled. He's leaning against the banister, half asleep. The kettle, in the kitchen, is whistling. I go to pour him a cup of tea and press it into his hands.

"I'm so sorry," I say.

"My brother is comin'," Julian says with a sigh. "What happened?"

I spill the whole story, my own reason for being there and how scared Joanna was. Julian pulls me close, and the last few hours hit me. Exhaustion runs through me. I yawn, covering my mouth.

"What about you?" Julian asks. He doesn't say the words out loud. One day I will tell him about my sister, but for now I let it pass. I want to cry, but nothing comes out. I'm just empty. Tired and empty.

"Sophie and Tommy wanted me to *get rid of it*. I can't do that," I say. I press a hand to my stomach. It still feels like nothing. The idea that a life grows inside of me is something I still can't wrap my head around. "I just have to tell him I did it, and then . . ." I trail off.

I don't know what's going to happen.

But I know I'm keeping the baby.

CHAPTER 47

1934

I spend more and more time at Julian's house. I'm worried about everything: the pregnancy, delivering the baby, how Tommy reacted. Julian sometimes comes home early from Sunset to stay with me.

I tell him I'm okay, that he can leave me alone, and he nods, but I don't think he believes it. It's nice being with him. We sit, listen to the radio. I read fan magazines, avoid reading Cheryl Lawrence's column, and lie on his couch. I've taken over a guest room, had some things delivered.

I write. I have so much free time that I fill one journal, and Julian buys me two more.

One evening, when all I can keep down is water and saltines, Julian sits at one end of the couch with my feet on his lap. I look at him and ask, "Are you happy at Sunset?"

"I suppose." He's smoking a cigarette and reading script pages, deciding on what he wants to do next. I feel a pang of envy. He has prospects.

I sit up, pulling my feet from his lap. He's decorated like a bachelor, the bare minimum. Francesca has well and truly moved out. I see photographs of her with younger men in the papers and magazines, and I throw them out before Julian sees them too. "Do you want to do another movie about two people falling in love?" Before he can answer, I continue. "I mean it. I keep thinking about Ingrid Belle and the film we saw. And how well it's doing at the box office. She's an Oscar contender. Everyone knows it."

"I'm not in acting for the statues. I'm in it for the stories," Julian says.

"Right. So aren't you tired of the same story over and over?" In the past few days, the idea has crept up on me. The moment I found out I was pregnant, I wanted to give my baby more than a woman who isn't in control of herself. "Don't you want to explore?"

He's looking at me now, and I fully have his attention. One arm over the back of the couch, his chin on his arm, his eyes big and warm and brown. "Go on."

I pick up my journal. One the last page, I have written *WESTON-DAVIES PRODUCTIONS.*

He takes the journal from me and looks at the page.

"I think we can really make something," I say. I'm getting ahead of myself, the cart before the horse.

He mulls it over, taking his time. "We're not producers."

"But we could be." I can't do it by myself. I know that. I need him. He's respected; people like working with him. I don't have the money; I don't have the connections. But Julian does. And there's no one I'd rather start a business with.

"I . . ." He trails off. He looks toward the pages of scripts in front of him.

"Tell me you want to spend another six months dancing constantly, and I'll drop the subject. But I think you know how great you and I could both be." I glare at him, not breaking eye contact, not letting him look away. "Think about how we could have control over what we do."

He's thinking it over. He frowns, then opens his mouth. Then he closes it. "We won't be able to do anything at Sunset," he says eventually. "I'll have to talk to people at Paramount. Maybe we could set something up with them."

And even though it's not certain, even though everything is just a possibility, it's something. And it's something I can hold on to. "Before you decide, I have to tell you a couple of things. Well, I have to tell you one thing and show you another."

"What?" Julian is instantly concerned.

I inhale. "I owe Sunset Studios two hundred thousand dollars." The number hangs in the air between us. "I can pay some of it but not all. And I want to buy my house, too, and I . . ."

Julian holds up a hand. "I'll deal with Sunset. You focus on keeping your house." He decides it quickly, and I don't know what he means by that. "What do you need to show me?"

"I want you to meet my family."

~

My mom and dad are sitting on the porch as we approach the house. Julian had one thousand questions on the train, and I ignored them all. Sometimes showing is better than telling.

"Momma. Daddy!" I call. Momma looks up at me and grins.

"Millie." My father is quiet, more stoic, but he hugs me first—and tightly. Momma looks Julian up and down.

"This is Julian John Weston," I say. "Julian, this is my mother and father."

His eyes move between them, their dark skin glowing from the sun, my momma's curly hair always unmanageable. He looks at me. Looks back at my parents. My father extends a hand. "Call me May," Momma says, as if she's ever been just May to anyone.

Julian is the picture of decorum: He doesn't say anything. But he puts two and two together. I hold my breath, watching for his reaction. He smiles, extending a hand. "Call me Julian." My mother falls in love with him instantly, says she thinks he's too thin.

"MILLIE!" Phyllis hangs out the kitchen window, yelling my name. Her hair tumbles over her shoulder, and for a moment, I think she's Joanna. "Millie! Come help with dinner, *please*!"

"Will you be okay?" I ask.

"I've got May to keep me company." Julian winks at her, and I think my mother actually giggles.

I wash my hands, put on an apron, while Phyllis peppers me with questions. "Is that *Julian John Weston*? Are you gonna marry him?"

"Julian is a friend, and you have to behave yourself or I'm never bringing him back here ever." She knows my threat has no legs. There's not much for me to do; Phyllis has already cooked enough food for an army.

All three of my brothers are at home too: Ralph, Walt, and Calvin. They're smoking cigarettes in the living room, but we get Walt to set the table.

By the time dinner is ready, the sun is setting, and we arrange ourselves around the table. Julian sits next to me, with Walt on his other side. Calvin, Phyllis, and Ralph are on the other side of the table. My parents sit at both ends. The radio is turned off, and my father makes me say grace. It's not something I do regularly; I stumble through it and catch Julian's quick smile as I do.

We pass dishes about; my mother clicks her tongue and fills my plate, then Julian's. I can tell he's trying not to laugh. Insults are flying—so are jokes—and I want to cry.

"So," Phyllis says. She thinks she knows everything. "Do you have something to tell us?" She's trying to be subtle.

I take a look at Julian, open my mouth. Before I can say anything, he speaks. "Your brilliant sister and I are going into business together." He's charmed my whole family. He's made it look so easy. Even Walt, the sensitive, quiet type, can't stop looking at him. "We're starting Davies-Weston, a production company." He flips our names. It's not what I proposed, but I like it.

We're going into business together, whatever that may mean.

"I've left Sunset," I say. "I want to grow as an actress." I can be better and bigger than anything Kenneth ever imagined for me.

Next to me, Julian and Walt are in the midst of . . . something. Walt's smile is small. Julian's pulling him out of his shell.

Phyllis sips from her water glass, but that doesn't stop her words from spilling from her. "Millie, next time, can you bring Tommy Ross? Please?" Just the mention of his name makes my heart stop.

"I'm not at Sunset anymore," I explain patiently. "I probably won't see him as much."

"Are you a Tommy Ross girl?" Julian pretends to be offended.

Phyllis laughs but can't look him in the eye. "I like to watch him dance."

"Well, Phyllis, now you've done it," I say.

Julian clears his throat, placing his napkin next to his plate as he rises. "I'm better than Tommy Ross, and I will prove it to you, if you'll rise." Phyllis, her eyes wide, does as she's told. "Lor—Millie?" I get up from my seat and walk the four paces from the kitchen table to the living room. I sit down at the piano. I'm rusty, and I can't do anything advanced, but I start playing a slow waltz. I can see Julian begin to ease Phyllis into the dance as I play.

It feels like home.

Phyllis can't take it seriously; she's laughing too hard to concentrate on the steps. Julian stops her, letting her stand on his feet as if she were a child. And they're whirling around the small space, Phyllis laughing hard as I play.

I finish the song, and after Phyllis stops laughing, she looks up at Julian, fluttering her eyelashes. "I'm sorry," she says. "You're better than Tommy Ross."

I catch Walt watching Julian with the same almost lovesick smile Phyllis is wearing.

CHAPTER 48

1934

In the following months, Julian and I pick our first project for Davies-Weston. *About Last Night* is a film noir, and Julian is directing. The film is this: A nightclub singer meets a patron who falls in love with her. To be together, she asks him to kill her husband. Then she sets him up to take the fall and gets away scot-free.

We start filming immediately so I can finish before I really begin to show. All my costumes are clingy, close to my body. Every morning, I stare at myself in the mirror, trying to see if I can see a bump. I keep my girdle on all the time. I can't risk anyone knowing.

Filming days are long, and they're capped by nights out at Cloud Nine or the Trocadero or the Cocoanut Grove. It means more dresses, more people looking at me. Every time Julian and I enter a place, the conversation turns to whispers about us.

Stories circulate about how we're taking on too much, how we're actors with big egos, how we will fail and quickly. Julian has banned all reporters, all magazines, all newspapers from set.

And even so, I feel better than I have in months. I let Jesse Weston check up on me, at Julian's insistence. Jesse says I need to eat more, and I try. I love the film, and Julian in the director's seat makes it easy to want to go to work every day. He usually picks me up, at three or four in the morning. We're on set all day, and then by eight or nine, we have to change to go out and be seen around town. It's all a game.

An exhausting game.

Even with everything going on, I still think about Tommy. I read reports from Sunset, about how *Taming of the Shrew* is going terribly, how he's in a terrible mood, throwing fits on set like a child.

I don't try to contact him, even though I want to. I have to focus on my future and on my baby.

Julian is leaning forward in his chair. We're now two months into filming, and I want to be done within the next few weeks. He's watching my costar, Oliver Black, and me, Oliver's arms around me. We're making *About Last Night* in conjunction with Paramount Pictures. We have access to their lot, their day players and costumes and makeup and everything. I have no idea how Julian managed it, but for the first time in a long time, the future seems bright. We have so much potential.

"Let's take this scene again," Julian says. "Oliver, back to your mark." I think we're making good time. Julian understands the time crunch we're on.

We run the scene again. My words spill from me as if they're second nature. I'm driven to make this film the best one ever, the best thing I ever do. *About Last Night* is the first time I really love acting, really see what I can be and what I can do.

It's a thrill to try something new. Julian is patient and understands how he and I want the film to look and feel. I'm wearing a black dress; Oliver wears a suit. He's good, green but enthusiastic. He approaches me in the scene; I blink up at him. He's slightly reminiscent of Tommy, same strong jaw and dancing brown eyes. He's not as tall or broad shouldered. But he's good looking.

"Cut. Print. Moving on," Julian says. He really is an excellent director. The set is a flurry with the crew bustling around Oliver and me.

"Good work," I say. Oliver smiles shyly. This film could be his big break too.

"Moving on, everyone. Three more scenes to shoot today," Julian says. He's so relaxed in the director's chair.

I'm exhausted. I'm happier than I have been in months. And that's what counts.

~

About Last Night is a shorter filming period than any of my films with Sunset. It's because there are no song and dance numbers. We're making good time, which is important, because if this film fails, Julian and I will both be out of money.

It's the middle of a filming day. We're in the second half of the film now, and it's a scene where I'm sitting across from Oliver Black. He's barely said two words to me off set, which is fine. I still think I'm a bit of a pariah.

Or he's read the articles about me and thinks I'm a whore.

I can't decide which is more likely.

We've been running the scene for the whole afternoon. Every time we do, Julian isn't happy with something. As a director, he's exacting, but kinder than Kenneth. From his chair, Julian groans. He's been in a touchy mood all day, and I can't help but think that maybe it's not us that's bothering him. He squeezes his eyes shut with a great flair for the dramatics.

"Can we do it again, *please*." He sounds exhausted. Just as exhausted as I feel. I exhale. I'm sitting on a couch, still wearing my girdle, my back straight, my posture flawless. Oliver is hovering near the entrance to this room, wearing a suit with his tie untied. "Once more." Julian leans forward in his chair.

We take it from the top again.

I start the scene standing. The skirt hem hits midcalf, and the bodice boasts a conservative neckline and a plunging back. It's a little bigger than it needs to be, and I'm hoping that between that and my girdle, no one can tell I'm pregnant.

"Action." Julian sits back again. He misses nothing. I'm a little lightheaded, have been all afternoon. I'm chalking it up to lack of food, and all I need to do is get through this scene and I can go home. I know Julian has plans for us tonight, but I know I won't be able to stand it.

Oliver comes in again, starting the scene. His voice is lovely, a perfect midrange that isn't too high or low, and his accent is clear as a bell. I could listen to him talk forever. He's staring at me, and I realize that he's finished his line. It takes me a moment to recall what I'm supposed to say, and it stutters from my mouth.

"Cut." Julian isn't angry this time. He stands from his chair. Oliver's eyes don't leave me.

And it's Oliver who catches me when I faint.

~

I wake up in my bed. The Weston brothers are both staring at me like I've grown an extra limb. Jesse's arms are crossed over his chest. "Lorelei," he says seriously.

I sit up, and Julian comes to my side, putting a pillow behind me and handing me a glass of water. "What happened?"

"You fainted on set," Julian said.

"Shit," I say.

"You need to rest," Jesse adds. His eyes are still on me, dark and somber, and I'm struck again by how similar he and Julian look. "Julian tells me you're still wearing your girdle."

"No one can know," I say.

"The baby has no room to grow. You have to eat too," Jesse says. I shake my head, start to protest, but I know that he won't listen. This isn't just about me anymore. "You're much smaller than you should be." He listens to the baby's heart. "You need to rest, Lorelei," Jesse says.

"Once I finish this film," I say.

"Now," Jesse counters. "You and this baby need it."

"Jess," Julian says, turning toward his brother. "I'll watch her."

"And you're a doctor now?"

"I played one in a film," Julian says. He raises an eyebrow, a deep frown on his lips. "I'll keep an eye on her."

I want to protest, say that I'm an adult woman who can take care of myself. But I remember I just fainted and am in no place to talk. "Pass me my journal, please," I say.

"We'll leave you to get some rest," Jesse says. He and Julian leave me alone after giving me my journal. I sit on my bed, pressing a hand to my stomach. I close my eyes. I don't think about the amount of money we're losing today. I know what Jesse said.

And I know what I have to do. It seems impossible to balance it all.

CHAPTER 49

1934

"I have to tell him." I'm sitting in bed, pages of a script around me. Julian is in a chair, his right leg on his left knee. He's reading reports of some sort. Jesse has mandated bed rest, and that means if I'm not on set, I'm in bed.

I don't think it's exactly what Jesse meant, but Julian has promised not to tell him.

Julian looks at me, his brow furrowed. It's the first thing either of us has said in an hour.

"I have to tell Tommy about everything."

He asked me to marry him. Then he came to my house with his wife to tell me to get rid of the baby. I don't know what he wants. I can't concern myself with that. I need to take care of myself and my child. I get to be selfish now.

I'm on the verge of crying every minute. I inhale. I hate the fact that I'm keeping this secret. I'm sitting cross-legged, without my girdle on, and every so often, Julian looks at my tummy. I'm big and tired.

"What would it change?" Julian asks. He leans forward, putting his papers on the bed. He moves the chair closer to me.

"I'm tired of hiding," I say. Isn't that it? Can't that be all? I think about how Tommy would react. I would hope that it would be positive, that he would love me still.

Does he love me, or does he love the baby I'm carrying?

I never thought I was in love with him. Lust, maybe. We were having fun.

Julian exhales. He doesn't respond for a long time, and I watch thoughts pass over his face. He's very expressive. He can't hide what he's thinking. "I don't think it'll help anything."

"What do you know about hiding?" I ask. But then I think about him and Walt at family dinners. Once I caught them on the porch, heads bent together, giggling like schoolboys. And Walt has been so bright these past few months. Happier. And I know Julian's the cause of that. Julian may not understand it all, but he does get some of it. "I'm sorry," I say. We never talk about his love life. We never talk about my race. Two things that are always off the table. "I shouldn't have said that." I inhale, closing my eyes. "I want him to know me. I know you two aren't friends."

"That doesn't matter," Julian says, even though I know it does. He frowns at the mere mention of Tommy. He knows Tommy's the dad, but Tommy isn't his favorite subject. "I want the best for you and the baby."

"I know," I say. "I do too."

Julian is quiet. He lights a cigarette, leaning back in his chair. He avoids my gaze. "He's never going to leave her." He says it so seriously, so quietly. "He's never going to be with you. You have to know that."

On some level, I do. I know that Tommy will never leave his beautiful blond wife and marry me. This was never supposed to happen. I press a hand to my stomach, closing my eyes.

The last thing I want to do is be Tommy's wife. I know how he treats Sophie. He'd treat me the same way.

"I still have to tell him." The thoughts run around my brain, gaining speed, and I can't seem to slow myself down or sort through my thoughts. "He has to know."

"Does he know you didn't go through with it?" Julian asks.

I shake my head. I'm hiding this baby from everyone except for Julian and Jesse.

I don't know what I'm going to do, but I know it'll be without Tommy.

A flutter spreads through my stomach, and I gasp. I sit up straight, and Julian leans forward. "What?" He's alert, ready to get up and call Jesse if we need to.

"I don't know." I press a hand to my stomach, and a flutter ripples through me again. The feeling is unnerving, and I think something's wrong.

Julian leans over, placing his hand, large and warm, over mine. "I don't feel anything."

"It's happening now," I say. I'm worried. "Call Jesse."

Julian considers it, moving to take my hand in his. "I think the baby is kicking." I stop. I take a deep breath, trying to let my panic wash away. "That's a good thing, Millie." He's taken to using my real name when we're alone. It reminds me that under the glossy veneer of Lorelei Davies, I am a real person. It doesn't always feel like that. Julian smiles at me. I try to smile back, but it comes out as a sob. It feels more real now. There's a life inside me.

And I know I made the right decision.

I feel the rumbling again and close my eyes. I make up my mind right there.

Tommy doesn't need to know at all.

~

None of my immediate family has ever visited me in Los Angeles. I know Phyllis would love it, want to soak up of every second of it. But I try to keep them away from Lorelei Davies.

It's more for me than for them.

So it is a surprise when there is a knock on the door, and I find Momma standing on my doorstep.

She's caught me on a day when I woke up with the urge to clean my whole house. I don't think I've ever had this drive in my life. I've always hired someone to do it for me, but I woke up at five in the morning and have been methodically cleaning every room. I'm working on tidying a smaller bedroom, directly next to mine.

There's a part of me thinking it could be the perfect nursery.

"Millicent Anne Dawson," Momma says. It's been so long since I've heard my middle name; I almost forgot what it is. "You're . . ." She trails off. I let her inside. I'm not wearing a girdle, and my tummy is on show. I worry that there are people lurking outside my house, and I can't be seen like this.

Momma and I sit on my couch. She makes me stand, turn in a slow circle to really take me in. "You didn't tell us."

Every time Julian and I visited my family, I hid it. I collapse next to my mother and close my eyes. "How far along are you?"

"Second trimester," I say. I'm doing my best to rest, to stay off my feet, Jesse's orders.

"You're so small," Momma says. I don't open my eyes or grace her with a response. I can feel her hand on my tummy. The kicks are stronger now; I can feel the baby shifting and moving. Julian can feel it too. I've been on my feet, and it's past noon. I'm hungry, and I'm tired.

"Momma," I say. I can't believe she's in my house. She can't believe I'm pregnant. I guess we're even. "I've been cleaning all day." I sit up, taking her hand. "Here."

The room I've cleared out is small, but it gets the morning light. The walls are currently white, but I think I can change the color, maybe a soft pink. I'm going to wait to decide and see if I can bribe Walt and Julian to do it for me.

"Millie," Momma breathes. She steps into the room, and I can see it: my baby growing up in this bedroom, right next to mine. All my old journals are stacked in the closet, and I don't know what to do with them. Momma doesn't ask me who the father of my baby is.

"Why did you come?" I ask.

Momma looks at me, blinking slowly. We have the same eyes, and I see myself reflected in hers. "I wanted to see you. I wanted to visit. I thought I should call, but I didn't know if you'd pick up."

We go back out to sit on my couch. I lean back, trying to let myself rest. I press a hand to my stomach. "Of course I'd pick up," I say.

"I had a feeling you needed me," Momma says. "I woke up, and I just . . ." She trails off, doesn't complete her thought. But I understand. I *did* need her.

The knock on the door interrupts us. I'm not expecting anyone else. Momma and I share a look. I start to tell her to ignore it, but I hear him. "Lorelei." It's Tommy. "You keep a key under the mat."

Before I can get up to open the door, it swings open. I'm standing, and through my day dress, he can see my tummy. He pales, focusing on me and not my mother. "You . . ." He trails off. The second surprise of the day.

"I couldn't do it," I say, not caring that my mother is right next to me.

His eyebrows knit together. He doesn't say anything for a moment. "I think we need to talk." I don't know why he came here. I haven't seen him since the night he asked me to get rid of the baby.

He crosses over to me, holding my face in his hands. He kisses me, then catches sight of Momma. "New housekeeper?" he asks. He doesn't let me respond. I hold my breath, hoping he won't see the slight resemblance we have. I actually think it's impossible to see that we're family unless you look closely. And he's not going to do that. He only really cares about himself. "I'm Thomas Ross. It's so nice to meet you."

I could cut in; I should. The words die on my tongue. Momma clears her throat. "May Dawson." They shake hands.

Tommy kisses me again. "I needed to see you. I couldn't take one more moment away from you. I've missed you." He's excited, boyish, and charming. Now is my chance to tell Tommy everything. I *can* feel it on my tongue. I can say this is my mother, that I'm a colored woman. He's looking at me expectantly. I can feel my mother watching me too.

"I'll go, Miss Davies," Momma says. Her voice is cold. She doesn't look at me, leaving quickly.

I thought she would understand, but it makes me feel terrible.

CHAPTER 50

1954

Thea and Sophie were both keeping distance from each other. Sophie hadn't tried to direct Thea's career at all since the awful Coca-Cola shoot.

They still took meals together. Thea didn't have any choice in that. She sat across from Sophie, watching her mother's every move. They didn't talk much, politely asking to pass dishes between them.

Since Tommy died, Sophie had stopped planning their elaborate menus. Most nights, they just sat there with water glasses between them.

Thea wondered: She spent all day in her dance studio, or at work, or with Amy. What did Sophie do all day?

"I know you're watching me." Sophie's eyes were turned to papers in front of her. Thea didn't know what she was reading. But it was, apparently, more interesting than her. Every so often, Sophie would pick up her fork or her wineglass in movements that were so absentmindedly graceful.

"Sorry," Thea said.

"Don't apologize." Sophie looked up at her, blue eyes cool. "Don't do it."

"Of course," Thea said. Sophie had taught so many of those little "lessons" growing up that it no longer fazed her. She had been raised to be Sophie's exact image: perfect posture, perfect appearance, perfect life.

Not unlike what Kenneth Webster had done to Lorelei.

"I hope you're not going to ask about your father," Sophie said, trying to read Thea's face.

"You had lunch with him at the office," Thea said. "The day he died. Why?"

Sophie exhaled, the dragged-out sigh of a woman who was on her last nerve. "We had lunch before their meeting. I wanted to talk about you and . . ." She trailed off. Sophie couldn't even say Lorelei's name. "I wanted to know what he did to Lorelei. I told him I loved him, that I would support him."

"Before?" Thea asked.

"Yes." Sophie was lighting a cigarette, tilting her head back to exhale smoke. She was so lovely. Thea remembered being four and five and six, watching her get ready for parties, the routine of hair and makeup and undergarments. She would watch as Sophie dressed, putting on an impossibly exquisite dress, and then Sophie would sit Thea on her vanity stool and do her makeup too. She thought her parents were royalty; that was how bewitching they were. Back then, all Thea knew was that she wanted to be that bewitching too.

Sophie would choose her pinkest lipstick and apply it to Thea's lips. She would tell Thea that she built her in her heart, that Thea made her a mother, and that she was the best thing that happened to her and Tommy.

She closed her eyes at the memory, gossamer thin. "What did you talk about exactly?" Thea asked.

"Thea," Sophie said. Her voice was whisper quiet. "I think you should let it rest. He killed her for us. For you." It was what she always said. Thea couldn't decide if Sophie was capable of murder. Sophie loved to gloss over unseemly things, imperfections.

"But I . . ."

"I know you want to know," Sophie said. She picked up her wineglass and took a sip. Questions bubbled up on Thea's tongue. She let them all die.

What Sophie wanted, Sophie got.

"Honey." Sophie put her glass down again. "I wish I did know. You have to believe that when he told me, I thought that our world was ending. Turns out that it was, just not the way I thought."

Every so often, Thea lost sight of what she and Amy were doing. They were in the middle of finding out what happened to Lorelei and if and how her father's death was linked. But it seemed to her that all they were doing was digging up the dead, pulling the curtain away from long-hidden secrets.

Did it matter what it was supposed to mean? Couldn't Thea make herself whoever she wanted to be?

The only person she wanted to tell about Lorelei's family—her family—was dead. She wondered how her father would react, knowing the truth about Lorelei after all these years.

She was tired of asking her mother and getting the bare minimum of an answer. She missed Tommy. During any normal dinner, they would be talking, gossiping, letting Sophie interject every so often. Thea was tired of going in circles with Sophie.

She sipped from her water glass, put down her fork. She'd have much better luck with Ilsa.

"Maybe we should move." Sophie was talking almost wholly to herself now, her eyes looking around the dining room. "We don't need this much space."

They'd never needed that much space. The house was lonelier now without Tommy.

Sophie pushed herself away from the table. Thea did the same. They spent an hour in each other's company, and the ending was always marked by Sophie rising from the table.

Thea always followed her lead.

Before they left the table, Sophie's eyes met hers. "Thea, stop asking questions. You have to learn that you don't get all the answers you want." Sophie's eyes were rimmed with red. She seemed exhausted.

A grieving woman.

Thea knew Sophie was putting on a performance.

~

Thea waited for her mother to disappear up the stairs. Then she finished Sophie's glass of wine and retired to her father's office. She put a record on, letting Billie Holiday fill the room. She sat down behind the desk, opened the drawer, and poured herself a glass of rye. She lifted it to her father, then took a sip.

She could feel Tommy with every heartbeat, every blink of her eyes. She could feel him watching her. She put the glass down on the desk, leaning forward on it. If she closed her eyes, inhaled, she could smell her dad's cologne.

Amy had given her copies of *The Courier*, defying Sophie's order of no news. Thea kept them in the office, and she was able to see, exactly, how her father's legacy had changed.

That party, the one before her birthday, was to laud Tommy for all his success, the awards, the films, the studio he'd built, and the money he'd made.

But with one suicide note, that had all changed.

Now the headlines disparaged him. His headshot—a photo of Tommy around thirty years old, his smile wide and his face unmarked by age, his brown eyes sparkling even in the black and white—ran with headlines calling him a murderer.

She picked the phone up, then pressed the receiver between her ear and shoulder. She dialed and waited.

"Amy Evans."

Thea guessed that Amy would still be at work. It was a good guess. Amy was spending more and more time at work, writing her column and working on the Lorelei story. "Theodosia Ross," Thea said. She could hear Amy bite back a laugh.

"I'm working on the first part of the story," Amy said. Thea could hear her writing in the background.

"I'm sitting at my dad's desk," Thea said. She didn't have a good reason to call. She was alone and didn't want to be. Even with her mother in the house, Thea didn't have anyone to talk to.

The side effect of being schooled at home, in ballet every free moment, modeling when she became a teen was that she didn't really have any friends. She was more alone than ever. Thea thought about calling Willa. She used to be able to talk to Willa.

Thea hadn't seen her since Tommy's celebration of life. She knew that they weren't meant for each other, that life would be so hard together. Willa saw their lives differently, and Thea couldn't bring herself to have a conversation with her. They hadn't talked, and Thea didn't think they ever really would. Thea wondered what Tommy would have had to say about her feelings about other women. It was better he didn't know.

"I was reading the papers you gave me," Thea said.

He would have hated to read the sort of things printed about him. Thea hated to read it. He had built his life from nothing, and someone had taken it away from him.

"I have to do something," Thea said. She felt *young* all of a sudden. "I thought you were wrong about my dad," Thea said. These past couple of weeks, investigating with Amy had totally changed her perspective. Deep down, Thea knew. There was no way Tommy Ross would kill himself. "I thought you were trying to see something that wasn't there."

"I . . . don't think I wanted to be right," Amy said softly. "Either way, it's awful." Connecting two murders, twenty years apart, was the hard part. Lorelei and Tommy were linked. Thea was too.

"How am I supposed to fix Tommy's legacy?" Thea asked. "What should I do?" She had been trying to ignore all the vile things that were being said about him.

The man in the papers wasn't the man Thea knew. It wasn't the man Tommy was.

She had to fix it.

Amy exhaled. "I've been thinking about that. I don't know."

Tommy had left her one million dollars. At the time, she hadn't known what she was going to do with it. But now? She would have to use it to repair Tommy's legacy. Amy's story would be one thing. Solving Tommy's and Lorelei's murders would be another.

It didn't feel like enough.

Thea sipped from her glass again, closing her eyes. She tried to picture what Tommy would do. What he wanted to do, what he stood for.

"I'll have to think of something," Thea said. She should hang up, go to bed. It was late, and she had an early morning.

But she drained the glass, listening to the quiet scratch of Amy's pen.

She could do it for Tommy.

CHAPTER 51

1954

Thea would never get used to the eerie calmness of Lorelei's house. She used the key Julian had given her, and she stepped in, bracing herself.

She closed the door behind her. She kicked her shoes off, letting her feet sink into the dusty carpet. She stopped, looking up at the line of Lorelei's theatrical posters. It was cold in the house; every hair on her arms was standing at full attention.

It was the way the house made her feel. When she stepped into it, a primal instinct told her to run. Maybe it was the fact that Lorelei had died in that house: her essence was still very much in it.

But Thea had been born in this house. Was it possible that her body remembered it? Remembered being here, then being ripped away from it, everything she had ever known? Sunlight danced through the window, dust particles trapped in the rays.

She moved to Lorelei's bedroom, going into the closet. She thumbed through all the dresses, the simple skirts, the blouses folded on shelves.

She and Amy hadn't gone through the whole house on their first visit. Once they had found the journals, they thought they hit gold. And they had, but Thea wanted to look around again. And with endless time on her hands, she did it.

All this work to build a narrative about Lorelei's life, and Thea still didn't know anything about her. Nothing concrete. Thea pulled down the hatbox filled with envelopes. She opened it, then passed through the piles of ripped-open envelopes. Some of the letters Tommy had written Lorelei were preserved in the journals. He had written to and about her so freely, in a way Thea could never see him talking about Sophie. He praised her charm, her humor, her talent. In one letter, Tommy was writing about her pregnancy and what he wanted for her. For them.

He was writing about Thea.

It was hard to imagine who Lorelei would have become. What she could have done. Thea sifted through the envelopes. She had also come here because she needed to get out of the house. She and Sophie were stalking around each other, and every small thing turned into a yelling match. She understood that Sophie was exhausted, grieving, and unsure.

Thea was, too, and it was upsetting that Sophie didn't see that at all. More than anything, Thea needed her mom.

She couldn't remember the last time she'd had this biological, primal feeling. All she wanted to do was crawl into Sophie's bed with her and sleep for days. All she wanted was her mom. Sophie had treated Thea like an adult since she was five, but she still wanted her mother. She wanted Sophie to tell her everything would be okay. She needed some support, now more than ever. She wanted to curl up in a ball and cry.

She was doing everything to not focus on the fact that she would never *really* get to know Lorelei. That option had been robbed from her when she was a week old.

Putting it all together made Thea feel small. Like she was just a pawn in someone's game. Like the outcome of her life didn't matter, that she was some trophy.

The only person she knew who was that competitive, who had such a drive to win, was her mother.

She sorted through the envelopes, unsure of what else to do. She would, maybe with Julian's permission, hire someone to clean the place, maybe sell some of Lorelei's things. That felt wrong too.

Now that she was used to it, the silence seemed almost friendly. Thea's fingers grazed something that wasn't an envelope. She fished it out from the box. It was a ring, a sapphire set among diamonds. She held it up, slipped it onto her left ring finger. It fit perfectly. She slid it off. Her heartbeat was reverberating through the empty room, the whole house, ruining her perfect silence. She sat on the dusty carpet, unable to move. The ring was beautiful, simple, the band a stunning silver.

Thea slid it on again, looking at how the sapphire danced in the daylight. It was simple, classic. Beautiful.

But was it Lorelei's?

~

Thea loved spending time at the Weston-Dawson house. She was sitting at the dining room table, across from Walter. Julian was between them, with a stack of papers in front of him for grading.

"Why do you make them write essays?" Thea had asked.

Julian leaned back in his chair. He was wearing the same cardigan he had been when Thea had sat in his class and round glasses she had never seen on him before. "I try to make them really connect with a performance. I want them to dissect what makes it so powerful," Julian said.

"And does anyone ever write about you?" Thea asked.

"At least two students per semester." Julian lit a cigarette, rolling his eyes with a sigh. "They always think I'll give them a higher mark."

Walter looked between them. "What did you want to talk about, Thea?" Julian's attention wandered back to his papers.

Thea reached into her purse and pulled out the ring. She handed it to Walter. "Was this Lorelei's?" Thea asked.

He held it up, the sapphire glinting in the light. He inspected it for a couple of moments, then handed it back to her. "It couldn't be," he said.

"How can you tell so quickly?"

He turned the ring toward her, and Thea could see a stamp on the band. **SOR 1930.**

Sophia Osbourne Ross. The year her parents were married.

Thea exhaled. "How did I miss that?"

Walter's smile was gentle, genuine. She liked that he never made her feel stupid for asking a question. "Hard to see. And Millie hated sapphires."

"She did?" Thea asked.

"And rubies," Julian said, his eyes still on his papers in front of him.

"She liked emeralds," Walter said.

Julian looked up at him, still sick with love after all these years. "Like the one you're wearing. She wore that the night she found out she was pregnant."

Thea reached up and touched the star pendant that sat at her throat. She never took it off. "She did?"

"She never told me where she got it, but I'd guess Tommy," Julian said.

Thea pressed the little star between her thumb and index finger. "I guess this could have been a phone call," she said sheepishly. The less time she spent at home, the better. Thea picked up the ring again, sliding it onto her finger. She watched the sapphire glimmer in the light. How did Sophie's ring end up among Lorelei's things?

"It's no problem," Walter said. "We've been together so long we know all of each other's stories. We need a new audience."

"Hey," Julian said. "Did I ever tell you about—"

"The time you and Jesse went to Vegas and gambled away a lot of money? Yes, and it's not a good story," Walt said, teasing.

"Jesse is my brother," Julian explained. "He helped deliver you. He died last year. Car accident."

Once again, a pang of longing. Her life would have been so much fuller if she had grown up around these men. She liked how easy it was to make them laugh, how thoughtful and kind they both were.

Different from Tommy, who tried his best, and a far cry from Sophie, who pushed Thea.

She liked watching Julian and Walter. She enjoyed being a part of their lives, knowing that she could go to them with any problem. She slipped the ring back into her purse. "What do you think Lorelei would have wanted?" Thea asked.

The two men shared a look. Julian put his pen down. "I think she would have liked to have lived."

"Aside from that," Thea said. She pulled her feet underneath her so she was leaning on the table.

Walter frowned, considering it. "I think she would have wanted to support other young actresses."

"Maybe," Julian said. He was leaning forward. "She would have wanted to make sure that other actresses didn't have to go through what she did."

"She'd want to be in control, at any rate," Walter added. He looked to Julian, who nodded. "Sometimes I felt like I never really knew her either. And just when I *was* getting to know her, she was gone. I knew Millie, but I never knew Lorelei."

Julian exhaled. "She would hate that I decided to teach. She would have had us keep working together forever."

Thea looked between the two men. She had ideas of what she wanted to do, how to give Lorelei the justice she deserved. She wanted to make sure both Lorelei and Tommy were remembered properly. Not as a crazy woman, not as a murderer.

And it was proving to be harder than she'd thought.

"Thea," Walter said after a moment. Julian had turned back to his papers, picking his pen up with great reluctance. "I think what you're doing is enough. I think she would be so proud of you."

As much as Thea wanted that to be true, she knew it wasn't. As long as the stories out there hadn't changed, she knew she was failing. And she had to do better.

CHAPTER 52

1934

The one photograph where I look pregnant is taken at the end of my eighth month. *About Last Night* moves to postproduction, and I choose a film to direct starring Julian, to give myself a break and to get off my feet.

I want to retreat from the public eye, but that would be bad for optics. Over the past few months, Julian and I have both fought to be seen as contenders with endless interviews and press.

No one thinks we can succeed.

We're having dinner. I'm to the point where I have to wear a girdle over a Spencer corset. I can barely breathe, and I'm not sure it's even working. It's just for special events, and dinner is always a special event.

Jesse is worried about my health. He tells me that the baby has had no room to grow, that it's putting me and him in danger.

He doesn't get it. What I have to do to keep our business running, our lives together.

I think about Joanna all the time. I write to my baby, Tommy's baby, and think about what could be.

Julian and I sit across from each other. We're seated in the center of the dining room. Some of the papers report we're having a torrid love affair. We let them think that. It's good for business. "Are you okay?"

Julian asks this at least twenty times a day. He shows more concern for me and my baby than I do. I don't think that's a good thing.

"I'm fine." I keep my voice low. I look around. We're surrounded by Hollywood bigwigs. I take a sip from my glass of water. "We're almost done with this film, right?"

Julian is quiet for a moment; he's considering it. The band is playing a slow Cole Porter song, and I'm reminded of my time on the Cloud Nine stage. "I think so. Why?"

"When we're done, I'm going away. To Europe, and I'm going to have my baby there. Then I'll bring him to be raised by my parents." It's a plan I've been mulling over for a while now, and I think it's the best thing for me and the baby. Going away is the only way I can keep my baby safe and keep my life.

"You can't," Julian says. He looks genuinely heartbroken at the prospect.

"It'll just be a few weeks. I'll take Phyllis with me," I say. "Then she can take the baby home, and I'll come back." I would take my mother with me, but we haven't spoken since I let Tommy think she was my maid. I deserve it. Julian, the traitor he is, has taken her side. And when I explained it to him, the look he gave me was one of cold betrayal.

Much like the one he's giving me now.

"But . . ." He leans back in his chair, perfect posture discarded for once. "If that's what you think is best."

"I do think it's best," I say. The band moves to a faster song. "Let's dance." There's no one else on the dance floor, but Julian obliges—he always does—and sweeps me up.

I'm in his arms. We're doing a foxtrot. "You can't leave," Julian says in my ear. He's a master of dancing and talking at the same time. I still have to concentrate, a little too much, on my steps. I can't respond, and he knows that. "I thought we were in this together."

"We are. In business together," I manage to reply. I knew he wouldn't be pleased with my plan. I'll have to raise this baby without a father. "I want you in his life. You're already his uncle."

"I want to be more than that." His reply is muted, and he spins me. The cameras flash, and I try to make sure that I'm smiling, but the photograph catches me looking almost heartbroken.

As we leave the dance floor, I spot Tommy and Ramona sharing a table. They're doing all they can to change the narrative around their own film. *Taming of the Shrew* went horribly. I can't help but be a little, a lot, overjoyed.

I know Tommy's been watching us. I feel a dull pull toward him. If this were seven months ago, we'd be sneaking off to the bathroom, and I'd let him rip my dress off.

But that's the past, and I'm looking toward the future.

I pick up my fork. I squeeze my left hand. "I know you're not happy about this. But I want my child to have stability. And I want him to have a family around him." I stop talking. I don't know how to phrase what I want to say next. "You'll always have a place in both of our lives. But he deserves a lot more than what I can give him alone."

Julian seems to understand this, and he doesn't mention it again. But he's upset, and I know he's processing everything.

Later, we take another turn around the dance floor, but the magic is lost. The night is ruined. And it's all my fault.

~

The next evening, Sophie Ross is at my door. Just Sophie. I've just returned home, in the middle of changing from my day clothes. I'm not wearing a girdle or a Spencer, and my stomach protrudes. She is wearing a glossy evening dress, a shawl wrapped around her shoulders.

She looks amazing. She always does.

She's clutching a copy of *The Courier*. Without saying anything, she holds it up. The paper is open to Cheryl's column with a photograph of Julian and me dancing the night before. The article asks who my baby's father is.

Cheryl suggests it's Kenneth Webster. I read the story earlier; then I threw the paper out.

"We need to talk," Sophie says.

I let her in. We sit across from each other at my kitchen table. For a while, we don't say anything. I should get dressed, but I'm so tired. My whole body aches, and I can feel the baby kick and shift. I think I'll call Julian and tell him I'm not leaving my house tonight.

"Are you sure this baby is Tommy's?" Sophie lights a cigarette. I'm leaning back in my chair, an arm under my bump. I feel so big, so heavy.

I swallow hard. I nod. I'm not sure I can summon the words to say anything to her. I look at the picture again, face up on my table. I look so sad—I can't bear to look at it.

"I want your baby." One thing I appreciate about Sophie is that she cuts right to the chase. "You're smaller than I thought you'd be."

"I've been hiding it best I can."

Sophie's all business. "We will take your baby. I'll give you money, and after you give birth, you leave Los Angeles."

"No," I say. "I already have a plan. This isn't just Tommy's baby; it's mine too. And I—"

"You think a baby wants a pill-addicted whore as a mother?" Sophie asks casually. "Don't you want to give your baby, my husband's baby, the best start in life possible? We'd give you money every year to stay away. This would be our child." She reaches into her purse and pulls out papers. Nothing official, but it's a list of rules, all neatly typed out. I can imagine her sitting at a typewriter, building the world she wants.

I open my mouth, then close it. "No." I stand firm. I almost let her walk all over me once, and I'm not going to let her do it again. She doesn't get everything she wants. She doesn't get anything. I sit up straight, and it takes some effort. I hold a hand over my stomach. I can feel the baby kicking, insisting that I make the best decision.

"Here's how this is going to go," I say. "I'm going to have the baby. I'm going to raise him with my family. This may be *your husband's* baby, but I'm his mother."

I see something in Sophie's eyes akin to deep sadness. She doesn't look at me; her eyes are fully on my tummy. My breasts and face are fuller. My hair is longer, glossier, shinier. I've continued the upkeep to be Lorelei Davies, and I've never felt healthier than I do right now at eight months' pregnant. Sophie's blue eyes rise from my body to my eyes. Then she looks away. "Four miscarriages. He just looks at you, and you get pregnant. We'll give you one million dollars."

"What does Tommy say?" The sum of money is almost enough to sway me. But I will never let Sophie near my baby, even if it means denying him his father.

"He doesn't know I'm here."

I realize this is the closest Sophie Ross will ever come to begging. We are such different women. We live such different lives. But I have something she wants.

A crueler version of me would wring her dry. I feel bad for her. She's a desperate woman. I'm standing my ground, and I'm not moving. "I think you should go now," I say. "This was a waste of both of our time."

Sophie rises and brushes invisible dust from the skirt of her dress. She picks up her wrap. "Thank you for hearing me out."

I close the door behind her. Then I go to my bedroom and write.

CHAPTER 53

1954

In the morning, Thea found Sophie where she always did: at the kitchen table, wearing a black button-down shirt tucked into a slim black skirt. In front of Sophie was an ashtray and a cup of coffee.

Thea sat down across from her mother. She was still in her leotard and tights from her morning warm-up.

"What, Thea?"

Thea leaned forward on the table, then straightened up before Sophie could chastise her for her posture. "I want to talk to you about something," Thea said. She had tossed and turned until her alarm went off; then her warm-up had been dotted with thoughts of Tommy and Lorelei.

Sophie looked up at her, her eyes cold and direct. "Say it, then."

"We should do something for Dad," Thea said. She cleared her throat. "I want to use some of the money he left me to make a donation or something somewhere." She hadn't worked out the finer details yet. She knew she had to do it. Had to repair his name. It was her name too. Thea was gutted she hadn't thought of it earlier.

Sophie's eyes narrowed. She was never as expressive as Tommy was. She hid everything she was thinking. "No."

"What?"

"No." Sophie repeated herself, cool and casual, as if they were discussing the weather.

"Why not?" Thea asked.

"Did you read what they're saying about him?" Sophie asked, as if Thea hadn't spoken. "I told you not to."

"I did it anyway." Thea raised her chin defiantly. Sophie's lips tugged into a frown. "I'm an adult, and you can't tell me what to do anymore."

This was the same track their conversations took every time. Sophie infantilizing her, Thea wanting to bite back. "I am trying to keep you safe," Sophie said with a sigh. Thea narrowed her eyes. A détente while Thea poured some coffee and Sophie lit another cigarette. "Your father wouldn't care about any of that. He would care that you and I are safe." Thea thought she heard Sophie's voice catch, the hint of a tsunami of tears yet to come.

"No," Thea said. "That's not what he would want."

"Who knew him better, Thea?" Sophie's voice was sharp.

"You did. Which is why I don't get why you wouldn't want to help clear his name," Thea said. "You were married for twenty-four years, and you don't care about him anymore."

"That's not true!" Sophie slammed the table with a flat hand, making Thea jump. She took a second, swallowed her anger, and continued. "I did everything for your father. I was the woman behind him. He's a murderer, Thea. You can't change something if it's true." Thea bit her tongue. Sophie continued. "You are still a child. I know we sheltered you, and maybe that was a mistake. There is so much of this world you don't understand."

"Then tell me," Thea said. Sophie didn't look at her. It was still early in the morning, and Thea was exhausted.

"No," Sophie said. She looked at Thea now, her gaze always discerning, always evaluating. "You need to grow up, Theodosia."

Was she telling Thea to *grow up* over mourning her father?

"I don't get how you're not feeling the same thing I am," Thea said.

Sophie sipped from her coffee cup, then put it back on the table before she responded. "I am." Her voice was soft. "You don't see it."

"Of course I don't," Thea said. Along with grief, she was living with rage. The fire threatened to consume her every moment of every day. And she was mad that her mother didn't see that.

Thea exhaled. The last thing she wanted to do was get into another long argument with her mother. She knew she couldn't make Sophie see her point of view. Sophie lit another cigarette. She leaned her head back, closing her eyes. "I have a headache," Sophie said. She pulled away from the table, standing up. "I'm going to bed. Don't disturb me."

"There is no chance of that," Thea said.

"Theodosia!" Sophie snapped, despite her apparent headache. "Can you please just go find something to do?"

"I'll be in my dance studio," Thea said, copying Sophie's tone exactly. "Don't disturb me."

It was more and more apparent that she and Sophie would clash over everything. Without Tommy there to moderate, all she and Sophie did was fight.

Nothing Sophie did made sense. Thea couldn't be bothered to try to understand where Sophie was coming from.

Thea decided to do what she wanted. Sophie couldn't stop her anymore.

CHAPTER 54

1934

When I was fourteen, I assisted my mother in one of my aunts' births. I was scared, tasked with staying by her side, holding her hand, and dabbing at her forehead with a damp towel.

What I really remember was Momma taking charge completely. She came in, gave orders to her sisters, and sat me right next to my aunt. I remember my aunt in the calm moments, sitting against the headboard of her bed, her legs spread apart, still making jokes with me.

But I also remember how being in that room felt. Simultaneously hours and seconds, then, by the morning, I was holding my baby cousin in my arms. My aunt was happy and exhausted.

I don't know how I'm going to be a mother. I'll be a part-time mother, I guess. My baby will be surrounded by love, surrounded by family.

I'm working on packing for Europe. I want to go. I'm at the end of my pregnancy, and Julian is okay with it. I haven't talked to my family yet, but I will, and Phyllis will come with me.

But the baby has other plans.

The pains start early. When I'm standing in my closet, I wet myself. It's not pee. My waters broke.

It starts easy. Mild cramping that builds to a wave cresting. I don't have a plan. I could call Julian or Jesse, but it doesn't feel desperate enough yet.

I can't stay still. I pace through my house, feeling pains surge through me, gradually getting closer together. They start vaguely uncomfortable and build to outright painful. Every so often, I have to stop, brace myself against the wall.

My one thought is that I want Tommy with me. I want him to hold my hand, dab at my forehead. I want us to experience this together.

I eventually settle on a mass of towels on my living room floor. I have a dish towel in my mouth to bite down on every time I have another pain. I'm scared, and I don't have anyone.

When the pains become unmanageable, I call Julian. I tell him to call his brother. Julian tells me to stay calm, that they'll be there as soon as they can.

I wait until I feel the urge to push. Each contraction rips me in half, and I'm in so much pain that I can't see straight. It's the worst thing I've ever gone through. I'm sweating, or crying, or both. Every time I think I can't bear the pain, it recedes, letting me catch my breath. I want to give up, I want to let myself go, but there will be a baby that needs me.

~

When Julian opens my door, I'm wrapped in my dressing gown, on my little nest of towels. I don't know how long it's been. It could've been hours of sitting, pushing, hoping. I'm just grateful to see Julian.

He has Jesse and Walter with him. Julian rushes to my side, holds my hand, tells me I can do this. He uses the dish towel I'm biting down on to wipe at my forehead.

Jesse kneels down and inspects me with direct intensity. "You're close. You should have called earlier."

"I'm fine," I say. Another contraction catches me, and I yowl, an animal in heat. Julian lets me squeeze his hand as much as I want.

Walt drifts for a moment, then picks up the phone to call our family.

Jesse looks up at me. "One more big push, okay?" he asks. I nod, and with the next pain, I give it everything I have. Jesse catches the baby, then clips the cord before giving me my child. "You have a girl," he says.

I blink at him, as if in a dream. "A girl." When she opens her eyes, I see she has Tommy's exact liquid warm-brown eyes. A rush of relief washes over me. I never thought it was Kenneth's baby.

I'm relieved to see it, all the same.

Jesse examines her, pronouncing her small but otherwise healthy. Walter kneels next to me. "You didn't tell us."

"I was going to. Momma knows," I say. He's looking at the baby, and I know he's thinking about Joanna. The baby is quiet; her eyes are closed. "Joanna May," I tell him.

"Can I?" Walter asks. He waits for me to nod before taking the baby from my arms. She is small. Walter looks at her with such bewilderment. He's already in love with her.

Julian waits for Walt to surrender baby Joanna; then he takes a turn. He coos to her, talks to her.

I'm in pain. I'm exhausted. She's been in the world for a few minutes, and she's already changed my life. I watch as Julian paces with her in his arms, staring down as he talks to her softly. He's twisting her name into a little song. I close my eyes. Walter sits down next to me. "She's wonderful," Walt says. I'm glad he's with me. "Phyllis is going to be so excited."

"If anything happens to me," I say, "you'll take care of her, right?"

"Of course. Nothing's going to happen." His voice is so soft. None of us are talking above a whisper, lest we wake Joanna May from her sleep.

I take my time, collecting things she'll need at my parents' house. When I get the chance, I call Tommy. I think he'll want to know.

And that is my final mistake.

CHAPTER 55

1954

When Thea got home from classes and teaching, she found Sophie sitting at the kitchen table.

"Mom," Thea said. Thea had stayed late at the studio, trying to put off this conversation. She almost wished she had Amy with her. Amy had offered to sit with her, give her some support.

But Thea was a big girl now, and she could do it alone.

"You missed dinner." Sophie sat, smoking, at the empty table. She had a notepad, and Thea realized it was almost Thanksgiving. The past couple of weeks had been long and short, and Thea didn't have anything to celebrate. Thea sat down across from Sophie. The house was big and hollow around them.

"I didn't miss anything," Thea said. Sophie's eyes flashed, and she looked toward her daughter. "I was working late."

"Right," Sophie said. "Ilsa left a plate in the oven for you." She seemed tired, older than Thea had ever seen her. She had dark circles under her eyes; her hair was flat and dull.

"I'm not hungry," Thea said. She reached into the pocket of her dress and pulled the ring out. She placed it on the table in front of Sophie. At the sight of the ring, Sophie turned green, but she kept her composure. "I want to know the truth. I know you're lying to me," Thea said. "First you said that Lorelei Davies was a—"

"That name again." Sophie's voice was full of venom. "You're just like him. He talked about her all the time and thought I wouldn't notice. He thought I wouldn't care."

"Mom," Thea said.

"You were supposed to be mine. She was never supposed to have you. I was willing to overlook everything else. Except for you." Sophie closed her eyes, exhaling softly. "You were supposed to be mine."

Her mother was dead.

Thea was sitting across from her kidnapper.

"What did you do?" Thea asked. She wanted to know exactly what had happened. Sophie took her time, lighting a cigarette.

She looked up and met Thea's eyes again. "What do you want me to say, Thea? That I killed Lorelei Davies? That I took you? That when your father wanted to tell you who your mother was, I killed him and framed him for the murder?" She raised her voice, and it echoed around them. Thea leaned back. She wanted Sophie to confess. She wanted the truth, but it didn't make her feel better, knowing it. She shouldn't have pushed. She should have left her life alone. "Of course I did."

Sophie killed *two* people. For her.

How was she supposed to feel about that?

"Did Dad know?" Thea asked.

"That I killed Lorelei? Of course not. But when he saw that necklace, he started to put it together."

"Why did you give it to me?" Thea's heart was in her chest. She couldn't breathe, her rib cage tight and heavy.

"Before your birthday, he said he was going to tell you. I needed to remind him I was in control," Sophie said. That was it. The drive Sophie had had Thea's whole life. Her competitive spirit, the need Sophie had to be singular, drove her to murder.

"Why make him confess?" Thea asked. The last piece of the puzzle. The one thing Thea couldn't figure out.

Sophie lit another cigarette, focused on her lighter. Seconds seemed to stretch into hours before Sophie answered. "He had no respect for me. He deserved it. Tommy and Lorelei would be out of our lives, and we could be happy together forever." It didn't make sense to Thea, but it did to Sophie.

It was always Sophie's world. Thea was just living in it.

"Mom," Thea said softly. "I . . ." She didn't know what to say. Her gut instinct was to apologize, even though she wasn't guilty of anything. "Why?"

"When you're in love, Thea, you'll understand." Sophie stabbed out her cigarette.

Fear and anger pulsed through Thea.

"I loved your father so much. I thought that we would be happy together forever," Sophie said. "But at the end of the day, the only thing that really mattered was you, Thea." Sophie leaned over, pressing her hand to Thea's cheek. They were quiet, orderly. They had yelled so much there was no point in more. This was what she'd wanted, in the worst way possible. "I meant what I said at Sal's. I wouldn't have done anything differently." Sophie rose from the table and leaned down, kissing Thea's forehead. "I won't apologize for any of it. I love you so much."

Thea didn't know what to make of any of it. She had the truth, and it wasn't what she wanted. She was Sophie's trophy. Sophie's prize for being Tommy's wife.

She had to call the police, but all she wanted to do was sleep forever.

She had to call *someone* with the truth. The police, then Julian, then Amy.

But she could call tomorrow. And figure everything else out later.

CHAPTER 56

1954

It was Thea who, upon waking the next morning, found Sophie in bed. It was Thea who called Julian and Walter, unsure of what to do.

The Ross house was surrounded by policemen. Walter and Julian waited while Thea explained the story again and again.

Her mother had confessed to two murders. Then she had gone up to her bedroom and poisoned herself, just like she had Lorelei and Tommy.

Harry was taken in, too, for assisting Sophie in the cover-up.

It was, frankly, unbelievable.

Thea called Grandmother Osbourne and the rest of her extended family. She watched as Sophie's body was taken away. Willa reached out. Thea didn't know, exactly, what to say to her. So she accepted Willa's condolences and hung up the phone as quickly as possible.

As the story of the double murder and suicide hit the papers, it was accompanied by a story by Amy Evans.

LORELEI DAVIES: A LIFE UNLIVED

The two-page story featured photographs Thea had never seen before, and Amy told the story of a woman given little choice in who she was.

Then she was murdered.

After Thanksgiving, a holiday Thea swore she'd never celebrate again, she donned a black dress and drove to the cemetery. On the passenger seat of the Corvette was a bundle of bright-red roses.

She parked, then slipped on a pair of silver cat-eye sunglasses. She clutched the roses to her chest. Lorelei's headstone was easy to find. The center of her row, the grave was now overflowing with an array of flowers.

Thea smoothed the skirt of her dress, pushed the older bouquets out of the way, and knelt. "Hi, Momma."

She put the roses down in front of Lorelei's headstone.

Lorelei Davies

1914–1934

Beloved daughter and friend

"I miss you so much, and we never met," Thea said. She was talking out loud; the nearest group of black-clad mourners were feet away from her. It was too hot to wear black. Her dress was sleeveless, and she could still feel perspiration pricking under her arms and at the back of her neck.

"I am so sorry. I . . ." Thea trailed off. She didn't believe that Lorelei was somewhere watching. She was this body in the grass under her knees. But still, there was something, in the November sun, the cloudless sky that just *felt* like Lorelei was with her.

This was Thea's first moment alone in days. Walter and Julian had insisted she practically move in. She'd returned to dancing full time. She spent time in Watts with Lorelei's family.

She did everything she could to not think about the deaths Sophie had left in her wake.

Julian had asked if Thea wanted company. Thea had declined. She wanted to see her mom on her own. Now that she was here, all she had was a marble headstone. Thea reached out, touching her fingers to the engraving of Lorelei's name. She had wanted this for so long—answers about where she came from—and now that she had them?

Thea was as unhappy as ever.

It wasn't what she had hoped for. Thea had hoped that her mother was out there somewhere, waiting for her. That she'd look in her eyes and see her face, her history. She had the Dawson family, but none of it felt like enough.

Lorelei had wanted her.

"I wish I had you," Thea said. "I can just picture how I'd have grown up surrounded by the Dawsons. I'm sorry you couldn't be there for me. I'm sorry the choice was taken from you. Dad loved me a lot."

She trailed off. She sat back on her heels. "All your films are playing now. A friend and I went to see the marathon, and seeing you on screen, you . . . I wish I was half that beautiful." Lorelei Davies was having a bit of a renaissance. Theaters played her films again, articles ran, and news stories aired about her life. People mourned this woman who had, up until recently, barely been remembered. The truth about her race was finally out, and Walter and Julian did interviews, separately, about the woman they knew versus the woman the public knew.

Julian and Walter said that it wasn't what Lorelei would have wanted. But it was what they had.

Both men kept Thea from the spotlight. The whole sordid affair was out, but Julian and Walter had decided that it wasn't the public's business who Thea was.

"I think you'd be proud of me. Julian tells me about how much he loved you and how much you wanted me," Thea said. She shifted so she was sitting cross-legged. She picked up a rose and placed it behind her ear. "I read Dad's script about you. He loved you so much. I don't know if he knew it then, but he knew it when he died." Was there a place where Tommy and Lorelei were back together? Were they happy? Were they watching her together? "*As Long as You're Mine*," Thea said. She had scoured the pages, following Tony and Lucy as they found each other and fell in love. The title haunted her, and Thea knew, one day, it would make a great film.

It would finish Tommy and Lorelei's story.

"Momma, I love you so much," Thea said. She had been sitting in silence for several minutes, trying to think of what to say. She had so many questions only Lorelei could answer.

The headstone wasn't talking.

"Thank you so much for trying to keep me safe," Thea said. "I know you loved me so much, and I hope I've done you proud."

She leaned over, pressing her lips to the headstone, warm from the midday sun.

Tomorrow would come, and another, and another. And Thea could come to understand.

CHAPTER 57

1934

Sophie Ross is many things. But she's no fool.

The touches and the looks between Tommy and Lorelei gave them away immediately. He talked about her constantly, in sweet ways no man talks about his coworker.

She saw them at every party and on screen. She saw how Lorelei looked at Tommy. She saw how Tommy looked at Lorelei.

He's never looked at Sophie like that.

She knew about the affair months before he confirmed it.

What gets her is the *baby*. The girl, born on October 31, 1934. Tommy's face is tight and drawn when he hangs up the phone.

Sophie feels something flare up in her when he does. He sits down at the table, telling her how the baby will be moved to Watts next week. She thinks about their marriage, how she would do *anything* to keep him, anything to keep her life with him. She wanted to be the one locked to him for life, the mother of his child, an unbreakable bond.

She can't take the fact that Lorelei Davies has won.

Sophie Ross is supposed to win. She won the husband. Biology didn't understand, nor did Lorelei Davies. Sophie's put up with so much.

She loves her husband. Together, they're the most incredible couple in the world.

Sophie decides to take matters into her own hands.

She waits until Tommy leaves on a trip. She packs for him, kisses him goodbye. The house is quiet. She insisted on this house, hoping to fill it with several tawny-headed children with her eyes and the cleft in his chin.

All she wanted was for him to love her.

Sophie goes to the garage and slides into the car. She doesn't have much time. She needs to make sure Lorelei is dead before Tommy returns.

She sits on Lorelei's street as the sun sets. It's early November. She thinks about Thanksgiving, inviting her own mother and siblings to join them.

And then they'll be able to meet *her* baby.

The night falls. Sophie removes her engagement ring, then presses it to her lips and puts it in the pocket of her dress. She can't risk it getting in the way. Then she pulls herself from the car, clutching her purse to her abdomen. The door is locked. There's a key under the mat. Tommy told her about it. Sophie can hear a baby wailing, a strong set of lungs. She lets herself in and closes the door behind her.

Sophie pulls the handkerchief from her purse, then pours chloroform all over it. She holds it in her right hand, ready.

It's Lorelei's singing that draws Sophie to her. She's in her bedroom, the baby on the bed. She's in the middle of changing the baby's diaper, humming softly. The baby has stopped crying. Sophie waits for Lorelei to finish, sigh, and stand up.

Then she wraps her arm around Lorelei's mouth and nose, pressing the handkerchief as hard as she can. There's a struggle, but Sophie is taller, stronger. She has the element of surprise. She hates to do this in front of the infant, but she won't remember any of it.

Sophie squeezes until Lorelei relents, goes limp, falls to the ground. Then she holds the handkerchief there a little longer, hoping Lorelei's dead. She folds the handkerchief, then puts it back in her purse. Then she turns to the baby. She's so small, smaller than Sophie could have imagined. She blinks up—her eyes are big and brown—and Sophie sees Tommy in them. She's so relieved she could fall to the floor. Sophie picks the baby up, and she starts screaming again. Sophie bounces to soothe her, rubbing a circle on the infant's back. The baby doesn't relent, and her scream almost punctures Sophie's eardrum.

Sophie paces slowly until the baby wears herself out.

Then she leans down and unclasps the star pendant necklace from around Lorelei's neck. She recognizes it. She thought Tommy was going to give it to her when she found it among his things.

She's holding the necklace and the baby. She has what she wants.

She goes home. Calls Harrison. She'll need his help.

What she doesn't know is that, during the struggle or when taking the necklace, her ring fell through a hole in her pocket.

~

The next day, Tommy is ushered home among reports of Lorelei Davies's suicide. Sophie and the baby, who has become Theodosia Adeline in the night, are awake when he comes home. She's listening to the radio. Lorelei Davies, aged twenty, a star of the screen, found dead in her bed. Reports say she killed herself in the middle of the night, overdosing on pills. Sophie doesn't know how Harrison managed it, but she's grateful. Now Sophie and Tommy can move on.

When Tommy finds them, in their bedroom, Sophie lying down with the baby next to her, he's overcome. "What?" he asks several times, the only thing he can think to say. He kneels next to the bed, looking at his daughter.

"She's ours, and that's all that matters," Sophie says. She's breathless.

"I love her." Tommy looks up at Sophie, his eyes wide with shock. She doesn't know if he's talking about her, Theodosia, or Lorelei.

It doesn't matter.

She could confess.

But she doesn't.

And as long as she can keep the secret, they'll be happy.

ACKNOWLEDGMENTS

I love this book so, so much. It was such a thrill to write and explore a world so different than my other series. First, thank you to myself. Writing books is hard, and it would never happen if I didn't do it. I wrote this one in a weird bit of turmoil in my life, and I am so proud of what it became.

Thank you so much to my agent, Travis Pennington, and my editor, Selena James, for taking me on (and Melissa Valentine for signing me)! Thank you to Jodi Warshaw, for helping me hone my skills and trust my instincts as a writer.

I hope my family didn't read this book, but your support means the world. Special thanks to my big brother, who patiently answered my unhinged medical questions for a plot point that got cut.

Thank you to Eva Bild for allowing me to steal your name and being my pregnancy consultant. All mistakes and dramatizations are my own.

To the Berkletes, a group that transcends publishing houses and countries and time zones: I love you so much. You are the most inspiring group of writers, and I am so proud to be one of you. Thank you so much especially to Lyn Butler and Elizabeth Everett, who were so sure I'd sell this book and didn't let me believe otherwise. Thank you, Melissa Larsen, for being my very favorite. Thank you to my sweet Italian mother, Ali Hazelwood. Thank you to Amy Lea for letting me steal your name and your story.

To everyone else who let me steal their name—Lauren (and for peer-reviewing my intimate scenes), Victoria (even though that scene got cut), Joanna, Willa, Rachel—thank you so much.

To the littlest Julian John: always reach for your dreams.

Hannah, Jessica, Khaya: Hi! My favorite musical friends. Thank you so much for getting me out of my apartment and also letting me hang with your pets!

Thank you so much, Lora Maroney, for always believing in me even when I doubted it. And for letting me yell about this book.

My sweetest July, my lovely honeybun: I love you so, so much. Thank you for listening to me explain this book to you in the vaguest ways.

To Vincent Briggs, my favorite pterrible dinosaur connoisseur: My lovely friend! Your friendship is wonderful. Thank you for helping me remember to eat.

To Sarah Strange: Please do not let Brenda and Trevor read this book. Love you.

Finally, to Black girls everywhere. I love you so much.

BOOK CLUB QUESTIONS

1. Why did you decide to pick up *As Long as You're Mine*? Did it live up to your expectations?
2. Were Lorelei and Tommy truly in love, even though he was married?
3. How do you think you'd react to being told a secret such as the one Sophie keeps from Thea?
4. How are Lorelei and Julian similar? How are they different? What makes their relationship work?
5. What makes Sophie and Lorelei similar? What does Tommy see in both of them?
6. What is the significance of the title of the book?
7. How do Lorelei and, to a lesser extent, Sophie, Ramona, and Thea hide who they are?
8. What makes Tommy, Sophie, Ramona, and Julian different in the 1950s from the 1930s?
9. When do you think Sophie told Tommy about Thea's connection to Lorelei?
10. How would this story be different if told from Sophie's perspective?

ABOUT THE AUTHOR

Photo © 2024 Calgary Academy

Born in Calgary but now residing in Toronto, Nekesa Afia holds a degree in journalism from Toronto Metropolitan University and a certificate in publishing from Centennial College.

A self-proclaimed midcentury-modern fan, Nekesa loves a Saturday afternoon spent in front of the classic movie channel. When she isn't writing, you can find her sewing, swing dancing, or actively trying to pet every dog she sees.

Nekesa Afia is also the author of the Harlem Renaissance Mystery series.